What re

CLOSE TO HOME

'WOW!!' ★★★★★
John, Netgalley reviewer

'The must-read book of 2018' ★★★★★
Tony, Netgalley reviewer

'One of the best crime thrillers to be published this year' ★★★★★
Joan, Netgalley reviewer

'I couldn't put it down' ★★★★★
Susan, Netgalley reviewer

'Brilliantly plotted, with as many red herrings as a Christie' ★★★★★
Amanda, Netgalley reviewer

'I did not, even for one second, see this coming' ★★★★★
Elizabeth, Netgalley reviewer

'It will keep you enthralled to the final chapter!' ★★★★★
Felicity, Netgalley reviewer

'Absolutely fantastic' ★★★★★
Claire, Netgalley reviewer

'The twist at the end is SO good' ★★★★★
Abby, Netgalley reviewer

'I was left blinking with astonishment!' ★★★★★
Stefanie, Netgalley reviewer

'A must-read ... worth more than five stars!' ★★★★★
Sue, Netgalley reviewer

CLOSE TO
HOME

CARA HUNTER

PENGUIN BOOKS

PENGUIN BOOKS

UK | USA | Canada | Ireland | Australia
India | New Zealand | South Africa

Penguin Books is part of the Penguin Random House group of companies
whose addresses can be found at global.penguinrandomhouse.com.

Penguin
Random House
UK

First published 2018
001

Copyright © Cara Hunter, 2018

The moral right of the author has been asserted

Set in 12.5/14.75 pt Garamond MT Std
Typeset by Jouve (UK), Milton Keynes
Printed in Great Britain by Clays Ltd, St Ives plc

A CIP catalogue record for this book is available from the British Library

ISBN: 978–0–241–28309–7

www.greenpenguin.co.uk

For Simon

Prologue

It's getting dark, and the little girl is cold. It had been such a nice day – the lights and the costumes and the fireworks like a shower of stars. It was magical, just like a fairy tale, but now, everything's been ruined, everything's gone wrong. She looks up through the trees and the branches seem to be closing in over her head. But not like *Snow White*, not like *Sleeping Beauty*. There's no prince here, no rescuer on a beautiful white horse. Only a dark sky and monsters in the shadows. She can hear noises in the undergrowth, the rustling of small animals and a heavier movement coming steadily closer, step by step. She wipes her cheek, where tears still linger, and she wishes with all her heart she was like the princess in *Brave*. *She* wouldn't be frightened being in the forest all alone. But Daisy is.

Daisy is very frightened indeed.

'Daisy?' says a voice. 'Where are you?'

More steps, closer now, and the voice is angry. 'You can't hide from me. I'm going to find you. You know that, don't you, Daisy. *I'm going to find you.*'

I'm going to say this now, before we get started. You won't like it, but trust me, I've done this more times than I care to punish myself remembering. In a case like this – a kid – nine times out of ten it's someone close to home. Family, friend, neighbour, someone in the community. Don't forget that. However distraught they look, however unlikely it seems, they know who did it. Perhaps not consciously, and perhaps not yet. But they know.

They know.

* * *

20 July 2016, 2.05 a.m.
Canal Manor estate, Oxford

They say homebuyers make up their mind about a house within thirty seconds of going inside. Well, take it from me, the average police officer takes less than ten. In fact, most of us have come to judgement long before we're through the door. Only it's the people we're judging, not the property. So when we pull up outside 5 Barge Close, I have a pretty good idea what to expect. It's what used to be called an 'Executive Home'. Perhaps still is, for all I know. They have money, these people, but not as much as they'd like, or else they'd have bought a genuine Victorian house and not this reproduction version on a raw new estate the wrong side of the canal. It's the same red brick, the same bay windows, but the gardens are small and the garages huge – not so much fake as downright forgery.

The uniform posted at the front door tells me the family have already done the obligatory search of the house and garden. You'd be amazed how many times we find kids under beds or in wardrobes. They're not lost, they're just hiding. And most of those stories don't have happy endings either. But it seems that's not what we're dealing with here. As the Duty Inspector told me an hour ago when he woke me up, 'I know we wouldn't normally call you in this early, but this late at night, a kid that young, it feels all wrong. And the family were having a party so people had started looking for her long before they called us. I decided pissing you off was the least of our worries.' I'm not, actually. Pissed off, that is. And to be honest, I'd have done the same.

'Out the back's a bombsite, I'm afraid, sir,' says the PC at the door. 'People must've been traipsing up and down all night. Bits of dead firework everywhere. Kids. Can't see forensics getting sod all out there, sir.'

Great, I think. Effing fantastic.

Gislingham rings the bell and we stand at the door, waiting. He's shifting nervously from one foot to the other. Doesn't matter how many times you do it, you never get used to it. And when you do, it's time to quit. I take a few last gasps of fag and look back round the close. Despite the fact that it's two in the morning, almost every house is glaring with light, and there are people at several of the upstairs windows. Two patrol cars are parked on the scrubby bike-tracked grass opposite, their lights throbbing, and a couple of tired PCs are trying to keep the rubberneckers at a decent distance. There are half a dozen other officers on doorsteps, talking to the neighbours. Then the front door opens and I swing round.

'Mrs Mason?'

She's heavier than I'd expected. Jowls already forming and she can't be more than, what, mid-thirties? She has a cardigan on over a party dress – a halter-neck leopard-print job in a dull orangey colour that doesn't go with her hair. She glances down the street and then wraps the cardy tighter about herself. But it's hardly cold. It touched ninety today.

'DI Adam Fawley, Mrs Mason. May we come in?'

'Can you take your shoes off? The carpet's only just been cleaned.'

I've never understood why people buy cream carpet, especially if they have children, but it hardly seems the moment to argue. So we bend over like a couple of schoolkids, undoing our laces. Gislingham flashes me a look: there are hooks by the door labelled with the family's names, and their shoes are lined up by the mat. By size. And colour. Jesus.

5

Odd, though, what exposing your feet does to your brain. Padding about in socks makes me feel like an amateur. It's not a good start.

The sitting room has an archway through to a kitchen with a breakfast bar. There are some women in there, whispering, fussing about the kettle, their party make-up bleak in the unflinching neon light. The family are perched on the edge of a sofa far too big for the space. Barry Mason, Sharon and the boy, Leo. The kid stares at the floor, Sharon stares at me, Barry's all over the place. He's got up like the identikit hipster Dad – cargo pants, slightly too spiky hair, slightly too garish floral shirt not tucked in – but if the look is landlocked at thirty-five, the dark hair is dyed and I suspect he's a good ten years older than his wife. Who evidently buys the trousers in this house.

You get all sorts of emotions when a kid goes missing. Anger, panic, denial, guilt. I've seen them all, alone and in combination. But there's a look on Barry Mason's face I've not seen before. A look I can't define. As for Sharon, her fists are clenched so rigid her knuckles are white.

I sit down. Gislingham doesn't. I think he's worried the furniture might not take his weight. He eases his shirt collar away from his neck, hoping no one notices.

'Mrs Mason, Mr Mason,' I begin. 'I understand this must be a difficult time, but it's vital we gather as much information as we can. I'm sure you know this already, but the first few hours really are crucial – the more we know, the more likely it'll be that we find Daisy safe and well.'

Sharon Mason pulls at a loose thread on her cardigan. 'I'm not sure what else we can tell you – we already spoke to that other officer –'

'I know, but perhaps you can just talk me through it again. You said Daisy was at school today as usual and after that she was here in the house until the party started – she didn't go out to play?'

'No. She was in her bedroom upstairs.'

'And the party – can you tell me who came?'

Sharon glances at her husband, then at me. 'People from the close. The children's classmates. Their parents.'

Her kids' friends then. Not hers. Or theirs.

'So, what – forty people? Would that be fair?'

She frowns. 'Not so many. I have a list.'

'That would be very helpful – if you could give it to DC Gislingham.'

Gislingham looks up briefly from his notebook.

'And you last saw Daisy when exactly?'

Barry Mason still hasn't said anything. I'm not even sure if he heard me. I turn to him. He's got a toy dog in his hands and keeps twisting it. It's distress, I know, but it looks unnervingly like he's wringing its neck.

'Mr Mason?'

He blinks. 'I dunno,' he says dully. 'Elevenish maybe? It was all a bit confused. Busy. You know, lots of people.'

'But it was midnight when you realized she was missing.'

'We decided it was time the kids went to bed. People were starting to leave. But we couldn't find her. We looked everywhere. We called everyone we could think of. My little girl – my beautiful little girl –'

He starts to cry. I still find that hard to handle, even now. When men weep.

I turn to Sharon. 'Mrs Mason? What about you? When did you last see your daughter? Was it before or after the fireworks?'

Sharon shivers suddenly. 'Before, I think.'

'And the fireworks started when?'

'Ten. As soon as it got dark. We didn't want them going on too late. You can get in trouble. They can report you to the council.'

'So you last saw Daisy before that. Was it in the garden or in the house?'

She hesitates, frowning. 'In the garden. She was running about all night. Quite the belle of the ball.'

I wonder, in passing, how long it is since I've heard anyone use that phrase. 'So Daisy was in good spirits – nothing worrying her, as far as you knew?'

'No, nothing. She was having a lovely time. Laughing. Dancing to the music. What girls do.'

I glance at the brother, interested in his reaction. But there is none. He is sitting remarkably still. Considering.

'When did you last see Daisy, Leo?'

He shrugs. He doesn't know. 'I was watching the fireworks.'

I smile at him. 'Do you like fireworks?'

8

He nods, not quite meeting my eye.

'You know what? So do I.'

He glances up and there's a little flutter of connection, but then his head drops again and he starts pushing one foot across the rug, making circles in the shagpile. Sharon reaches out and taps him on the leg. He stops.

I turn to Barry again. 'And the side gate to the garden was open, I believe.'

Barry Mason sits back, suddenly defensive. He sniffs loudly and wipes his hand across his nose. 'Well, you can't be up and down opening the door every five minutes, can you? It was easier to have people come in that way. Less mess in the house.' He glances at his wife.

I nod. 'Of course. I see the garden backs on to the canal. Do you have a gate on to the towpath?'

Barry Mason shakes his head. 'Fat chance – council won't let you. There's no way he got in that way.'

'He?'

He looks away again. 'Whoever it was. The bastard who took her. The bastard who took my Daisy.'

I write 'my' on my notepad and put a question mark next to it. 'But you didn't actually *see* a man?'

He takes a deep breath that breaks into a sob, and he looks away, tears starting again. 'No. I didn't see anyone.'

I shuffle through my papers. 'I have the photo of Daisy you gave Sergeant Davis. Can you tell me what she was wearing?'

There's a pause.

'It was fancy dress,' says Sharon eventually. 'For the children. We thought that would be nice. Daisy was dressed as her name.'

'I'm sorry, I'm not with you –'

'A daisy. She was dressed as a daisy.'

I sense Gislingham's reaction, but don't allow myself to look at him. 'I see. So that was –'

'A green skirt, green tights and shoes. And a head-dress with white petals and a yellow centre. We got it from that shop on Fontover Street. It cost a fortune, even just to hire it. And we had to leave a deposit.'

Her voice falters. She gasps, then clenches her hand into a fist and pushes it against her mouth, her shoulders shaking. Barry Mason reaches across and puts an arm round his wife. She's whimpering, rocking backwards and forwards, telling him it's not her fault, that she didn't know, and he starts to stroke her hair.

There's another silence, then suddenly Leo edges forward and slips off the sofa. All his clothes seem slightly too big for him; you can barely see his hands for his sleeves. He comes over to me and gives me his phone. It's showing a still from a video. A still of Daisy in her green skirt. She's a beautiful child, no doubt about that. I press Play and watch for about fifteen seconds as she dances for the camera. She's brimming with confidence and exuberance – it radiates off her even on a two-inch screen. When the video stops, I check the tag – it's only three days old. Our first piece of luck. We don't always get something as up to date as this.

'Thank you, Leo.' I look up at Sharon Mason, who's now blowing her nose. 'Mrs Mason, if I give you my mobile number can you send this to me?'

She waves her hands helplessly. 'Oh, I'm hopeless with those things. Leo can do it.'

I glance at him and he nods. His fringe is a bit too long, but he doesn't seem to mind it in his eyes. They're dark, his eyes. Like his hair.

'Thanks, Leo. You must be good with phones for someone your age. How old are you?'

He blushes, just a little. 'Ten.'

I turn to Barry Mason. 'Did Daisy have her own computer?'

'No way. The things you hear about with kids online these days. I let her use my PC sometimes as long as I'm in the room with her.'

'So no email?'

'No.'

'What about a mobile?'

This time it's Sharon who answers. 'We thought she was too young. I said she could have one for Christmas. She'll be nine by then.'

So that's one less chance of tracking her down. But this I do not say. 'Did you see anyone with Daisy last night, Leo?'

He starts, then shakes his head.

'Or before that – was there anyone hanging around? Anyone you saw going to or from school?'

'I drive them to school,' says Sharon sharply. As if that settles it.

And then the doorbell rings. Gislingham flips his notebook shut. 'That'll be SOCO. Or whatever we're supposed to call them now.'

Sharon looks at her husband, bewildered. 'He means forensics,' says Barry.

Sharon turns to me. 'What are they here for? We haven't done anything.'

'I know that, Mrs Mason. Please don't be alarmed. It's standard procedure in a – when a child goes missing.'

Gislingham opens the front door and lets them in. I recognize Alan Challow straight away. He started on the job a few months after I did. Hasn't aged that well. Too little on top, too much round the waist. But he's good. He's good.

He nods to me. We don't need the pleasantries. 'Holroyd's just getting the kit from the car,' he says briskly. His paper suit is creaking. It's going to be hell in that thing when the sun comes up.

'We'll go upstairs first,' he says, pulling on his gloves. 'Then start outside as soon as it's light. No press yet, I see. Praise be for small mercies.'

Sharon Mason has got unsteadily to her feet. 'I don't want you poking about in her room – touching her things – treating us like criminals –'

'It's not a full forensic search, Mrs Mason – we won't be making any mess. We don't even need to go into her room. We just need to take her toothbrush.'

Because it's the best source for DNA. Because we might need that to match to her body. But this, again, I do not say.

'We will be making a more extensive search in the garden, in case her abductor has left any physical evidence that might help us identify him. I trust we have your agreement to do that?'

Barry Mason nods, then reaches up and touches his wife's elbow. 'Best we just let them do their job, eh?'

'And we'll be arranging for a Family Liaison Officer to attend as soon as possible.'

Sharon turns to me. 'What do you mean, *attend*?'

'They'll be here to make sure you're kept informed as soon as we get any news, and to be on hand in case you need anything.'

Sharon frowns. 'What here? In the *house*?'

'Yes, if that's OK with you. They're fully trained – there's nothing to worry about, they won't be at all intrusive –'

But she's already shaking her head. 'No. I don't want anyone here. I don't want you people spying on us. Is that clear?'

I glance at Gislingham, who gives a minute shrug.

I take a deep breath. 'That is, of course, your right. We will designate a member of our team to be your point of contact, and if you change your mind –'

'No,' she says quickly. 'We won't.'

* * *

Oxford's News @OxfordNewsOnline   02.45
BREAKING Reports coming in of considerable
police presence on the Canal Manor development –
no further details as yet . . .

Julie Hill @JulieHillinOxford   02.49
@OxfordNewsOnline I live on Canal Manor – there
was a party last night and the police are here
now questioning the neighbours

Julie Hill @JulieHillinOxford   02.49
@OxfordNewsOnline No one seems to know what's
happening – there are about 15 police cars

Angela Betterton @AngelaGBetterton   02.52
@JulieHillinOxford @OxfordNewsOnline I was at the
party – it's their daughter – apparently she's gone
missing – she's in my son's class

Julie Hill @JulieHillinOxford   02.53
@AngelaGBetterton Oh that's awful, I thought it
must be drugs or something @OxfordNewsOnline

Oxford's News @OxfordNewsOnline   02.54
@AngelaGBetterton What's the little girl's name and age?

Angela Betterton @AngelaGBetterton 02.55
@OxfordNewsOnline Daisy Mason. Must be 8 or 9?

Oxford's News @OxfordNewsOnline 02.58
BREAKING Reports coming in of possible child
#abduction in the Canal Manor development.
Sources say an 8-yr-old girl is missing from her home

Oxford's News @OxfordNewsOnline 03.01
If you hear more on the Oxford #abduction tweet us
here – bringing you Oxford local news and more
throughout the night

* * *

Just after three the media team ring me to say the news is out, and we may as well make the best of it. Twenty minutes later the first outside broadcast van arrives. I'm in the kitchen; the family are still in the sitting room. Barry Mason is lying back on an armchair, his eyes shut, though he's not sleeping. When we hear the sound of a vehicle drawing up he doesn't move, but Sharon Mason rises from the sofa and looks out of the window. She sees the reporter get out, and then a man in a leather jacket with a mike and camera. She stares a moment then glances in the mirror and reaches a hand to touch her hair.

'DI Fawley?'

It's one of Challow's team, halfway down the stairs. A girl, but I think she must be new because I don't recognize her voice. I can't see her face either, what with the hood and the mask. Contrary to what they'd have you believe on telly, forensic fashion is far more chicken-packer than TV CSI. They drive me crazy, those sodding shows – the last thing a real forensics officer would ever do is contaminate a crime scene by flicking their bloody hair extensions about. The girl beckons to me, and I follow her up to the landing. The door in front of us has a neat plaque announcing

✿ ✿ ✿ **Daisy's Room** ✿ ✿ ✿

and a piece of paper stuck to it with Blu-Tack saying

KEEP OUT!!

in large untidy capitals.

'We've got what we need,' she says. 'But I thought you would want to see the room. Even if we don't go in.'

When she pushes open the door I understand what she means. No kid's room ever looked like this outside of a sitcom. Nothing on the floor, nothing on the surfaces, nothing shoved under the bed. Comb precisely parallel with the brush. Soft toys sat in a line, staring at us with their small beady eyes. The effect is more than a little disconcerting. Not least because the boisterous, bubbly child I saw on the video footage simply doesn't fit with a room as preternaturally neat as this. Some empty rooms echo with the people who once inhabited them. But this is the emptiness of absence, not presence. The only sign she was ever here is the Disney poster on the far wall. The princess from *Brave*, alone in the forest with her defiant bright red hair, and across the bottom in big orange letters CHANGE YOUR FATE. Jake loved that film too – we took him twice. It was a good message for kids – that it's OK to be yourself; you just need the courage to be who you really are.

'Horrible, isn't it?' says the girl beside me, breaking into my thoughts.

At least she has the tact to keep her voice down.

'You think so?'

She's taken her mask off now and I can see her wrinkle her nose. 'Talk about over the top. I mean, absolutely *everything* matching like that? No one likes their name *that* much, believe me.'

And now she mentions it, I see it. It's all daisies. The whole bloody lot. Wallpaper, bedspread, curtains, cushions. All different, but all daisies. There are plastic daisies in a green pot, and a bright yellow daisy headband hanging on the dressing-table mirror. Glittery daisy hairslides, a daisy lampshade and a daisy mobile hanging from the ceiling. It's not so much a bedroom as a theme park.

'Perhaps she liked it that way?' But even as I'm saying it I'm not buying it.

The girl shrugs. 'Maybe. What do I know – I don't have kids. Do you?'

She doesn't know. No one's told her.

17

'No,' I say.

Not any more.

* * *

BBC Midlands Today

Wednesday 20 July 2016 | Last updated at 06:41

Police appeal for help in search for missing Oxford girl, 8

An 8-year-old girl has gone missing from her home in Oxford. Daisy Mason was last seen at midnight on Tuesday in the garden of her family home, where her parents Barry and Sharon Mason were holding a party.

Daisy is described as blonde with green eyes, and was wearing a flower fancy dress with her hair in bunches. Neighbours say she is outgoing but sensible, and is unlikely to have gone willingly with a stranger.

Police say that anyone who sees Daisy or has any information about her should contact the Thames Valley CID incident room on 01865 0966552.

* * *

By half seven the forensics team have nearly finished in the garden, and uniform have started another search of the area in and round the close, every movement watched, now, by a bank of hungry TV cameras. There's the canal as well, but I'm not even going to think about that. Not yet. Everyone is going to assume this girl is still alive. Until I say so.

I stand on the tiny patio looking down the back garden. There are scraps of burnt-out firework littered across the flower beds, and the dried-up summer turf has been trodden to scrub. That uniform was right: chances of a decent footprint, or anything else remotely useful, practically zero. I can see Challow down by the back fence, bent double, picking his way along the undergrowth. Above his head, a balloon is caught in the bushes on the towpath, its silver streamer rippling gently in the early air. As for me, I'm desperate for a fag.

The canal curves slightly here, which means the Masons' garden is a little longer than most of those in the close, but it would still be pokey for that many people. I can't decide if it's the swing in the corner, or the crappy pampas grass, or just the lack of sleep, but it's unnervingly like the garden we had when I was growing up. Boxed in with all the other identically dreary houses in a dismal ribbon development that owed its entire existence to the Underground – a stop on the final stretch, thrown down randomly in what had once been meadows, but were long since concrete by the time we lived there. My parents chose it because it was safe, and because it was all they could afford, and even now I can't argue with them on either score. But it was horrible, all the same. Not a place of its own at all, just 'south' of the only thing resembling a real town for miles around. The same town I went to myself – to school, to my mates' houses, and later, to pubs and to meet up with girls. I never brought a single friend home; I never let them see where I really lived. Perhaps I shouldn't be so hard on these Canal Manor people: I know what it's like to feel you're on the wrong side of the glass.

At the bottom of the Masons' garden the barbecue is still smouldering, the metal giving tiny clicks as it cools. The chains of the swing are bound together tightly with duct tape, so it can't be used. There's a stack of garden chairs, a gazebo (folded) and a trestle table with a gingham cloth (also folded). Underneath, there are green cool boxes labelled BEER, WINE, SOFT DRINKS. There are two wheelie bins on the patio behind me, the one for recycling gaping with cans and bottles, the other stacked with black bags. It occurs to me – as it should have done straight away – that Sharon Mason has done all this. The tidying, the folding up. She went round this garden making it presentable. And she did it after she knew her daughter was gone.

Gislingham joins me from the kitchen. 'DC Everett says nothing useful from the house-to-house so far. No one we've spoken to who was at the party remembers seeing anything suspicious. We're collecting their camera photos though – should help with the timeline. There's no CCTV on the estate but we'll see what we can find in the surrounding area. And we're checking the whereabouts of known sex offenders within a ten-mile radius.'

I nod. 'Good work.'

Challow straightens up and waves us towards him. Behind the swing, a fence panel is loose. It looks solid from a distance, but push it hard enough and even an adult could squeeze through.

Gislingham reads my thoughts. 'But could someone really get in, take the kid and get out without anyone noticing? In a garden this size, with that many people about? And the kid presumably struggling?'

I look around. 'We need to find out where the gazebo was and how big it is. If they put it across the bottom of the garden, it's possible no one would've been able to see that hole in the fence, or anyone going through it. Add to that the fireworks –'

He nods. 'Everyone looking the other way, lots of bangs, kids screaming –'

'– plus the fact that most of the people here were parents from the school. Bet you any money the Masons had never met some of them before. Especially the fathers. You'd need balls of steel, but you could walk in here and pretend to be one of them and you might just get away with it. And people would actually *expect* you to be talking to the kids.'

We start up the lawn towards the house. 'Those

photos you're collecting, Chris – it's not just a timeline we want from them. Start ticking off their names. We don't just need to know where people were, but *who they are.*'

* * *

At 7.05, out in the close, DC Everett is ringing at another door. Waiting for it to open, waiting to fix her professional smile and to ask if she can come in and speak to them for a moment. It's the fifteenth time she's done it now and she's telling herself not to be irritated that she got lumbered with the house-to-house, while Gislingham gets to be inside the only house that matters. At the heart of things. After all, you can count on the fingers of one hand the times a child abduction turned on What the Neighbours Saw. But to be fair, some of these people were actually in the Masons' garden when their daughter went missing. Though considering how many potential witnesses were in that small space, Everett's had little of any real use thus far. It was 'a nice party', 'a pleasant-enough evening'. And yet at some point in the middle of it a little girl disappeared and nobody even noticed.

She rings again (the third time) and then steps back and looks up at the house. The curtains are pulled back but there are no signs of life. She checks her list. Kenneth and Caroline Bradshaw, a couple in their sixties.

They could easily be on holiday before the schools break up. She makes a note next to their name and goes back down the drive to the pavement. One of the uniforms comes up to her, slightly out of breath. Everett's seen her about at the station, but she's only just out of training at Sulhamstead and they've never actually spoken. Everett's trying to remember her name – Simpson? Something like that. No – Somer. That's it. Erica Somer. She's older than most new recruits, so she must have done something else first. Rather like Everett, who has a false start in nursing to her name. But she keeps that one quiet, knowing that all it would do is give her male colleagues one more excuse to make her the one to break bad news. Or knock on bloody doors.

'There's something in one of the bins – I think you should see,' Somer says, gesturing back from where she came. She's straight to the point, no nonsense. Everett warms to her at once.

The bin in question is on the corner where the close turns in from the side road. A forensics officer is already there, taking pictures. When he sees Everett he nods, and the two women watch while he reaches into the bin and pulls out what's lying on the top. It unpleats like a snakeskin. Flaccid, empty, green. Very green.

It's a pair of tights, ripped at one knee. And small enough for a child.

*   *   *

Interview with Fiona Webster, conducted at
11 Barge Close, Oxford
20 July 2016, 7.45 a.m.
In attendance, DC V. Everett

VE: Can you tell us how you know the Masons, Mrs Webster?

FW: My daughter Megan is in the same class as Daisy at Kit's, and Alice is the year above.

VE: Kit's?

FW: Sorry – Bishop Christopher's. Everyone round here just calls it Kit's. And we're neighbours, of course. We lent them the gazebo for the party.

VE: So you're friends?

FW: I wouldn't say 'friends' exactly. Sharon keeps herself to herself. We talk at the school gate, like you do, and sometimes I go jogging with her. But she's far more disciplined about it than I am. She goes every morning, even in the winter, after she drops off the kids at school. She's worried about her weight – I mean she hasn't actually said so, but I can tell. We had lunch once in town – more by accident than anything – we bumped into each other outside that pizza place on the High Street and she couldn't really say no. But she ate next to nothing – just picked at a salad –

VE: So she doesn't work, then, if she runs in the mornings?

FW: No. I think she did once, but I don't know what. It'd drive me mad, being stuck indoors all day, but she seems totally absorbed in the kids.

VE: So she's a good mum?

FW: I remember all she talked about at that lunch was what great marks Daisy had got for some test or other, and how she wants to be a vet, and did I know which university would be best for that.

VE: So a bit of a pushy parent?

FW: Between you and me, Owen – my husband – can't stand her. You know that phrase about sharp elbows? He says she has *scythes*. But personally I don't think you can blame anyone for wanting the best for their kids. Sharon's just a bit more obvious about it than most of us. In fact I think the Masons came here in the first place for the schools. I don't think they can afford to go private.

VE: These houses aren't exactly cheap . . .

FW: No, but I just get the feeling things are a bit tight.

VE: Do you know where they lived before?

FW: Somewhere in South London, I think. Sharon never talks much about the past. Or her family. To be honest I'm a bit confused why you want to know all this – aren't you supposed to be out there looking for Daisy?

VE: We have teams of officers searching the area and checking local CCTV. But the more we know about Daisy, and the family, the better. You never know what might prove to be significant. But let's talk more about last night. What time did you arrive?

FW: Just after seven. We were one of the first. The invite said 6.30 for 7, and I think Sharon had actually expected people to come at half past. She was really on edge when we got there. I think she might have been worried no one would turn up. She'd gone to huge trouble about it all – I told her, everyone would have been happy to pitch in and bring stuff, but she wanted to do everything herself. It was all laid out on the tables in the garden, under cling film – that stuff is so horrible, don't you think, I mean –

VE: You said she was on edge?

FW: Well, yes, but only about the party. She was fine later, once it got going.

VE: And Barry?

FW: Oh, Baz was the life and soul, as usual. He's always very sociable – always finds something to say. I'm sure the party was his

idea. And he dotes on Daisy - the usual
dads and daughters thing. He's always
picking her up and carrying her about on
his shoulders. She did look very sweet in
that flower get-up. It's sad when they grow
out of the dressing-up phase - I wanted
Alice to wear fancy dress last night but
she point-blank refused. She's only a year
above Daisy but now it's all crop tops and
trainers.

VE: You must know Barry Mason pretty well?

FW: I'm sorry?

VE: You called him 'Baz'.

FW: [*laughs*] Oh Lord, did I say that? I know
it's awful, but that's what we call them,
well some of us. 'Baz 'n' Shaz'. Short for
Barry and Sharon, you know? But for God's
sake don't tell Sharon I called her that -
she absolutely hates it - blew her top once
when someone let it slip out by mistake.

VE: But Barry doesn't mind?

FW: Seems not to. But he's pretty easy-going.
More so than her. Not that that's difficult.

VE: So when did you last see her - Daisy?

FW: I've been racking my brains about that.
I think it was just before the fireworks.
There were lots of little girls running
about all night. They were having a whale
of a time.

VE: And you didn't see anyone talking to her –
    or anyone you didn't recognize?

FW: There weren't many people there I didn't
    know. I think they were all from the
    estate. At least, I don't remember anyone
    from the other side.

VE: The other side?

FW: You know. Over the canal. The posh lot. You
    don't get them slumming it over here very
    much. But in any case, as far as I remember
    Daisy spent the whole time with her friends.
    Adults are pretty dull when you're that age.

VE: And your husband – Owen? Was he there?

FW: Why do you want to know that?

VE: We just need to know where everyone was –

FW: Are you suggesting *Owen* had something to do
    with it, because I can tell you right now –

VE: Like I said, we just need to know who
    everyone was at the party.
    [*pause*]
    It's possible we may have found the tights
    Daisy was wearing. Do you remember if she
    still had them on when you last saw her?

FW: I'm sorry, I really can't remember.

VE: And she didn't fall over or hurt herself at
    the party, as far as you saw?

FW: No, I'm sure I'd have remembered that. But
    why do you ask that – what difference does
    it make?

* * *

At 8.30 I'm in the car, parked round the corner in Waterview Crescent, which is definitely one notch up on the property pecking order – three-storey town-houses, and even, would you believe, a couple of stone lions on plinths at the entrance. I'm eating a pasty someone has brought over from the petrol station on the main road. I can feel my arteries clog just looking at it. But there's a press conference scheduled for ten, and if I don't eat anything I'm going to be light-headed. And while I'm at it, the car is a Ford. In case you're wondering. And I don't do bloody crosswords either.

There's a tap on the driver's window and I wind it down. It's DC Everett. Verity, her name is – I told her once, with a name like that she was destined for this job. And she won't give up looking for it either – the truth, I mean. Don't let that stolid appearance fool you – she's one of the most ruthless officers I've ever had.

'What is it? What did Fiona Webster have to say?'

'Plenty, but this isn't about that. The old dear at number thirty-six. She saw something. A couple of minutes after eleven, she says. She's sure because she was about to phone the council nuisance line about the noise.'

I remember what Sharon Mason said about people

reporting you. Perhaps I misjudged her – you're not paranoid if your neighbours really are shits.

'So what did this Mrs –'

'Bampton.'

'What did Mrs Bampton say?'

'She says she saw a man walking away from the Masons' house with a child in his arms. A girl, and she was crying. In fact more like screaming, the old lady says. That's why she went to the window in the first place.'

I'm shaking my head. 'It was a party. How do we know it wasn't perfectly innocent – that it wasn't one of the fathers on his way home?'

If I'm pushing back it's not because I doubt what she's saying, it's because I really don't want this to be true. But her cheeks are pink – she's on to something. 'Mrs Bampton says she couldn't see the man's face at that distance, so she can't give us a description.'

'So how does she know it was a girl he had with him?'

'Because she was wearing fancy dress. She was wearing a *flower outfit.*'

* * *

Thames Valley Police @ThamesValleyPolice   09.00
Can you help find Daisy Mason, 8? Last seen on
the Canal Manor estate #Oxford Tuesday midnight.
Any info call on 01865 0966552
RETWEETS 829

BBC Midlands @BBCMidlandsBreaking   09.09
There will be a police press conference at 10 a.m.
this morning about the disappearance of 8-yr-old
Daisy Mason
RETWEETS 1,566

ITV News @ITVLiveandBreaking   09.11
BREAKING: Oxford police to detail the search to
find 8yo #DaisyMason at 10 a.m. Will give details
of sighting of possible suspect
RETWEETS 5,889

*   *   *

For the first fifteen minutes, the press conference was
pretty uneventful. The usual questions, the usual
non-answers. 'Early stage of the investigation' – 'Doing
everything possible' – 'Anyone with information'. You
know the drill. The audience was edgy – knowing this
could be big, but lacking an angle and going in circles.
The possible sighting had provoked a momentary
flurry, but without either a photo or a description it
wasn't adding up to much. One of the usual suspects
tried to elbow herself into the limelight with a pretty
crass attempt to make it personal ('DI Fawley, are you
really the appropriate officer to lead a child abduction
investigation?'), but everyone else steered clear. I was
checking my watch – they'd just about had their allot-
ted quarter of an hour – when someone at the back got

up. Looked about seventeen. Sandy hair, pasty skin rapidly going very red as everyone turned to look at him. Not from one of the nationals, I knew that. Probably some intern for the local not-much-more-than-ad-sheet. But I underestimated him, and I should have known better.

'DI Fawley, can you confirm that you found an item of clothing near the scene that may belong to Daisy? Is that true?'

It was as if the air had been electrified. Two dozen people suddenly fizzing with attention.

I hesitated. Which is, of course, always fatal.

There were hands in the air now, the sound of furious tapping at tablet screens. Six or seven people were trying to cut in, but Pastyface was standing his ground. In both senses.

I noted, in the nanosecond it took me to reply, that he deliberately hadn't detailed exactly what we'd found. But it's not because he doesn't know. It's because he wants to keep that bit of the scoop to himself.

I took a deep breath. 'Yes, that is true.'

'And this – *item* – was covered in blood?'

I opened my mouth to reply, to set him straight, but it was too late. The room was in uproar.

* * *

At 10.15 DC Andrew Baxter sets up a flip chart at the front of the church hall on the Banbury Road that's been commandeered for the search teams, and props up a large-size map of North Oxford. The immediate area has been covered, and with the number of locals turning up and phoning in, asking if they can help, the next phase needs proper organization.

'Right,' he says, raising his voice above the din. They can hear the police helicopter over their heads. 'Listen up. We need to be clear who's doing what so we don't end up chasing our tails or falling arse over tit. Feel free to choose your own cliché if those don't hit the spot.'

He picks up a red marker pen. 'We've divided the next search areas into three zones. Each team will have at least a dozen police officers, and a trained Search Adviser whose responsibility will be to collate evidence and make sure an overenthusiastic Joe Public isn't doing more harm than good.'

He takes the pen and draws a line round a section of the map. 'Team one, under Sergeant Ed Mead, will take the Griffin School, all hundred bloody acres of it. Most of it's open space, thankfully, but there's still quite a number of copses and wooded areas, and the undergrowth along the east side of the canal. The school's whipped in a bunch of sturdy sixth-formers to pitch in — the head of PE used to be in the army so I'm sure he knows the drill. No pun intended. Team two, under Sergeant Philip Mann, will take the towpath alongside Canal Manor and the nature reserve to the west of the canal. Volunteers from the local wildlife trust will meet you there – apparently some birds are still nesting so they'll be on hand to ensure we don't do any unnecessary damage. There are also residential narrowboats along that stretch, and we need to question the owners.'

He draws more lines on the map. 'Third team, under Sergeant Ben Roberts, will take the recreation ground, the car park by the level crossing and the college sports grounds off the Woodstock Road. Plenty of locals happy to help there too.'

He snaps the top back on the pen. 'Any questions? Right. Keep in touch by phone, and we'll convene another meeting if the search needs to be widened or if the helicopter turns up something. But let's hope that won't be necessary.'

* * *

I'm halfway out of the press room when my phone rings. It's Alex. I stare at it, wondering whether picking up is a good idea. I have one of those bland factory-decided pictures on the screen. Trees and grass and sky. I didn't choose it – I didn't really care what it was, I just had to get rid of what I used to have. That picture of Jake on Alex's shoulders I took last summer, the sun behind them making his dark hair glow red. I'd just told him he was getting a bit too big for piggyback and he was grinning at me and doing it anyway. The picture always made me think of a poem we read once at school, 'Surprised by Joy'. That's what Jake looked like in the picture, surprised by joy. As if his own happiness has taken him unawares.

I pick up the call.

'Hello, Adam? Where are you?'

'I'm at the station, a press conference. Something came up – I didn't want to wake you –'

'I know – I heard – it was on the news. They said there's a child missing.'

I take a deep breath. I knew we'd face something like this sooner or later; it was just a matter of time. But knowing something will happen doesn't always make it easier when it does.

'It's a little girl,' I say. 'Her name is Daisy.'

I can almost hear her heartbeat. 'The poor parents. How are they holding up?'

It should be a straightforward question, but I don't have a straightforward answer. And that, more than anything else so far, brings home to me how puzzling the Masons are.

'It's hard to tell,' I say, opting for flat honesty. 'I think they're more in shock than anything. But it's early days. There's no evidence of harm. Nothing to say we won't find her safe and well.'

She says nothing for a moment. Then, 'I sometimes wonder if that's worse.'

I turn away and lower my voice. 'Worse? What do you mean?'

'Hope. Whether that's worse. Worse than knowing. At least we . . .'

Her voice dies.

She's never talked like this before. *We've* never talked like this. They wanted us to – they told us we had to. But we just kept putting it off. Off and off and off until we couldn't talk about it at all. Until now. Of all times. She's crying now, but quietly, because she doesn't want me to hear. I can't decide if it's out of pride or because she doesn't want me to worry. I glance up and one of the DCs is beckoning to me.

'Sorry, Alex, I have to go.'

'I know, I'm sorry.'

'No, *I'm* sorry. I'll call you later. I promise.'

* * *

19 July 2016, 3.30 p.m.
The day of the disappearance
Bishop Christopher's Primary School, Oxford

The bell is ringing for home time and children are streaming noisily out of their classrooms into the sunshine and the overheated cars their parents have waiting at the gate. Some run, some skip, one or two straggle, and some of the older kids gather in groups, talking and sharing things on their iPhones. Two of the teachers stand on the steps watching them go.

'Nearly the end of term, thank God,' says the older of the two as she scoops up a trailing sweatshirt and restores it to its owner. 'I can hardly wait – this one seems to have been more than usually exhausting.'

The woman next to her smiles ruefully. 'Tell me about it.' Some of her own class are filing past now, and one of the girls stops to say goodbye. She's a little tearful, because her family are going on holiday the following day and her teacher won't be coming back next term. She likes her teacher.

'Have a nice time in South Africa, Millie,' says the woman kindly, touching her lightly on the shoulder. 'I hope you get to see the baby lions.'

Millie's classmates catch her up and follow her out. A couple of boys, a tall girl with plaits and one who looks Chinese. And last, in a wild rush, a blonde girl with a pale pink cardigan tied round her shoulders, carrying a Disney Princess bag.

'Slow down, Daisy,' calls the teacher as she hurtles down the steps. 'You don't want to fall over and hurt yourself.'

'She's in high spirits today,' observes the older woman as they watch the girl run to join the two girls ahead.

'The family are having a barbecue tonight. I expect she's just a bit overexcited.'

The older woman makes a face. 'I wish I was still young enough to get excited about soggy lettuce and over-cooked burgers.'

Her colleague laughs. 'They're having fireworks too. You're never too old for those.'

'OK, you have me there. I'm still a sucker for the pyrotechnics. Even at my age.'

The two women exchange a smile, then the younger one turns and goes back into the school while the other lingers for a few minutes watching the playground. In the weeks to come this moment will come to haunt her; the little blonde girl, standing in the sunlight at the school gate, talking happily to one of her friends.

* * *

'So who the fuck's been talking to the press?'

10.35. The incident room is hot. The windows are open and someone's dug an ancient electric fan out of some storeroom or other. It hums as it moves, slowly, left to right, right to left. Some people are perched on desks, others leaning against them. I look at them, slowly, left to right, right to left. Most of them have no problem meeting my eye. One or two look embarrassed. But that's it. If ten years of interrogation have taught me anything, it's when at a wall, stop pushing.

'I gave strict instructions not to make any reference in public either to the tights or what we found on them. And now the family have to hear about it on the bloody news. How do you think that's going to make them feel? The information came from someone in this room and I fully intend to find out who it was. But I'm not going to waste valuable time doing that now. Not with Daisy Mason still missing.'

I turn back to the whiteboard. There's a map with coloured pins stuck in it, and a clutch of blurry photos, obviously culled from phones, pinned along a rudimentary timeline. Most of the pictures have names attached; one or two have question marks. And next to them, Daisy herself. It strikes me for the first time, looking at the shots, how like her mother she is. How like and yet how unlike. And then I wonder why I'm so convinced of that, since I've never even met her.

'Where are we with this supposed sighting?'

Someone behind me clears their throat. 'We've got CCTV from every camera within two miles.'

The voice is Gareth Quinn's. You know the look. Sharp suit and blunt razor. Acting DS, while Jill Murphy's on maternity leave, and determined to make every minute of it count. I find him irritating, personally, but he's not stupid and that look of his is useful when you need someone who doesn't look too much like a copper. It won't surprise you to learn he gets called 'GQ' by the station wags, a name he affects – a little too theatrically – to despise. I hear him come up behind me.

'The canal is to the east of the estate here,' he says, 'so you have to go over one of these two bridges to get out, and neither have cameras. But there *is* a camera on the Woodstock Road going north here,' pointing at a red pin, 'and one here on the ring-road roundabout. If he wanted to get away quickly, he'd have gone that way, rather than south through the city.'

I look at the map, at the expanse of open land stretching to the west: three hundred acres uncultivated for a thousand years, and even in this weather, half underwater. It's no more than five minutes from the Canal Manor estate, but you'd have to cross the railway line to get there.

'What about Port Meadow – are there any cameras on the level crossing? I don't remember ever seeing any.'

Quinn shakes his head. 'No, and in any case the crossing's been closed for the last two months while they build a new footbridge and re-lay part of the line. The work's being done after hours, and there was a whole crew there last night. The old footbridge has been closed off prior to demolition, so no one could have got across to Port Meadow that way.'

'So if that's a non-starter, what are the other options?'

Quinn points at a green pin. 'Given we found the tights here, the suspect's most likely route would seem to be Birch Drive and then up to the ring road, like I said. It also tallies with where that old biddy says she saw Daisy.'

He steps back and tucks his pen behind his ear. It's a tic of his, and I spot a couple of the lads at the back do the same – they're taking the piss, but there's no malice in it. He's one of them, but he's also a DS now, at least for the time being, and that makes him fair game. 'We've been through the footage on all the cameras on that route,' he continues, 'but we can't find sod all.

There wasn't much traffic at that time of night, and the drivers we've spoken to so far have all checked out. There's one or two we haven't managed to track down yet, but none of them are men alone in cars. And there's definitely no one on foot with a small child or carrying anything that could remotely be a small child. Which means one of two things: either that old buzzard on the close didn't see what she thought she saw –'

'– or Daisy is still on the Canal Manor estate.'

I can't be the only one who thinks, in that moment, of Shannon Matthews, hidden by her mother to scam money from sympathy, while the police moved heaven and earth to find a girl who was never missing in the first place. And didn't one of the neighbours say the Masons were short of cash? But that's as long as the thought lasts. Not just because the Masons aren't that stupid, but because, even if they are, the timing just doesn't add up.

I take a deep breath. 'OK, let's step up the search along the towpath and anywhere else on the estate a body could have been hidden. But *discreetly*, please. As far as the press is concerned, this is still a missing person, not a murder. OK, that's it for now. Reconvene at six unless there's a new development.'

* * *

'I think we've found who it was, sir.'

It's 3.00 p.m., and I'm in my office, on the point of

leaving for the estate, and fresh – if that's the word – from a royal bollocking from the Superintendent about what happened at the press conference. The person at the door is Anna Phillips, on secondment from the software start-up on the business park, who are ticking the box on local community involvement by helping to pitchfork us flat-footed plods into the twenty-first century. She, by contrast, wears very high heels. And a very short skirt. She's a great hit in the station, which will come as no surprise at all. Alex had her hair cropped like hers when we first met – it made her look mischievous. Playful. All the things she's lost, these last few months. I've done a double-take a couple of times since Anna arrived, but then I see her smile and know I'm mistaken. I can't remember the last time I saw my wife smile.

'Sorry – I'm not with you. Who what was?'

If I'm a bit sharp it's because I still have words like 'incompetence' and 'consequences' reddening my ears. And because I can't find my car keys. But she seems unfazed.

'The leak. Gareth – DS Quinn – asked me to see if I could find out where it came from.'

I look up. So it's 'Gareth', is it? She's gone slightly red, and I wonder if he's told her he's got a girlfriend. It wouldn't be the first time he'd developed convenient amnesia on that one.

'And?'

She comes round to my side of the desk and logs on

to the web. Then she types in an address and steps back, allowing me to see. It's a Facebook page. The most recent post is the still from the video of Daisy we released to the press. That doesn't bother me – the more people who share that the better. But what does bother me is everything else. Shots of uniforms on doorsteps. Several of Challow's team going into the Mason house. One of me, snatching a fag, which isn't going to go down that well with the Super either. Judging by the angles, the pictures have all been taken from inside one of the houses on the close. And when Anna scrolls down there's a post logged seven hours ago saying that the police have found a pair of bloodstained green tights, which they think are the ones Daisy was wearing when she disappeared.

'The page belongs to Toby Webster,' she says, answering before I ask.

'Who?'

'Fiona Webster's son. The neighbour DC Everett interviewed this morning. I think she asked her about the tights. That must be where he got it from. He's fifteen.'

As if that explains it. Which I suppose, at one level, it does.

'It wouldn't have taken much for that reporter to find this,' she continues. 'In fact, I'm surprised more of them didn't.'

Which is code for 'I think you owe your team an apology'. Which I clearly do.

'And there's something else –'

The phone rings again and I pick it up. It's Challow.

'You wanted a rush done on those tights?'

'And?'

'It's not hers. The blood. No match to the DNA on the toothbrush.'

'You're sure – it can't possibly be Daisy Mason's?'

'DNA doesn't lie. But you know that.'

'Fuck.'

But he's already put the phone down. Anna is staring at me, an odd look on her face. If she's that exercised by swearing she's not going to last long here.

'I've been looking at the photos again,' she begins. 'The ones at the party.'

'Sorry, I have to go. I'm already late.'

'No, wait – it'll only take a minute.'

She bends again to the PC and opens up the file of images from the shared server. She selects three of the pictures, then opens a still of Daisy from the video and lines it up carefully next to the others.

'It took me a while to spot it, but once you do, it's really obvious.'

Obvious to her, perhaps, but not to me. She's looking at me expectantly but I just shrug.

She picks up a pen and points. 'These three on the right are the only ones of the party that have Daisy in them. At least all we have so far. But none of them are very clear – she's either got her back to us or she's partially hidden behind someone else. But there's one thing we definitely can see.'

'Which is?'

She points at the video still from three days before. 'Look at how long the dress is here – definitely well above her knee. And then look at the other three pictures.'

And now I see. I see very clearly. The girl wearing the dress at the party must be at least two or three inches shorter than Daisy Mason. It's not Daisy at all.

It's *another child*.

* * *

Oxford's News @OxfordNewsOnline   15.18
Canal Manor #abduction update – sources say police have found bloodstained garments. Anyone with info shd contact @ThamesValleyPolice #FindDaisy

Elspeth Morgan @ElspethMorgan959   15.22
That poor family. I can't imagine what they're going through #FindDaisy

BBC Midlands @BBCMidlandsBreaking   15.45
#MidlandsToday at six will have the latest on the disappearance of #DaisyMason. @ThamesValleyPolice earlier released a photo of her

William Kidd @ThatBillytheKidd   15.46
If you know where Daisy Mason is pls call the police #FindDaisy #DaisyMason

Anne Merrivale @Annie_Merrivale_ 15.56
Am I the only one who thinks there's something
odd about this #DaisyMason thing? How can a child
disappear from her own garden + nobody see?

Caroline Tollis @ForWhomtheTollis 16.05
@Annie_Merrivale_ I agree – I said to my OH the
moment we heard – there's more to that than
meets the eye #DaisyMason

Danny Chadwick @ChadwickDanielPJ 16.07
What parents let their kid stay up 2 gone midnight?
They obvs weren't keeping proper tabs on her – only
got themselves to blame #DaisyMason

Angus Cordery @AngusNCorderyEsq 16.09
@Annie_Merrivale_ @ForWhomtheTollis
@ChadwickDanielPJ You mark my words – it'll be
one of the parents. Always is #DaisyMason

Anne Merrivale @Annie_Merrivale_ 16.10
@AngusNCorderyEsq It is odd that neither of them
have appeared in public yet @ForWhomtheTollis
@ChadwickDanielPJ #DaisyMason

Elsie Barton @ElsieBarton_1933 16.13
@AngusNCorderyEsq @Annie_Merrivale_
@ForWhomtheTollis @ChadwickDanielPJ God I'd
hate to have your suspicious minds #FindDaisy

Anne Merrivale @Annie_Merrivale_   16.26
@ElsieBarton_1933 You have to admit the whole
things sounds very odd #DaisyMason

Elsie Barton @ElsieBarton_1933   16.29
@Annie_Merrivale_ All I know is a little girl's missing
and we should focus on finding her not making
accusations about her parents #FindDaisy

Angela Betterton @AngelaGBetterton   16.31
@AngusNCorderyEsq @ChadwickDanielPJ
@Annie_Merrivale_ @ForWhomtheTollis You don't
know what you're talking about – you don't even
know the family #FindDaisy

Danny Chadwick @ChadwickDanielPJ   16.33
@AngelaGBetterton I know I'd keep a bloody
sight better watch on my own kid. And what makes
you such an expert anyway? #DaisyMason

Angela Betterton @AngelaGBetterton   16.35
@AngusNCorderyEsq I was at the party – both
parents were there all night – there's no way either
of them was involved #FindDaisy

Caroline Tollis @ForWhomtheTollis   16.36
@AngelaGBetterton Is there any news on the
bloodstained tights – have the police confirmed
that? #DaisyMason

Anne Merrivale @Annie_Merrivale_   16.37
@ForWhomtheTollis There was nothing on the
news. But it proves someone harmed her that
night, doesn't it? #DaisyMason

Caroline Tollis @ForWhomtheTollis   16.39
@Annie_Merrivale_ Poor baby, I think she's
already dead #DaisyMason

Anne Merrivale @Annie_Merrivale_   16.42
@ForWhomtheTollis I know. I think the only
mystery now is who killed her #DaisyMason

*   *   *

When I push open the door to the incident room the
air is dense with energy. Everyone turns to look at me
as I go to the whiteboard and point a finger at one of
the photos from the party.

'As you've probably heard by now, it's looking very
unlikely that the girl in this picture is Daisy Mason.'

The noise level begins to rise and I raise my voice.
'What you don't yet know is that I have just had con-
firmation from the lab that the blood on the tights was
not – repeat *not* – that of Daisy Mason. Which means it
probably came from this girl, in the picture. And if old
Mrs Bampton did indeed see a man carrying a child,
that too was almost certainly this other girl and *not*
Daisy Mason.'

It hits me then, as it sometimes does. You can't pre-pare for it, can't prevent it – you never know what random association of words or ideas will do it – but suddenly your carefully closed-down brain is awash with unwanted memory. Me carrying Jake, his sleeping head nestled against my chest, smelling the shampoo in his hair and the summer garden on his skin – the warmth, the weight of him –

I'm suddenly horribly aware of the stillness in the room. They're staring at me. Some of them, anyway. The ones I've known longest are looking anywhere but me.

'Sorry – as I was saying, I don't think we have two missing kids here – I suspect it's just a simple case of mistaken identity. Looking at the rips on the tights, the blood was probably nothing more sinister than a grazed knee. *But* we still need to find that other girl and make sure she's OK. And we need to establish how she got the flower outfit – it's possible the two kids switched costumes, so she may be able to tell us what Daisy was really wearing that night. In the meantime, Everett – can you go back through all the photos from the party with Anna Phillips and see if you can find any other blonde girls that might be Daisy.'

Gareth Quinn gets to his feet – he has his tablet in his hand and he's frantically scrolling down. 'I think I might know who the girl is, boss. I'm sure one of the cars on the CCTV was a four-by-four belonging to a family on the close. Yep, here it is – David and Julia

Connor. They have a daughter called Millie who's in Daisy's year at Kit's, and they were on the party list but apparently left early because they were driving down to Gatwick to catch a flight really early this morning – we have the family on camera heading towards the ring road at 11.39 p.m. That's why we haven't been able to talk to them yet, and to be honest it wasn't a high priority up to now. But I've left a message on David Connor's mobile to call me.'

He goes up to the map and then turns to me, pointing, his eyes eager. 'The Connor house is here – number fifty-four. They'd have had to walk right opposite Mrs Bampton's on the way back from the Masons. I think it was *David Connor* the old lady saw, carrying his daughter home.'

There's an odd sensation in the room now – I've seen it before – the breakthrough that isn't really a breakthrough because all it does is close off a possibility, rather than getting you any closer to the truth. A sense that pieces are slotting together, but you're still no closer to seeing what picture they make. But there's a piece here now that's suddenly looking very dark.

It's Gislingham who comes right out with it, Stating The Bleeding Obvious being his usual stock-in-trade. But hey, every team should have one. Especially in this job. 'So is this what we're really saying,' he says. 'That the Masons saw this other girl running about in that get-up all night and didn't twig it wasn't really their daughter?'

'The headdress thing does cover most of her face,' begins Everett. 'I mean, we didn't realize it wasn't her and we've been staring at the pictures hard enough.'

'But we're not her parents,' I say quietly. 'Believe me, I'd know my own kid even in a ski mask and a plastic sack. You just do. You know how they move – the way they walk –'

The way Jake moved, the way Jake walked. Time stutters. Just for a fraction, avoids the chasm, then moves on.

'But also how they *talk*, surely,' says Gislingham. 'If the Masons had actually spoken to that girl they'd have known at once –'

'Which means one of two things,' interrupts Quinn. 'Either they didn't speak to their own daughter at all that night, which is scarcely credible, or there's something much more worrying going on here.'

'It's not just them,' I say quietly. 'It's Leo as well. He must have known it wasn't Daisy at the party. The parents might claim they were too preoccupied, but he's a watching sort of a kid. *He knew.* So why didn't he tell them – why didn't he tell *us*? Either he's hiding something or he's frightened of something. And right this moment, I'm not sure which is worse.'

'So what do we do now, boss? Tell the Masons about Millie Connor? Bring them in for questioning?'

'No,' I say slowly. 'Let's get them to do a TV appeal for their daughter. I want to see how they handle it. All three of them – make sure the boy is there too. There's no harm doing an appeal anyway – after all, she could still be out there somewhere, and it may have nothing at all to do with the family.'

People start to shift, stand, pick up phones, but I haven't finished yet.

'And I know I don't have to say this but, I don't want *anyone* outside this room to get the slightest hint that the girl at the party wasn't Daisy. Make sure the Connors know that as well. Because it's possible we have a whole different timeline here from what we've been assuming. It's possible Daisy Mason was never at that party at all.'

* * *

Phone interview with David Connor
20 July 2016, 6.45 p.m.
On the call, Acting DS G. Quinn and (listening)
DC C. Gislingham

GQ: Thank you for phoning, Mr Connor, and our apologies for disturbing your holiday.

DC: No problem – I'm sorry I wasn't able to get back to you before. It's such a shock, hearing what's happened. My wife saw it on BBC World News in the hotel room.

GQ: Were you aware that the flower costume your daughter wore at the party was the one Daisy Mason should have been wearing?

DC: I wasn't but it seems my wife was. Millie
    had some of her friends round after school
    the afternoon before –

GQ: So Monday afternoon?

DC: Er, was it Monday? Sorry – I'm a bit jet-
    lagged. You're right, it must have been
    Monday. Anyway, Julia says they all brought
    their fancy dresses over and tried them on.
    And then tried each other's on – you know
    what girls that age are like. It seems that
    at some point in the ensuing chaos Daisy
    decided that she preferred Millie's costume,
    and Millie said they could swap.

GQ: Do you know if Daisy's mother was aware the
    costumes had been switched?

DC: I have no idea. Let me ask Julia . . .
    [*muffled noises*]
    Julia says Daisy assured her that her
    mother wouldn't mind. But obviously she
    doesn't know if Daisy actually spoke to her
    about it.

GQ: We found the tights in a bin on the estate
    but the blood on them doesn't match
    Daisy's –

DC: Ah yes, sorry about that. Millie fell over
    and as it was getting late and she was a
    bit whiny we decided to call it a day. The
    tights were a write-off so we just ditched
    them. Apologies if it caused you a problem.

GQ: What costume was your daughter originally
    going to wear, Mr Connor?

DC: A mermaid, so my wife tells me. I never saw
    it but apparently it had a flesh-coloured
    top thing and a tail with shiny blue and
    green scales.

GQ: And any sort of headdress or mask?

DC: Hang on a minute.
    [*more muffled noises*]
    No, nothing like that.

GQ: So if Daisy had been wearing that costume
    at the party it would have been obvious she
    was there?

DC: I guess so - are you suggesting -?

GQ: Merely establishing the facts, Mr Connor.
    Did you see Daisy last night?

DC: Now you come to mention it, I don't think I
    did. I mean, on the news it said she was
    there - that she went missing afterwards,
    so I just assumed - Christ, that changes
    things a bit, doesn't it?

GQ: And is there anything Millie can tell
    us - anything she might have heard or seen
    at the party?

DC: To be honest we're not getting much sense
    out of her at the moment - she's just crying
    all the time and refusing to talk about it.
    I don't really want to push it. But when she
    calms down I'll get Julia to ask her - I'll

54

```
          call you back if there's anything that
          might help.
GQ:       Thank you, Mr Connor. And may I remind you
          not to discuss this conversation with
          anyone else. That's very important.
          Particularly the press.
DC:       Of course. And please let me know if there's
          anything else we can do. We all have to
          pull together to find the bastard who did
          this, don't we?
```

* * *

18 July 2016, 4.29 p.m.
The day before the disappearance
The Connor house, 54 Barge Close

Julia Connor fills half a dozen glasses with juice and carries the tray up to her daughter's room. She can hear the noise the children are making all the way up the stairs; the neighbours can probably hear it halfway down the street. Inside, the carpet is buried in clothes and costumes.

'I hope you all know which costumes belong to who,' says Julia, putting down the tray. 'I don't want to get into trouble with your mums.'

Three of the girls are in front of the long mirror, lavishly admiring themselves. A pink princess, a flower, a butterfly.

'Who is the fairest of them all?' demands the

princess of her reflection, as her gold cardboard crown slips over one eye. 'Don't you think I look absolutely *beautiful*?'

Julia smiles to herself, wishing she'd had half that kid's confidence when she was their age. Then she closes the door and goes back down to the kitchen, where she turns the radio on and starts chopping vegetables for dinner. They're playing an old Annie Lennox track, so she turns up the volume and sings to herself. *Sisters are doing it for themselves.* It's so loud, in fact, that she doesn't notice the sudden commotion upstairs. So she never hears the wailing cries of '*I hate you! I wish you were dead!*'; she never sees the girl in the flower outfit pinned against the wall or the other child who is furiously attacking her, jabbing at the small pale face in its blank petal mask.

* * *

By six, the search team is running on empty. The towpath has been taped off to the public for over a mile north from the estate, and they've been along it, inch by inch, using poles to part the undergrowth, and collecting anything that might even conceivably be evidence in plastic bags. Sweet wrappers, beer cans, a child's shoe. Why, wonders Erica Somer, straightening her aching back and checking her watch, is there only ever *one* shoe? Do those who lose them limp home half shod? And how exactly does a shoe get lost anyway – you'd hardly fail to notice it was missing. And then she shakes her head at the pointlessness of even thinking about it, and blames it on low blood sugar.

A few yards further on, six or seven conservation volunteers in waders are making their way through ditches half filled with rotting leaves and rubbish chucked by the day boaters. After so many hot days, the water levels are low and the smell is high. They've already covered the nature reserve a hundred yards behind. Erica never even knew it was there, despite growing up less than five miles away. But hers wasn't the sort of school that went in for field trips or nature study days; the teachers had enough on their hands keeping a lid on the chaos. She had no idea there was somewhere so wild so close to the centre of the city. So wild, so overgrown, half flooded and unpathed. She saw three water rats and a family of moor hens and – suddenly – out of nowhere – a rearing, hissing beating of whiteness and wings as a male swan rose up in defence of his hidden young.

But all these hours later, what do they have to show for it? Beyond the backache and the glorified litter pick, nothing. No one saw anything – neither those living on the water, nor those backing on to it, several of whom were having barbecues in their gardens at the time the Masons were having their party. Two or three even remembered the fireworks, but none of them saw a little girl. It's as if she vanished into thin air.

At 7.25 she gets a call from Baxter.

'You can knock off. We're going to get frogmen in tomorrow morning.'

Erica frowns. 'Really? If it was my budget I wouldn't bother. The water's not that deep – not like a river – and with all the boat traffic, the water's constantly being disturbed. If she was here, we'd have found her by now.'

'Look, I'm not disagreeing – between you and me I suspect it's as much for PR as anything. The ACC wants to prove to the world we're leaving no stone unturned. Hence the bloody helicopter.'

'The press must be loving that.'

'Yeah,' says Baxter. 'I rather think that's the idea.'

* * *

I take my seat for the second press conference exactly twenty-four hours after I did so for the first one. A lot can change in a day. Daisy's face is all over the internet, and they tell me #FindDaisy is trending on Twitter. It's now, officially, a Big Story, which means the Super is chairing proceedings and we're in the media suite at Kidlington, though even here it's standing room only for the hacks. There's a live feed to Sky News and at least a dozen other cameras, and in among them, unobtrusive, Gareth Quinn and Anna Phillips with a digital hand-held. I want to make sure we get all of this, every single frame.

At precisely 10.01 we usher the Mason family on to

the dais to the clatter of flashlights. Leo Mason looks green in the glare – for a horrible moment I think he might actually be sick, right there in front of the cameras. As for his father, he immediately pushes his chair back as far as it will go, which is about as obvious a 'tell' as I've ever seen. I just hope for his sake he never decides to take up poker. When I went round last night to tell them about the appeal he kept asking if it was really necessary, what it would achieve, whether that sort of thing ever works in bringing someone back. Safe to say I've never had a parent try to argue me *out* of publicity for their missing child. And this is his little princess, his adored daughter. And I actually don't think he's faking it. Not that part of it, anyway. Which only serves to make it more perplexing. As for Sharon, she hardly said a word the whole time I was there. I kept on talking but I knew she wasn't taking any of it in. And now, looking at her, I can see what had suddenly become so preoccupying – she was wondering *what to wear.* Clothes, make-up, jewellery – everything about her is matching, immaculate. She looks like she's here for a job interview, not to beg for her baby back.

At 10.02, the Super clears his throat and reads from the paper in front of him. We've had to be more than usually careful what we say, given what we now know. We can't afford to lie outright, but we can't afford to tell the whole truth either.

'Thank you for coming, ladies and gentlemen. Mr and Mrs Mason are going to give a short statement about the disappearance of their daughter, Daisy. This is all we will be saying at this conference today. Our priority is to find Daisy safe and well and return her to her family. We do not have any further information we can share with you at present, and neither the family nor DI Fawley will be answering questions. I appreciate your understanding in this matter, and I would ask you to accord the family the privacy they need at this difficult time.'

Flashlights, people shift forward in their chairs. They're not interested in what the family say – everyone says the same things if a kid is missing – but they do very much want to hear *how* they say it. They want to gauge what sort of people the Masons are. Do they stand up to the scrutiny? Do they sound convincing? Do we like them? It's about character, and credibility. And, needless to say, that great English obsession, class.

The Super turns to his left, to Barry Mason. Who opens his mouth to say something but then buries his head in his hands and begins to sob. We can just about hear him mumbling something about his 'little princess'. A word which is really starting to get on my tits. I make a conscious effort to keep my expression impassive, but I'm not sure how well I'm succeeding. As for Leo, his eyes widen and he shoots an anguished glance at his mother, but she's looking at the cameras, not at him. Under the table, out of sight of everyone but me, he creeps a hand on to her leg, but she does not move, makes no sign.

The Super coughs. 'Perhaps you could read the statement, Mrs Mason?'

Sharon starts, then reaches her hand to her hair. Just as she did when she saw the TV crew arrive at the house. And then she turns direct to camera. 'If anyone knows anything about where our little girl is,' she says, 'please, please come forward. And Daisy – if you're watching this, you're not in any trouble, darling – we just want you to come home. We miss you – your dad and me. And Leo, of course.'

And then she reaches to put an arm round her son, drawing him close. Into the circle.

* * *

I watch the footage with Bryan Gow, the consultant we bring in for things like this. You'd probably call him a profiler, but these days they're wary of anything that smacks of prime-time procedural. Bryan himself, ironically enough, is straight out of central casting: trainspotter, mainstay of his local pub quiz team and amateur mathematician (don't ask me how that works – it's always struck me as the ultimate contradiction in terms).

We run the tape all the way through, and then he asks to see it again.

'So what do you think?' I say eventually.

He takes off his glasses and rubs them on his trousers. 'To be honest, where to start. The father definitely doesn't want to be there, and I don't believe all that theatrical sobbing.'

'Me neither. In fact, I suspect it's just an excuse to put his hands over his face.'

'I agree – he's hiding something. But it isn't necessarily to do with the child. I would look into his background. It's possible he's having an affair or involved in something else that means he doesn't want his face on TV.'

'He runs a building firm,' I say drily. 'I imagine there are plenty of people he might be avoiding. And the boy?'

'Harder to read. He's troubled by something, but it could just be the trauma of his sister going missing. Again, I'd check into his behaviour recently. See if something else has been going on that pre-dates the disappearance. How he's been at school.'

'And Sharon?'

Gow makes a face. *'Curiouser and curiouser, said Alice.* Did she come straight from the hairdresser or is that just how it looks?'

'I got Everett to ask her about that – casually, so as not to spook her. Apparently she said, "You don't want them to get the wrong impression."'

'Them?'

'I noticed it before. She's clearly paranoid about what other people think, but never actually defines who "they" are.'

Gow frowns. 'I see. Rewind to where she talks about her daughter.'

Sharon Mason's face appears, close up, and then freezes, her mouth slightly open.

'Have you heard of someone called Paul Ekman?'

I shake my head.

'But you've seen *Lie to Me*?'

'No, but I know which show you mean. The one where he works out who's telling the truth just from their body language?'

'Right. That character is based on Ekman. His theory is that there are certain emotions that can't be faked, because you can't consciously control the muscles in your face that express them. So with sorrow, for example, it's all about the space between the eyebrows. If you're really miserable, not just pretending to be, your brows will be drawn together. It's surprisingly hard to fake that convincingly for more than a minute or two – I know – I've tried. If you look at people in TV appeals who turned out later to have committed the crime themselves, you'll see exactly what I mean. It's the brows that give them away – the top half of the face doesn't match the bottom. Try googling Tracie Andrews next time you're online. Classic example. And now look at Sharon Mason.'

And there it is. There may be tears welling in her eyes, and a quiver to her lip, but her brow is smooth. Untroubled.

I get up to leave, but he calls me back.

'I would anticipate things getting nasty in cyberspace,' he says, putting his glasses back on. 'In cases like this, people often base their judgements on the sort of visual clues we've just been talking about, even if most of them don't know they're doing it. I suspect the Masons are in for trial by Twitter. Whether they deserve it or not.'

I call the St Aldate's incident room on my way out. Everett tells me there's no child in a mermaid costume in any of the photos taken at the party, which means we're going to have to recalibrate the whole investigation. We need to establish when Daisy was last seen, by whom, and where. We need to confirm exactly what she was wearing. We need to question the Masons. And once that gets out, the shit is really going to hit the fan.

* * *

ITV News @ITVLiveandBreaking   10.02
Watch live: Missing Daisy Mason – family make appeal #FindDaisy
RETWEETS 6,935

Scott Sullivan @SnapHappyWarrior   10.09
#DaisyMason Watching the police appeal – dad looks as guilty as hell – and whats with the mother – cold as ice

Indajit Singh @MrSingh700700700   10.10
Not finding daisy mason parents at all convincing &

why wont the police let the press ask questions?
Suspicious

Scott Sullivan @SnapHappyWarrior   10.11
#DaisyMason Parents will be arrested by the end
of the day – just u wait. Seen it all before

Lisa Jenks @WorldsBiggestManUFan   10.12
@SnapHappyWarrior Cant believe your being
judge and jury & they haven't even found her – are
you for real? #FindDaisy

Scott Sullivan @SnapHappyWarrior   10.12
@WorldsBiggestManUFan Are YOU for real! Anyone
can see somethings not right. Look at the other
kid – scared stiff

Danny Chadwick @ChadwickDanielPJ   10.14
Never seen a dad cry more than the mum at one of
these things. I knew there was more to this than
meets the eye #DaisyMason

Rob Chiltern @RockingRobin1975   10.15
#DaisyMason I hope the police have searched
the bloody house – I smell a police fuck up.
Wouldn't be the first time

Lilian Chamberlain @LilianChamberlain   10.16
@RockingRobin1975 The parents don't know where

she is. No wonder they look traumatised. People react differently to stress . . .

Lilian Chamberlain @LilianChamberlain 10.16
@RockingRobin1975 . . . They're not suspects. Just parents. My heart goes out to them #FindDaisy

Caroline Tollis @ForWhomtheTollis 10.17
Have the police thought to question the brother? #justsaying #DaisyMason

Garry G @SwordsandSandals 10.19
U know what I think? – father murdered her. Nailed on #DaisyMason

* * *

We'd asked the Masons to stay at Kidlington after the appeal. We gave them some guff about procedures and paperwork and parked them with Maureen Jones, who's drawn the short straw as Family Liaison Officer, but the real reason was to avoid carting them in for questioning in full view of the world. And especially that nosy little sod with the overactive Facebook page.

I take Quinn with me and look in on the Super on the way, at his request. And even though I make a big show of being in a hurry, he asks if he can have a private word and tells me to shut the door, so I know what's coming. But first, the bad news.

66

'I'm not asking for a warrant for a forensic search of the Mason home. At least not yet. The CPS will want more than circumstantial evidence and unanswered questions before they go to a magistrate.'

'Oh for God's sake –'

'I know where you're coming from, but this whole case is already turning into a media circus, and I am not about to fuel it with pictures of blokes in white suits carrying out teddy bears. As far as I've been informed, we don't even know for certain where the Mason girl was last seen. It's quite possible she was abducted walking home from school.'

'But Sharon Mason said she always picked the children up by car. Which narrows the chances of someone else taking Daisy to somewhere south of sod all.'

'Fair enough, but until you've established that for an absolute fact, I'm blocking a warrant application. Who knows – we may not even need one. Have you actually asked the parents for their permission?'

'I just can't see them agreeing. Sir. They won't even let us have Family Liaison in the house, which in itself –'

'– is not even remotely close to reasonable grounds for suspicion. Ask them – politely – if we can do a search. And then we'll talk. Right?'

I sigh. 'Right.'

I turn to go but he gestures to the chair then sits back and puts his fingertips together, composing his face into what HR no doubt call 'Suitable Empathy'.

'You sure you're OK taking this one on, Adam? I mean, I know you're more hands-on than most DIs, but it's not going to be easy, especially after –'

'I'm fine, sir. Really.'

'But losing your child like that. I mean, in those circumstances. Anyone would be affected. How could you not be.'

I open my mouth, then close it again. I find myself suddenly, deeply, violently angry. I look down at my hands and will myself not to say something I might regret. Like how bloody dare he sit there and casually prise open pain I've spent months appeasing. There are livid marks on my palms now where the nails have dug into the flesh. Deep red wheals. I can't look at them without feeling sick.

When I look up I realize he's still watching me. 'And what about Alex?' he says, still probing. 'How is she bearing up?'

'Fine. Alex is fine. Please, I just want to get on with the job.'

He frowns – a frown that comes with the caption 'Appropriate Concern'. I'm starting to wonder if he's been sent on some sort of training programme.

'I know that,' he says, 'and no one is suggesting for a moment that your work has been anything other than first rate. But it is only – what – six months since it happened? That's not long, not for something like that. And this is the first time you've had to deal with a child –'

I get to my feet. 'I appreciate the thought, sir, but it's really not necessary. I'd much rather concentrate on finding Daisy Mason. Time is not on our side. You know the stats as well as I do, and it's nearly thirty-six hours already.'

He hesitates, then nods. 'Well, if you're sure. But we may get some kickback in the press. They're bound to dig it all up again. Are you prepared for that?'

I make a face which I hope comes over as 'Complete Contempt'. 'They'll soon find something better to do. And in any case there's nothing to find.'

'No,' he says quickly. 'Of course not.'

Quinn shoots me a quizzical glance when I emerge.

'Admin,' I say, and he's too smart to push it. I start off down the corridor. 'Where are we with the school?'

'Everett and Gislingham are there now. Thought Chris could use some female back-up on that one.'

'Still nothing from the search teams?'

'Nada. We're widening the perimeter but with no intel about where to look it's needle-in-a-haystack stuff.'

'Intel', by the way, is another word that really gets on my tits.

At the family room, I pause at the door.

'Separately or together?' says Quinn.

'On their own. But I want to be in both.'

'So him first, then?'

'Right,' I reply, 'him first,' as I knock on the door,

which is opened by Maureen Jones, who steps back to let us pass.

I know the police are supposed to make more of an effort these days, but this is hardly my idea of a reassuring environment. It's a step up from Interview Room One at St Aldate's, I'll admit that, but with the cheap furniture pushed back against the walls it looks depressingly like a doctor's waiting room, which only reinforces the overwhelming sense that you only come here to get bad news. Barry Mason is sitting back on the settee, his eyes shut and his legs apart. He's sweating. His skin looks oily, as if it's covered with a fine layer of grease. But it's chill today, for July. Sharon is on one of the hard-back chairs, her feet exactly together, her handbag on her lap. It's one of those replica designer jobs. The brown ones with the cream pattern. The chair is so uncomfortable I'd expect her to be fidgeting, but she's perfectly still. She doesn't even look up when we come in. Leo does. And then after a moment he gets up from the floor where he's been sitting playing with a train and backs slowly towards his mother, his eyes all the time on mine.

I clear my throat. 'Mr Mason, Mrs Mason, thank you for waiting. I have some information I can now share with you. We wanted to be absolutely sure, before we said anything.'

I pause. A cruel, deliberate pause. I know what they must be thinking, but I need to see how they react.

Sharon brings her hand slowly to her face and Barry gasps, the tears already coursing down his face. 'Not my little princess,' he wails. 'Not my Dais–'

Leo grips his mother's sleeve, his eyes wide with pure terror. 'What are they talking about, Mum? Is it about Daisy?'

'Not now, Leo,' she says, not looking at him.

I can't hold the pause any longer. Not with any decency. They're expecting me to sit down, but I don't.

'What we have ascertained,' I begin slowly, 'is that Daisy was not at the party on Tuesday.'

Barry swallows. 'What do you mean, she *wasn't there*? I *saw her* – we all did –'

Sharon turns to her husband and grips his arm. 'What are they saying – what do they mean, she wasn't there?'

I slip a glance to Leo, who has dropped his gaze to his scuffed shoes. His cheeks are flushed. I was right – he knew all along.

'We've spoken to Millie Connor's parents and they've confirmed that *she* was wearing the daisy outfit at the party. Not Daisy. As far as we can tell, your daughter was never there.'

'Of course she was!' cries Sharon. 'I told you – I *saw her*. And don't try to tell me I don't know my own daughter. I've never heard such – such *rubbish*.'

'I'm afraid there's no room for doubt, Mrs Mason. And as I'm sure you will realize, this changes the whole

71

investigation. We will now have to go back through the events of that day and establish a definitive last sighting of your daughter: when Daisy was last seen, where and who by. We will also have to widen our enquiries beyond the guests at the party to Daisy's schoolmates, her teachers and anyone else she may have come into contact with in the days leading up to her disappearance. And as part of that process, we will have to interview you again, to ascertain exactly where you were during the day on Tuesday. Do you understand?'

Barry's eyes narrow. It's as if a switch has flipped. Or perhaps a tap turned off is the better analogy. Because there are no tears now. 'Are we under arrest?'

I look at him steadily. 'No, Mr Mason, you are not under arrest, we are interviewing you as what we call "significant witnesses". We have a special suite here, for interviews like that, and you should be aware that we will be videoing the conversation. It's important we capture everything you can tell us. So if you could come with me now, Mr Mason, we'll then talk to Mrs Mason afterwards.'

Sharon refuses to look at me. She shifts her position on the chair and her chin lifts with a sharp, defiant little movement.

'We would also like your permission to conduct a forensic search of your home.'

Barry Mason looks at me, openly hostile. 'I watch TV. I know what that means. You think we did it but you don't have enough evidence to get a warrant. *Do you.*'

I refuse to rise to the bait. 'A search of that kind might provide invaluable –'

But he's already shaking his head. 'No way – absolutely no bloody way. I'm not having you lot fitting me up for something I didn't do.'

'We don't *fit people up*, Mr Mason.'

He snorts, 'Yeah, right.'

We stare at one another. Impasse.

'I've arranged for an appropriate adult to attend,' I say eventually. 'They should be here in the next ten minutes.'

'Oh, fuck off,' snaps Barry. 'If I need someone to hold my hand I'll call my bloody lawyer.'

'Not for you,' I say evenly. 'For your son. We need to interview Leo as well, and he'll need someone present to protect his interests. And I'm afraid that can't be either of you.'

As I show Barry through the door and reach to close it I hear the sound of retching and turn to see Leo being violently sick against the wall. Maureen is on her feet at once, reaching for the box of tissues, putting her arm round his shoulders, telling him it's OK. The last thing I see before I close the door is Sharon Mason reaching into her bag for a wet wipe and bending to clean some infinitesimal spatter from her shoes.

* * *

BBC Midlands Today

Thursday 21 July 2016 | Last updated at 10:09

Daisy Mason: Police extend search to Port Meadow

Oxford police are using a helicopter to help in the search for 8-year-old Daisy Mason, who was last seen on Tuesday night. The ancient Port Meadow site to the west of the city extends for over 120 hectares and has never been cultivated. As Detective Inspector Adam Fawley told the BBC, 'It's a huge open expanse, with heavily wooded areas around the boundaries. Using a helicopter to support our teams on the ground will help us carry out the search far more quickly and efficiently.' DI Fawley refused to confirm whether the helicopter is fitted with an infra-red camera, but stressed that the police are still treating the investigation as a missing person inquiry.

Owners of the allotments adjoining Port Meadow have also been asked to check their sheds and outbuildings.

If you have information about Daisy contact Thames Valley CID incident room on 01865 0966552.

*   *   *

Amy Carey @JustAGirlWhoCant   10.41
I live north of Port Meadow – I can see the helicopter
looking for Daisy Mason. Fingers crossed they find
her soon #FindDaisy

Danny Chadwick @ChadwickDanielPJ   10.43
This gets weirder the longer it goes on – are the
police suggesting an 8YO could have got across
the railway line in the dark? #DaisyMason

Amy Carey @JustAGirlWhoCant   10.44
@ChadwickDanielPJ I thought it odd too – you
can't even get on to Port Meadow from here any more.
You have to go all the way round by Walton Well

Samantha Weston @MissusScatterbox   10.46
I can't see this ending happily. RIP poor little
angel x #DaisyMason

Amy Carey @JustAGirlWhoCant   10.47
There are literally 100s of people out helping with
the search #FindDaisy

Scott Sullivan @SnapHappyWarrior   10.52
#DaisyMason Like I said – it'll be the parents.
Bet the father was abusing her – he looks the type

Jenny T @56565656Jennifer   10.53
@SnapHappyWarrior That's a disgusting thing to
say. Trolls like you make me sick #FindDaisy

Scott Sullivan @SnapHappyWarrior   10.54
@56565656Jennifer How many times does this have
to happen before idiots like you see whats in front of
their faces? #DaisyMason

Jenny T @56565656Jennifer   10.54
@SnapHappyWarrior Look at that picture of Daisy
taken 3 days before she went missing. That's not
the picture of an abused child #Happy

Kathy Baines @FulloftheWarmSouth   10.55
#DaisyMason I don't understand this at all. All I
know is its really heartbreaking. So so sad

Jimmie Chews @RedsUnderTheShed   10.56
I heard chance of finding a kid dead is 80% if it goes
over 24 hrs. This #DaisyMason thing was always
going to end in Tragedy

J the Kid @Johnnycomelately   10.56
It's a sad reflection on our modern media world that
everyone always suspects the parents. As if your
child going missing wasn't bad enough

Kathy Baines @FulloftheWarmSouth   10.59
@Johnnycomelately I agree – I wish people wouldn't
sensationalize everything. It's so horrible already
#DaisyMason

JJ @JampotJamboree88   10.59
I don't believe any of it it doesn't add up v
suspiscious #DaisyMason

Kevin Brown @OxfordBornandBred   11.00
#FindDaisy #DaisyMason #Oxford
#DaisyWhereAreYou #Missing

Eddie Thorncliffe @EagleflyoverDover   11.01
Just caught up with that #DaisyMason TV
appeal – absolutely NO WAY those parents are
innocent. Horrible body language

Lilian Chamberlain @LilianChamberlain   11.02
Twitter can be vile sometimes. Leave those poor
parents alone. They're going through enough. Shut
up and let the police do their job #FindDaisy

Scott Sullivan @SnapHappyWarrior   11.03
@LilianChamberlain Can't believe anyone can be that
bloody naive. Just you wait, you'll see I'm right
#DaisyMason

* * *

The interview suite is marginally more comfortable than the family room, but it is only marginal. The main difference seems to be a couple of framed prints of golden retrievers. I wonder – not for the first time – if it's supposed to be some sort of subliminal message. Barry Mason strides in with that archetypal alpha male gait of his – shoulders back, hips open. Alex calls it the walk of the cock. He looks up at the video camera on the wall, making sure I see him doing it, then pulls one of the fake leather armchairs as far from the table as he can realistically place it, sits down and hoists one foot on to the other thigh.

'What I want to know,' he says, without waiting for me or Quinn to sit down, 'is why you're wasting time with me when you should be out there looking for my daughter.'

I take my own seat and Quinn follows.

'We are "out there", Mr Mason, as you put it. We have over a hundred officers searching for Daisy. No effort is being spared –'

'If that's true, how come you haven't found her? I can't believe no one saw *anything* – not in a poxy little place like that estate. Everyone's always nosing about in other people's business. You can't be questioning the right people – you can't be looking in the right places.'

There's a part of me that can't help agreeing with him, much as I dislike the man. I've never known an abduction case like this. No sightings, no leads, nothing. It's as if someone waved a magic wand and Daisy vanished into thin air. Which is, of course, complete nonsense. But in a case like this, nonsense and rumour will expand to fill any vacuum, and right now, we haven't a single reliable fact to put in their place.

'As I said, Mr Mason, there is a huge team on this case. Bigger than any I can remember in the ten years I've been working here. But until we know precisely *when* Daisy disappeared, the risk is that you're right – that we are indeed looking in the wrong place. And only you can help us with that. You and your wife.'

I have him there and he knows it. He stares at me, then shrugs and looks away.

I reach for my notebook. 'So, you told us just now you were unaware that the girl at the party wasn't your daughter. I have to tell you I find that very hard to believe.'

'Believe what you sodding like. It's the truth.'

'You didn't talk to her that night? You didn't pick her up? One of the neighbours said you often carried her about on your shoulders.'

He makes a face at my stupidity. 'Haven't done that for months. She says it makes her look like a baby in front of her friends. And she's too heavy to cart about these days. Not since I did my back in last Feb. Never been right since.'

Which makes three complex answers to one simple question. Liars always overkill, at least in my experience.

'And you didn't speak to her at the party? Use her name? Not the whole night?'

'I was doing the barbecue. You never done that? If you take your bloody eyes off it for a minute it either goes out or burns the lot. I remember seeing her running about, but now you come to mention it, I don't think I did talk to her. Not up close. I called out to her at one point asking if she wanted some sausages but she just giggled and ran off.'

And yet you didn't realize it wasn't your daughter's laugh. I can hear it, even now, and I've only heard it once, on a cheap mobile phone.

'How much did you have to drink?'

He bridles. He knows that wasn't a non sequitur. 'I had a couple. It was a bloody barbecue, for God's sake. I wasn't driving.'

I make a note or two. Purely for the sake of the pause.

'So when do you remember seeing Daisy before that?'

'Must have been about 5.30. That's when I got in. I was supposed to take the afternoon off but there was an emergency at one of my sites in Watlington. Burst pipe – half a ton of tiling under water. Client was having kittens. And then the traffic was awful coming back.'

Three answers. Again.

'But Daisy was definitely in the house when you got home?'

'Yup. The music was on upstairs. That Taylor Swift thing. She's always playing it.'

That, at least, rings true. It was what she was dancing to on the video. I glance at Quinn, who edges forward in his seat. 'Did you go up, sir?'

'To her room? No – Sharon was pestering me to set up the barbecue. Having a go at me for being late. I just called out hello to Dais and went out to the garden. Didn't even have time to change.'

He seems to have no idea of the implications of what he's saying.

'So,' I say, 'you never actually saw your daughter or heard her voice?'

He flushes. 'Well, no. At least I don't think so. I think she called out but I can't be sure.'

'Which means your last sighting of her would have been at breakfast that morning? No contact after that?'

Clearly not. Now, finally, he looks shaken.

'None of this makes any sense,' he says at last. 'Where is she?'

'That, Mr Mason, is what we're trying to find out.'

Out in the corridor again, I tell Quinn to check out the Watlington story. 'Shouldn't be too difficult to verify he really was where he says he was. I know I'm biased when it comes to the tossers in his profession, but I don't believe a bloody word that bloke says.'

Quinn makes a face and I can't really blame him; he's probably had enough of my builder stories. The sink in that bloody extension still drips.

'Right, boss. And shall I get Mrs Mason?'

'She can wait a few more minutes. I'm going to have a fag.'

* * *

5 July 2016, 4.36 p.m.
Two weeks before the disappearance
The Connor house, 54 Barge Close, first-floor landing

Mille Connor and Daisy Mason are playing with Millie's soft toys. Daisy has the look of a child who's been let into the secret about Santa Claus but told not to spoil it for the little ones. Millie, by contrast, is deep into an immensely complex made-up story involving Angelina Ballerina, Peppa Pig and a one-eyed teddy bear. Every now and then Daisy makes a suggestion, then sits back and watches what Millie does. She smiles to herself every time this happens, whether her ideas are incorporated into the story or not, as if that doesn't really matter. A moment later there's the sound of a key in the door and after a couple of false starts Julia Connor eventually pushes the front door open and dumps three large carrier bags on the floor. Her face is red and her hair wet. She's wearing gym gear.

'Millie!' she calls. 'Are you home? Do you want some juice?'

Millie puts her head round the banisters. 'No thank you. I'm just up here on my own playing.'

'Is your brother not back yet, then?'

Millie shrugs. 'He said he was going to play football after school.'

Julia Connor smiles. 'I remember now. That team from High Wycombe, wasn't it? Let's hope he wins. Otherwise he'll be even more bad-tempered than usual, playing in the rain.'

She picks up the bags again, and takes them through to the kitchen, where she turns on the radio and starts unpacking the shopping.

It must be at least half an hour later that the front doorbell rings. The two little girls start and exchange a glance, then Daisy edges back further out of sight and Millie creeps forward to where she can see down the stairs. There's a figure shadowed against the frosted glass. Julia Connor comes through from the kitchen, wiping her hands on a tea towel.

'Oh, it's you,' she says as the door opens. 'Must be ages since we last –'

'I'm so sorry to trouble you, Mrs Connor –'

'Oh, *Julia*, please – you make me sound like my mother-in-law.'

'This is so embarrassing, but have you by any chance seen Daisy? She was supposed to be home by four o'clock sharp and she's still not back, and it'll be getting dark soon. Her father will be so worried.'

Julia is a picture of concern. 'Oh dear, how awful. But I'm sure there's nothing to worry about. She probably just stopped off at a friend's on the way home and lost track of the time. Have you tried calling round?'

Sharon Mason flutters her hands, seemingly in despair. 'I never seem to know who her friends are these days, never mind have their numbers. I can't remember the last time she brought someone home. You were the only person I could think of.'

Julia reaches out and touches her hand. 'Let me ask Millie for you – she might know.'

Millie looks up at the sound of her name but Daisy immediately grips her arm and puts her finger to her lips. Then she shakes her head slowly, her eyes all the while intent on Millie's face.

'Are you still up there, Millie?' calls her mother. 'Did you see Daisy after school today?'

Millie stands up and goes to the head of the stairs, where the two women can see her. 'No, Mummy. I don't know where she is.'

Julia turns to Sharon with an apologetic look. 'I'm so sorry, I really don't know what to suggest. Perhaps you can give me your number and I can call you if I hear anything? And such a shame about your evening out too.'

Sharon frowns. 'What evening out?'

Julia flushes. 'Well, the handbag – the shoes. I just thought you must be going out. Sorry – I didn't mean anything by it.'

'Of course I'm not going out. My little girl is *missing.*'

Julia opens her mouth, then fails to find anything to say. But she dutifully writes down Sharon's number before watching her step carefully down the uneven gravelled drive and back down the close. Then she shuts the door again and returns to the kitchen. Upstairs on the landing, Millie turns to Daisy. 'You're going to be in awful trouble.'

'It's OK – I'll go down in a minute when your mum's not looking and let myself out.' She smiles broadly. 'Don't worry. She won't even notice.'

* * *

Amy Cathcart is sitting in the Hill of Beans coffee shop in the centre of Newbury, watching the TV on the wall behind the bar, waiting for her friend to arrive. She's twenty-seven, blonde, petite, GSOH, likes children and animals, and enjoys long country walks. At least that's what her profile says. In reality she's rather closer to middle height, walking bores her and her sense of humour is wearing thin. Right this minute the culprit is Marcia, who's a quarter of an hour late, but her job, the world and herself are all equally wearying. Equally disappointing. That very morning she'd had an invite to yet another wedding, in yet another fancy hotel. Her wardrobe is gaping with outfits she can't wear a second time with the same crowd, and she's getting mighty tired of being that person on the far left of the group shot whose name no one can remember ten years on.

Marcia pushes through the door, her eyes still on her phone. She tucks a wisp of perfectly red-gold hair behind her ear as she stares at the screen, presses a couple of times, then finally looks up.

'Amy! So sorry I'm late. Been on the phone all morning. Bloody copywriters – never do what they're asked. They're all too busy thinking they're the next Dan Brown to focus on the sodding brief.'

They kiss and Marcia hitches herself up on the stool. 'What you having?'

'Americano. But it's my turn.'

Marcia flaps dissent away. 'Least I can do. So tell me – what have you been up to? Met anyone interesting?'

It's six months since Amy joined the dating site, and it's been – to put it charitably – a mixed bag. She's beginning to think she might be at a difficult age – there seems to be precious little between the slightly-too-desperate divorced and the never-been-married-and-you-can-see-why. Last Christmas her mother gave her a magnet for the fridge that said: 'Men are like a box of chocolates – leave it too long and all that's left are the nuts.' Which is exactly the sort of catty and irritatingly accurate thing she'd expect her mother to come out with. Though this time, it might just be different.

'Well,' she begins, 'there is a guy I've been emailing. We haven't met yet, but he sounds more promising than most of them. Not that that's saying very much.'

'Name, age, income, baggage?' It's Marcia's standard catechism.

'He's called Aidan. He's thirty-nine and he works in the City. Divorced but no kids, thank God.'

The coffees arrive and Marcia stirs through the froth on her cappuccino and licks the spoon. 'So when are you going to see him?'

'Possibly next weekend. He's got some big take-over he's working on, so he hasn't had a lot of time. Though he's sent me loads of texts. Sometimes when he's actually in one of the meetings. About how boring it is and how all the banker types are playing "my dad's bigger than your dad". Though I'm not getting my hopes up – not till I meet him. I mean, remember Mr Licky?'

Marcia's opens her eyes wide. 'Oh Lord. Fate worse than actual death. So go on – show me some of those texts.'

Amy starts to say no – it's too soon – they're private – but Marcia's having none of it. 'Come on, it isn't actual *sexting*, is it?'

'No, of course not –'

'Well then, where's the harm? Gimme. Come on, give it here.'

Amy hands over her phone and sits back as her friend scrolls through the messages. She pretended to mind but actually she rather likes having one up on Marcia for once. Marcia's never had trouble finding men, and has an enviable track record as dumper, not dumpee. Surely it must be Amy's turn eventually. Even if Mr Right is too much to hope for, at least a relation-ship that gets off the ground before it crashes and burns.

But that's exactly what happens. Right there, at precisely 10.06, as she lifts her cup to her lips and her eyes to the TV screen.

*　　*　　*

Interview with Sharon Mason
21 July 2016, 11.49 a.m.
In attendance, DI A. Fawley, Acting DS G. Quinn

AF: Our apologies for keeping you waiting, Mrs Mason. Would you like a cup of tea?

SM: No thank you. I had some earlier. It was disgusting. It tasted like you made it with evaporated milk.

AF: As we explained earlier, we're trying to pin down exactly when Daisy was last seen, and where. You told us that you weren't aware that the daisy costume was being worn that night by Millie Connor?

SM: I was busy. Sorting out the food, doing the drinks. People always ask for something you haven't got. And it was dark - there were children running about all over the place. I just assumed it was her. You'd have done the same.

AF: Actually, Mrs Mason, I'm not sure I would. But we're not here to talk about me. Do you know what happened to the mermaid costume

88

Daisy swapped with Millie? Have you seen it
in the house?

SM: No, I've never clapped eyes on it. It's
certainly not in her room.

AF: And did Daisy wear her usual uniform to
school that day? Have you checked if *that*
is in the house?

[*pause*]

SM: No. I haven't looked.

AF: Perhaps you could do that, Mrs Mason. Given
that you won't allow us to conduct a proper
search ourselves.

[*pause*]

GQ: What time did you pick the children up from
school?

[*pause*]

SM: Actually, I didn't.

AF: I'm sorry? Are you saying you didn't collect
them after all? You specifically told us
you'd picked them up –

SM: No I didn't. I *said* I drive them to school.
And I do. There and back. I just didn't do
it on Tuesday.

AF: Do you realize how serious this is – how
much time we've wasted? If you'd told us
Daisy came home alone –

SM: She wasn't alone. Leo was with her. I told
them both that morning they'd have to walk
for once.

AF: And why didn't you tell us this before?
[*pause*]

SM: I knew you'd only get the wrong idea. That you'd start blaming me. And it's not my fault. I can't be in two places at once, can I? Do you know how much work a party like that creates? Barry was supposed to help me - he *said* he'd take the afternoon off, but then he called and said he'd be late. As usual.

GQ: What time was that - the phone call?
[*pause*]

SM: I'm not sure. Perhaps about four.

GQ: We can easily check with the phone company.

AF: And you'd told Leo that morning that he had to walk his sister home?

SM: Yes, I told both of them at breakfast. I told Daisy to make sure to find Leo, and not run off on her own.

GQ: Was she in the habit of doing that?

SM: Not in the way *you* mean. She was always very sensible. But she's interested in things. Animals and such. Insects. She gets distracted sometimes, that's all.

AF: I gather she wants to be a vet when she grows up? That's a long training.

SM: Daisy knows how important it is to work hard at school and get a good job. She's extremely bright. She got 97 out of 100 in a

maths test last term. The next best after
that only got 72.

AF: So to get back to Tuesday afternoon. What
time did the children get home from school?

SM: Daisy came in about 4.15. I was in the
kitchen. The door slammed and she went up
to her room.

AF: You saw her?

SM: No. Like I said, I was busy. She was really
banging about upstairs so I guessed there
must have been some sort of squabble on the
way home.

AF: Do the children argue a lot?

SM: Sometimes. No more than other people's
children, I daresay.
[*pause*]
Perhaps a bit more lately.

AF: So why's that?

SM: Who knows, with children. You could drive
yourself mad working out why they do this
and that.

AF: Has it been one child rather than the other
who's been acting up?

SM: Oh, Leo. Definitely Leo. Adolescent boys can
be so moody.

GQ: He's ten years old.
[*pause*]

SM: Barry thinks he might be worried about his
SATs.

AF: But that's a whole year away. He's only in
    Year 5 now, isn't he?

SM: He's not as clever as Daisy.
    [*pause*]

AF: I see. So going back to Tuesday afternoon.
    Daisy gets back at 4.15. When did you next
    see her?

SM: I called out and asked her if she wanted
    anything but she didn't answer. I assumed
    she was sulking.

AF: So you didn't actually *see* her? Not then,
    and not earlier, when she got home?
    [*pause*]

SM: No.

GQ: What time was that, when you called up to
    her?

SM: I don't remember.

AF: So when did she come down for the party?

SM: People had started arriving by then. It was
    all a bit chaotic. I remember seeing her
    running about with her friends. Like I
    told you.
    [*pause*]

AF: I see. And what about Leo? Was he with
    Daisy when she got back from school?

SM: No. I saw him later.

AF: How much later?

SM: I don't know. About a quarter of an hour.
    Something like that.

AF: So about 4.30. What had happened, Mrs Mason?
Why did they not come back together?
[*pause*]
Mrs Mason?

SM: He said they'd had an argument and Daisy
had run off.

GQ: What was this particular argument about?

SM: Like I said, no doubt something and
nothing. I couldn't get a word out of him.

AF: So you didn't go upstairs and talk to Daisy
about it?

SM: No, of course not. I told you already. She
was obviously OK, wasn't she? She didn't
need me fussing over her. She was always
saying she hated that. And in any case, I
don't see what difference it makes.
[*pause*]
What? What are you looking at me like that
for? It's not my fault. Whatever it was
that - that - *happened*, it must have been
after that, mustn't it? Someone must have
taken her at the party.

AF: We've already established she was never *at*
the party, Mrs Mason.
[*pause*]
The first guests arrived at about seven, I
believe?

SM: Yes. Around then. Though they were invited
for earlier. People can be so rude.

AF: So your contention is that sometime between
4.15 when she got home, and seven when the
first guests arrived, your daughter
disappeared from under your nose – from her
own bedroom?

SM: Don't you dare take that tone with me. What
do you mean *my contention* – it's not *my
contention*, it's *what happened*. She was in
her room. There was music on – it was still
on when I got back. Ask Barry – he heard it
too – when he finally deigned to show his face –

AF: Hold on – what do you mean *when I got
back*?

[*pause*]

SM: Well, if you must know, I popped out for
twenty minutes. I had to get mayonnaise. I
bought some the day before, but when I went
to make the sandwiches I realized someone
must have broken the jar. And since no one
had bothered to tell me about it, I had to
go out again.

AF: Why on earth didn't you tell us this before?

SM: Barry doesn't like leaving the children in
the house alone.

AF: So you didn't want him to know that's what
you'd done.

[*silence*]

Is there anything else you haven't told us,
Mrs Mason?

[*silence*]

So when exactly was this shopping trip of
yours?

SM: I didn't notice the time.

AF: But before your husband got back.

SM: He got in about fifteen minutes later.

AF: And the front door was locked?

SM: Of course the *door was locked* –

AF: And what about the side gate?

[*pause*]

SM: I'm not sure.

GQ: You said that it was open during the party.
And presumably it'd been open the night
before as well, when Mr Webster brought
round the gazebo. Did you lock it after he
left on Monday?

SM: I can't remember.

GQ: What about your husband? Did he help Mr
Webster with the gazebo?

SM: He wasn't there. He was home late. Again.

GQ: And the patio door – was that open when you
went to the shops for the mayonnaise?
[*pause*]

SM: I think so, yes. I was only popping out for
a minute.

AF: So you left the house open and the side
gate possibly unlocked. With two young
children alone in the house.

SM: You can't blame me. It's not my fault.

```
AF:   So whose fault was it, Mrs Mason?
      [pause]
      This mayonnaise, where did you buy it?
SM:   I couldn't find any. I tried that funny
      little place on Glasshouse Street but they'd
      run out, and then I went to the Marks on
      the ring-road roundabout but they didn't
      have any either.
GQ:   It must have taken you more than twenty
      minutes to do all that. Parking, going in,
      driving, parking again, driving back. I'd
      say half an hour minimum, even forty
      minutes. Especially at that time of day.
AF:   More than enough time for someone to get
      into the house and take your daughter.
SM:   I told you. The music was still on upstairs
      when I got back.
AF:   But you have no idea if she was there to
      hear it. Do you, Mrs Mason?
```

* * *

When Everett and Gislingham get to Bishop Christopher's the bell has just gone for lunchtime and two hundred kids are hording out of the doors.

'Where do they get the bloody energy?' yells Gislingham over the din.

'Carbohydrates,' grins Everett. 'You know, that stuff Janet won't let you eat any more.'

'Don't remind me,' he grumbles, eyeing his gut rue-fully. 'Man cannot live by low-fat cheese alone, Ev. Not this one, anyway.'

He stops a moment and looks around at the whoop-ing, shrieking children. 'They don't seem to be that upset about their fellow pupil, do they? I suppose it'd be different if this was a secondary school. They'd have counsellors, educational psychologists – the works. I suppose this lot are too young to understand.'

Everett follows his gaze. 'Most of them, yes. But those girls over there – they know something's hap-pened. I bet they're in her class.'

Three girls are sitting on the same bench, their heads close together. Two have hair in long plaits and another looks Chinese. As they watch, one of the girls starts to cry, and Everett sees the teacher on duty make her way across to them and sit down next to the girl in tears.

Inside the school the corridors echo with the silence. Gislingham stops a moment and takes a deep breath. 'How is it all schools smell the same?'

'A fruity little blend of sweaty socks, farts and chip fat, layered with ripe undertones of sick and disinfect-ant. Oh yes, quite unmistakeable.'

Everett looks around and spots a map of the site on the wall opposite. 'So which way to the headmistress's office, I wonder?'

Gislingham makes a face. 'Blimey, that takes me back. Spent more time there than in class. Could have found my way with my eyes shut.'

'It never ceases to amaze me that you ended up a copper, Gislingham.'

He shrugs. 'I think they decided it was probably better having me on the inside pissing out.'

The head's office is at the back of the building, overlooking a small square of dried-out scrubby grass, a chicken-wire fence covered in honeysuckle and a row of spindly poplars.

Alison Stevens gets up to greet them. She's an elegant black woman, deftly dressed in an outfit designed to convey the optimum combination of authority and approachability: navy skirt just below the knee, soft powder-blue cardigan, tiny round earrings.

'DC Everett, DC Gislingham, please – take a seat. This is Daisy's form teacher.'

The young woman leans forward to shake their hands. She's probably no more than twenty-five, red hair in loose corkscrew curls, a thin flowered dress over bare brown legs. Everett sees Gislingham square his shoulders a little. Men, she thinks, they're all the bloody same.

'Kate Madigan,' she says in a soft Irish accent, her eyes concerned. 'I can't even imagine what the Masons must be going through. It must be every parent's worst nightmare.'

Alison Stevens clears her throat. 'I've had the caretaker download the CCTV from the camera at the gate. Here's the footage you need.'

She taps her keyboard, then swings the laptop round

to face them. The screen shows the time as 3.38 p.m. Daisy is at the gate talking to the Chinese girl they just saw in the playground, and another girl is standing a few feet away. Daisy has a school bag in one hand.

Gislingham glances at Everett. 'Shit. Did anyone think to check if that bag is in the house?'

'I don't think so. And they're not about to let us in to look for it now. Not from what I hear.'

'Who are the other girls?' continues Everett, glancing at Kate Madigan.

'The one with the blonde hair is Portia Dawson. Her parents are consultants at the university hospital. The other is Nanxi Chen. She's American. Her father is a professor. Politics, I think. They've only been here since Christmas.'

'Daisy keeps some pretty high-powered company, judging from this,' says Gislingham.

Alison Stevens looks at him warily, not sure if he's impugning or merely inferring. 'It's the nature of the catchment, Detective. Lots of our children have parents who are academics. One of them is a Nobel Prize winner.'

'I think we just saw Nanxi outside,' says Everett. 'Could we speak to her before we go?'

'I will call her mother and check that's OK.'

'And Portia Dawson?'

'Her parents have kept her off since Wednesday. She's apparently very upset. And as it's the end of term she wasn't likely to miss very much, so I didn't object. I'll give them a call.'

On the screen Daisy talks to Nanxi until her mother arrives to collect her at 3.49. It's 3.52 when Leo appears. His head is down and his hands are in his pockets. He doesn't speak to Daisy, as far as they can tell. She watches him go past and waits until he's halfway down the road before hitching her bag over her shoulder and following him out of sight. It's the last time they see her. And it's the only camera between the school and the Canal Manor estate.

'Mrs Stevens,' says Everett. 'Is there anything else you can tell us about Daisy? How has she been recently – anything troubling her as far as you know?'

'I think Kate would be better able to talk about that than me.'

Gislingham turns to the teacher. 'Anything you can tell us would be really helpful, Miss Madigan.'

Everett groans inwardly; Christ, he's even clocked she's not wearing a ring.

Kate looks at a loss. 'I can't tell you how devastated we all are. I've had children in tears all morning. Daisy is such a nice little girl – bright, well-behaved. Very popular. A joy to teach.'

'But?'

'What do you mean, *but*?'

'Sorry, I just thought I could hear a "but" coming, that's all.'

Kate Madigan glances at the head, who nods.

'Well,' she continues, 'I have noticed her marks have been sliding a bit recently. Nothing dramatic – she's still easily in the top third. But she has seemed rather quieter than normal. A bit preoccupied, shall we say.'

'Have you spoken to her about it?'

'I did try. In passing, like you do, so as not to unnerve her. But she said everything was fine.'

'And you believed her?'

Kate looks troubled. 'I did wonder, I suppose. From one or two things she'd said before, I suspect she wasn't that happy at home. Nothing – *serious*,' she says quickly. 'Nothing that suggested she was in any way at risk.' She blushes. 'I used to talk to her a lot about books. I don't think the Masons are very interested in that sort of thing. But I do know she was looking forward to the party.'

'The last time *I* spoke to her she was in very good spirits,' interjects the head. 'She told me how excited she was about what she was going to do in the holidays.'

'I wish I could help more,' says Kate, 'but to be honest, I've only had the class for a few months – I don't know any of the children that well.'

'Kate is the supply teacher we were sent when Kieran Jennings broke his leg skiing at Easter,' says the head. 'We were very glad to get her and we're very sorry she's going.'

'Going?' says Gislingham.

Kate Madigan smiles. 'Back to Ireland. I've got a job in Galway. Nearer my family.'

'So,' says Everett, a touch briskly, 'you were concerned about Daisy.'

Again Kate Madigan looks across at the head teacher. 'No, I wouldn't use a word as strong as that. I'd noticed a slight change, that's all. A *very slight* change. I told Alison about it, and she was going to brief Kieran when he comes back, so he could keep an eye out. There was absolutely nothing specific. If there had been, we'd have taken it further.'

For the third time in as many minutes, the two women exchange glances.

Everett doesn't need nudging again. 'There's something else, isn't there? Something you're not telling us.'

Alison Stevens takes a deep breath. 'To be honest, Detective, it wasn't Daisy we were worried about.'

* * *

The social worker is a man. Don't know why that surprises me, but it does – somehow I always assume it'll be a woman. But when I watch him with Leo on the video feed, I realize a bloke is actually a much better idea. In five minutes they're on football, and in ten we've established that Chelsea are going to win the League again next season, Wayne Rooney is overrated and Louis van Gaal has funny hair. When I open the door and go in to join them, Leo's looking more like a normal kid than I've ever seen him.

'So, Leo, I just need to ask you a couple of quick questions about Tuesday afternoon, is that OK?'

He stiffens and I curse inwardly.

'It's nothing to worry about. You want to get your sister home safe, don't you?'

He nods then, but he doesn't do it straight away, and he doesn't look at me either. He reaches across and picks up the can of Coke Gareth Quinn gave him and starts playing with it. You don't need to be a child psychologist to work out there's some sort of displacement going on here. Or that the truth – whatever it is – is troubling him. And yet here am I, crashing in with my lead boots on. 'You walked home from school with Daisy that day, am I right?'

He nods. 'Mum was too busy.' His head is still down. I can scarcely see him behind the heavy dark fringe.

'Did you walk home together all the way?'

He nods again.

'Are you sure? Because we thought you might have had some sort of a fight.'

He looks at me now. 'Who told you that?'

'Your mum. She said you and Daisy came home separately. She thought you must have had an argument.'

Back to the Coke can again. 'She saw some stupid butterfly and she wanted me to take a picture of it, but I wouldn't.'

'Why not? Doesn't seem much to ask. Because she didn't have a phone herself, did she?'

'Mum wouldn't let her.'

'So why didn't you take the picture?'

He shrugs. 'Dunno.'

'So what happened then?'

'I left her there looking at it. I told her we had to get home because of the party and Mum would be angry, but she wouldn't come. So I left her there.'

'I see.'

I leave a pause, then, 'So you support Chelsea, do you?'

He flashes me a quick look, then nods. He has beautiful violet-blue eyes, and incredibly long lashes. There's something elfin about his face I can't put my finger on.

'One of my DCs supports Chelsea. Mad about them, he is. Who's your favourite player?'

'Eden Hazard.'

'He's the Belgian one, yes? Where does he play?'

'He's in midfield.'

'Is that where you play?'

'Dad says I'd be better off sticking to defence. He says I'm not quick enough for midfield.'

'Does your dad take you to games?'

'No. He says it costs too much and takes too much time to get there.'

'London's not that far away, surely?'

A shrug. 'I went once with Ben and his dad. We beat Stoke three—nil. It was really good. He got me a scarf.'

'Ben's your best friend?'

Another shrug. 'He used to be but he moved.'

'So who's your best friend now?'

Silence.

I'm beginning to realize just how lonely this kid is. Part of me wants to reach out and hold him and make it all better. But I can't. Because the other part of me is about to make it worse. Sometimes, I bloody hate this job.

'Leo, I've got a bit of a problem and I need you to help me with it.'

He's staring intently at the empty can now, and his right leg is jigging up and down. I exchange a glance with the social worker.

'You see, my problem is that your mum says Daisy got home quite a bit before you on Tuesday. Which doesn't really make sense if you say you left her behind looking at the butterfly. Do you see what I mean?'

A pause and a nod – barely a movement at all. His cheeks are red now.

'You just need to tell me what happened, that's all. You're not in any trouble.'

The social worker leans forward and puts his hand gently on Leo's arm. 'It's OK, Leo. You can tell the police officer. It's always better to tell the truth, eh?'

And that's how it all comes out.

* * *

Gislingham pushes open the door of the Year Four classroom. The afternoon sun is streaming in through the windows, falling slantwise on a poster of the alphabet in animals, and a banner saying WHAT WE ARE GOING TO DO IN THE HOLIDAYS. Under it the children have written things and stuck pictures to them, cut out of magazines. Two or three are going to Disneyland, one to New Zealand. Daisy appears to be most excited about going on a ferry for the first time, and Nanxi Chen will be visiting her cousins in New York. But at this precise moment she's sitting with Kate Madigan and Verity Everett, in the far corner of the room.

Gislingham beckons to Everett, who gets up and comes over. He lowers his voice. 'I left a message for the boss. They're interviewing the boy right now.' He glances at his watch. 'Sod it, I'm supposed to pick up Janet in twenty minutes. It's her eighteen-week scan.'

He doesn't say, but Everett knows it's their first child, and at forty-two, after three miscarriages, she's going to want him there.

'Don't worry,' she says. 'You go and I'll finish up here. Alison Stevens says the Dawsons can see us at two so I'll go round after this and meet you later.'

'You OK getting to the house?'

She smiles. 'It's only a ten-minute walk. I think I can manage.'

If Everett had worried about getting Nanxi Chen to open up, it's soon obvious that she has rather the opposite problem on her hands. Nanxi has the confidence of a child twice her age, and a full-on American frankness to go with it. Daisy Mason, in her opinion, is 'super-smart' and 'really sassy'. She does the best hand-stands in class (Kate Madigan smiles sadly at this) and tells the most awesome stories, though Portia is better at drawing, and Daisy's no good at dancing at all, even though she thinks she is. Millie Connor is best at that, but she's a bit stupid otherwise (a mild rebuke and a blush from teacher at this one).

'And what are you good at, Nanxi?' asks Everett.

'Oh, math. My dad wants me to go to MIT like he did.'

Everett has no idea what MIT is, but she gets the picture.

'So how has Daisy been at school recently? Was there anything worrying her at all?'

Nanxi considers for a moment. 'Well, I suppose there was one thing. But it was a secret. She only told us because we're her BFFs.'

Everett does her best not to look overeager. 'What secret, Nanxi?'

The girl looks doubtful suddenly, as if she's realized she's already said too much, but Kate Madigan encourages her. 'It's OK, Nanxi – I'm sure Detective Everett won't tell anyone.'

'Daisy didn't tell me what it was. She said one day she was meeting someone and it was a secret. She seemed really excited at first, but then she said it was nothing and she wasn't going to see them again.'

'And she didn't tell you who it was she'd seen? A grown-up? Another child?'

A vigorous shake of the head.

'And was she upset after she saw this person?'

Nanxi considers. 'No, not upset. She wasn't crying or anything. I think she was just mad.'

Which, as Everett reminds herself, means something very different in America.

'Was Daisy happy at home, Nanxi?'

Nanxi makes a face. 'Like, *seriously*? Have you *seen* that house?'

Kate intervenes quickly. 'Now, Nanxi, that's not a nice thing to say. We don't judge people by how much money they have, do we?'

Nanxi looks as if money's the only reliable yardstick you're ever likely to get, but she doesn't say anything.

'What I really meant was whether Daisy was happy with her family?'

'Well, Leo's kinda weird. A bit wimpy kid. And her mom's always on at her about her marks.'

'And what about her father? Everyone says they're really close.'

'I guess so, only –'

'Only?'

'He used to be, like, her hero or her Prince Charming or something. But she doesn't talk about him like that any more. She doesn't even call him Daddy.'

'So what does she call him, Nanxi?'

The girl looks at Everett, a world of knowing suddenly in her eyes. 'She calls him the He Pig.'

* * *

A few minutes later, when Everett gets up to go, she finds herself in front of a pinboard of drawings entitled OUR FAIRY TALES. Perhaps it's Nanxi's reference to Prince Charming, but something makes her look closer.

Most of them are a predictable mix of Once Upon a Time and Harry Potter – boy wizards and green dragons and long-haired princesses in towers not much taller than they are. She notices in passing that Nanxi's right and Portia is clearly the most talented artist in the class, but the drawing that really strikes her is Daisy's. She calls Kate Madigan over.

'Were there stories that went with these pictures?'

Kate smiles. 'How perceptive of you. Yes, we did the stories first and then I got them to draw a picture of what they'd written.'

'Do you have the stories?'

'Yes, I think they're still in a pile somewhere.'

She goes over to the desk. It's heaped with little presents still in their gift-wrap.

'The kids obviously like you,' says Everett, reading a couple of the messages. *To the best teacher in the world. We will miss you xxxx*

'What? Oh, that. Yes, it is nice when they bring you things. I haven't opened them yet. It seems, you know, not the right time.'

She's found a pile of essays now, and starts flicking through them, a coil of red hair slipping forward over her shoulder. She gets to the end, frowns, then looks up, a little flustered.

'Now that's odd, so it is. Daisy's doesn't seem to be here.'

It's Everett's turn to frown. 'Really? Where else could it be?'

Kate Madigan looks bewildered. 'I suppose it could be at home. I did take them back to the flat to mark them. But I don't see how that one could have got separated from the rest.'

'Could someone have taken it – from here, I mean? Could someone have come into the classroom?'

'Well, I suppose it's possible. The room isn't locked during the day. But why on earth would anyone want it?' She looks really distressed now. 'I don't understand – it's only a fairy story.'

Everett doesn't understand either. But it's nagging at her all the same.

* * *

Find Daisy Mason Facebook Page

We've decided to put this page together so we can all share any info about Daisy and perhaps help find her. So show your support by adding a daisy to your avatar, both here on FB and on Twitter, and we'll try to make a 'daisy chain' strong enough to bring our little angel home.

Lorraine Nicholas, Tom Brody, Alice Shelley and 33 others liked this

TOP COMMENTS
John Stoker Let's get this Daisy Chain linking up. Who knows – someone may even see it and remember

something. Wouldn't it be great if social media could make a positive difference for once, rather than just all that horrible trolling there's been on Twitter ✿
21 July at 14.32

Jan Potts This is a great idea – and I agree, those Twitter trolls make me sick to my stomach ✿
21 July at 14.39

Find Daisy Mason And remember everyone – call Thames Valley CID if you have any information at all. Even something that might not seem relevant. 01865 0966552
21 July at 14.56

* * *

The Dawson family live only a mile away from Barge Close, but it's like another town entirely. Verity Everett pauses on the pavement opposite to get the measure of the place before she knocks on the door. Four storeys, including a lower ground, and even from where she's standing she can see two of the rooms upstairs are lined with books. The front is weathered red brick and recently renovated stone, and there's a line of black railings above a low wall and a neatly gravelled drive. The street is lined with trees that must have been planted when the houses were built, more than a century before.

The door is opened by a pretty woman in an apron who explains that she's only here to clean, and Mrs

Dawson is out in the garden. Everett makes her way down a flight of stairs into a huge kitchen running front to back and out into a garden dotted with apple trees. Portia's mother sees her coming and makes her way up to meet her, a wicker basket over one arm. She's tall and slender, with thick brown hair in a stylish asymmetrical cut, and a long cream tunic over khaki capri pants. The sort of woman who can make you feel dowdy, even when she's deadheading the geraniums. Everett doesn't have an outfit that expensive, even for best.

'You have a beautiful house, Dr Dawson.'

'Oh, Eleanor, please. I get enough doctoring at the hospital.'

She's clearly used that line before, but the smile that goes with it seems genuine.

'The garden is nice, isn't it?' she continues. 'Though you should have seen it when we moved in. Complete building site. Which is exactly what it was, of course. The whole house had to be gutted. The Victorians might have built to last but these places are like fridges in the winter so we had to strip it back to the brick and start again with proper insulation. I was battling plaster dust for months.'

I rather suspect it was your cleaner who did that, thinks Everett, but she doesn't voice the thought.

'Well, it looks lovely now.'

'That's very sweet of you. Let's go down to the summerhouse. Portia's been there reading. We're all so distraught about Daisy. Such a beautiful little girl and so bright – I remember her asking me once who

Leonardo was. And she wasn't talking about ninja turtles, either.'

She smiles. 'Listen to me, rattling on. I should have asked – would you like tea?'

Everett's about to trot out the usual no, but suddenly decides, to hell with it. 'Yes, that would be great.'

'Just let me ask Amélie to put the kettle on and I'll be with you.'

Her French accent is perfect. And when the tea arrives, there are slices of lemon on a dish and milk in a jug. No cartons for the Dawsons, clearly.

Portia is sitting on a swing seat, a copy of *Black Beauty* on the chair beside her, and a large tabby cat on her lap. It doesn't look like she's been doing much reading. She'd looked sturdy on the CCTV but she doesn't look so now. There are dark circles under her eyes and Everett guesses she hasn't been eating much.

'This is Detective Constable Everett, darling,' says Eleanor Dawson, setting down the tray. 'You remember? She wants to ask you about Daisy.'

'Is that all right with you, Portia? It won't take very long.'

'It's OK,' says the girl, stroking the cat, which blinks its amber eyes for a moment before settling again with a sigh.

'We've had a look at the footage from the CCTV outside the school gate, and it shows that you and Nanxi were probably the last people who saw Daisy before she left for home that day. Is that right?'

'I think so.'

'Were you all looking forward to the party?'

'I wasn't going.'

'Really, why not? I thought all her class were invited. And you're her best friends.'

Portia blushes. 'Daisy forgot to tell us which day it was, and by the time she remembered Mum already had something else that day. Nanxi couldn't go either.'

And if both her closest friends were absent, thinks Everett, that may explain why none of the children at the party seem to have noticed Daisy wasn't there.

'Did you go to the Connors' house the day before, Portia? When the girls were trying on their costumes?'

Portia glances at her mother. 'Yes, for a little while. I didn't stay very long.'

'What about Daisy's house? Did you go there often? Do you know Daisy's family?'

Portia looks away. 'We used to come here instead. She said it was because it was closer to school but I think she liked my house better than hers.'

'I see. When I spoke to Nanxi, she said Daisy had met someone recently, but it was supposed to be a secret. Do you know who that was?'

Portia shakes her head. 'She talked about it. She was really happy, to start with. But after she said she didn't want to talk about it any more. That if we were really her best friends we wouldn't ask her. I'm sorry. I just don't know anything.'

The girl is starting to look anxious and, seeing her

mother's concerned glance, Everett elects to change tack.

'What's the best thing about having Daisy as a friend?'

Portia brightens a little. 'She's really clever. She helps me with school stuff. And she does these – what do you call them – when you try to sound like someone else?'

'Impersonations.'

'She's really good at them. She does one of her mother. And of famous people on the telly.'

'TV,' says Eleanor Dawson quietly. 'We say "TV".'

'Do they make you laugh, the impersonations?'

Portia looks away. 'Sometimes.'

'And what's the worst thing?'

Portia opens her mouth, then stops. 'She listens,' she says eventually, her face red.

'You mean she eavesdrops?'

'Sometimes she hides and you don't know she's there and she listens to what you say.'

'I see,' says Everett as her phone starts to ring. She gets up with an apologetic gesture and moves quickly to the shade of an apple tree that's probably older than her flat. It's Gislingham.

'Boss wants us all back at the station in an hour.'

'OK, I'm pretty much done. How did it go – the scan?'

She can almost hear him beaming. 'All OK. And it's a boy.'

'Brilliant, Chris. I'm really pleased for you.'

'We're just finishing here so I'll come and pick you up after I drop Janet at home.'

'Give her my love. And tell her not to let you bully her into calling the baby something he won't forgive you for. Like Stamford Bridge.'

'Coming from someone called Verity Mabel, I'd call that pretty rich.'

But she knows he's smiling.

* * *

At 3.30, I push open the door to the St Aldate's incident room. I could hear the noise halfway down the passage, but as soon as they see me the room falls silent. Silence with the fizz of expectation. They have the bit between their teeth now.

I go to the front and turn to face them.

'Right, I'm sure a lot of you have got wind of what's happened today, but we all need to be on the same page, so bear with me. First, the appeal. We've had over a thousand calls so far, and the usual crop of supposed sightings halfway across the country but nothing that looks particularly promising. Yet. Certainly no authenticated sightings of Daisy after she left the school gate at 3.52 that afternoon, and contrary to what the Masons originally led us to believe, Sharon Mason did *not* pick the children up from school, so Daisy and Leo had to walk back. Mrs Mason has also just called me to confirm that her daughter's school uniform is missing. All of which means we cannot *completely* discount the possibility that Daisy was abducted on her way home. On the other hand, we haven't located the mermaid costume yet either, and given she can't have been wearing both at the same time something clearly isn't adding up. Likewise both parents insist that when Daisy came home from school that afternoon she went upstairs and put on her music. Both say they heard it, but neither of them actually *saw* her. So that isn't adding up either. And I'm afraid there's something else we need to factor in as well.'

I take a deep breath. 'Sharon Mason now says she went out for up to forty minutes that afternoon, leaving the children alone in the house –'

'For Christ's sake, now she bloody tells us.'

'Look, I'm as frustrated as you are, but there it is. She didn't want her husband to know, apparently, which is why she didn't tell us until we got her alone. She thinks it was just after 4.30 that she left, because that's when Leo got home. She says she went first to the Glasshouse Street parade and then the M&S on the ring-road roundabout, but their CCTV is out of action and no one remembers her. Which may prove something or absolutely nothing. The important point for all of you is that the children were alone, and the side gate and patio doors were probably both open. So in theory Daisy could have just wandered off on her own, though if that was the case the odds are we would have found her by now, given the number of people we have looking. The other possibility is that someone could have taken her. Either from outside the house, or even – just conceivably – from inside.'

'Come on,' says a voice at the back. Andrew Baxter, I think. 'The chances of a random paedophile happening to swing by in that *precise forty minutes* –'

'I know, and I agree with you. The odds are vanishingly small. In fact there's only one way that would make sense and that's if someone was already watching the family and saw their opportunity when Sharon went out. Possibly someone Daisy knew, and would have let into the house. And that may not be as far-fetched as it sounds. Everett – can you share what you got from Daisy's friends?'

Verity Everett stands up. 'I just got back from speaking to Nanxi Chen and Portia Dawson. They both confirmed that Daisy had met someone recently and that it was a big secret. Neither could tell me who it was, but both said Daisy was angry afterwards and wouldn't speak to them about it.'

'And you're sure,' says Baxter, 'that they meant angry, not upset?'

Everett stands firm. 'Definitely angry. And there's something else. The kids in Daisy's class wrote fairy stories this term, and Daisy's has gone missing. The teacher's going to have another look for it. And yes, it could just be a complete coincidence, but we'll need to check that no one's been in that classroom who wasn't supposed to be there. Because it's just possible there's something in that story that could identify the person she'd been meeting. Something that person doesn't want anyone to see.'

'So,' I say, looking around the room, 'we urgently need to find out who that person was. And given Daisy Mason seems to have been pretty closely monitored most of the time, my guess is the only place she could have met anyone without her parents knowing is at the school. So I need someone to go through the CCTV at Bishop Christopher's for the last six weeks. Every break-time, every lunchtime. Extra brownie points for volunteering or else I just pick a victim.'

I scan their faces. 'OK, if there's no takers it's your turn to get the short straw, Baxter.'

'He won't mind,' quips Gislingham. 'He's an Aston Villa fan. He's used to watching a screen for hours and nothing happening.'

'What about the boy?' says someone else at the back, over the ensuing laughter. 'Leo – what's his story? Surely he would have heard if someone got into the house?'

I wait for the noise to die down. 'Good question. Bloody good question, in fact. When we first questioned Leo he said that Daisy got distracted by a butterfly on the walk home and he went on without her. Which didn't tally with what Sharon said about Daisy getting home first. So we pushed him a bit more and got a different story entirely. What he says *now* is that some of the older boys have been bullying him at school, and they caught up with him and

Daisy on the way home on Tuesday and started to have a go. Pushing him about, making fun of his name. They call him "Nuka the puker", apparently. Nuka's a character in *The Lion King*. For those of you who haven't seen it. The mangy one.'

'Christ,' says Baxter. 'It's all a bit bloody poncey, isn't it? It was Zit-face and Fat-bum when I was at school.'

More laughter. Baxter, for the record, is rather on the chunky side, but at least the zits are long gone.

'Doesn't surprise me,' says Everett drily. 'The sort of kids you get at that school – that's definitely the sort of smart-arse thing they'd come out with.'

'The point is,' I say, raising my voice, 'Leo says Daisy ran away when the bullies caught up with them, and that's why she got back before he did. Sharon Mason claims to know nothing about any of this, incidentally. According to this latest version of events, Leo went straight to his room when he got back and shut the door, so *in theory* he may not have heard anyone come into the house. He says he was annoyed with Daisy because she ran off and left him on his own, and he kept out of her way at the party for the same reason, which is why he didn't realize the girl in the daisy outfit wasn't her. I'm not sure I buy that, but he wouldn't budge on it, however much I pushed him. What *does* ring true is that Daisy and Leo had some sort of row on the way home.'

'Could it actually have *been* him?' says Baxter. 'If they had a row on the way home, could he have attacked her? Kids that age can be pretty volatile – she might have fallen over, hit her head –'

'In theory, yes, but if he did, where's the body? There's no way a child of ten could hide a body so well we haven't found it. Even if he had plenty of time, which he didn't.'

'OK,' says Baxter, though I can tell he's not completely convinced. 'But even if we discount him as a suspect, how much of this new story of his can we really believe? Some kids that age don't even know the difference between truth and lies.'

Boys that age, I think. Boys Jake's age.

'I don't think he's lying.' It's Gislingham, loudly, into the silence. 'Not about the bullying, anyway. Leo's form teacher, Melanie Harris, says she thinks it's been going on most of this term – his clothes were torn a couple of times and he had grazes on his hands, but they could never catch the kids responsible and Leo kept insisting he had just fallen over or something. Without an official complaint there wasn't much they could do. But he's definitely been acting up.'

Quinn considers. 'Didn't Sharon say he'd been moody?'

But Gislingham is shaking his head. They've been doing this low-level needling for weeks – ever since Quinn got bumped up to DS. 'I think this is more than just moody. He's had temper tantrums, been disruptive in class. A couple of weeks ago he went for another kid's eye with a pencil – the head teacher suspected it was one of the boys who've been bullying him. Leo didn't do the kid any actual damage, which is probably the only reason he got away with it. They got Sharon Mason into the school about it but she refused to take any of it seriously. Kept saying "boys will be boys", apparently, and "children are so mollycoddled these days" and stuff like that.'

The more I hear about Sharon Mason, the less I understand her. For someone so superficial, she's curiously opaque. There's something going on here, but I sure as hell don't know what it is. 'Did you look at the CCTV for the period after Leo and Daisy left, to see if anyone was following them?'

'I checked frame by frame for the half hour after, but there wasn't anything obvious. A few boys did leave heading in the same direction, but that doesn't prove anything. Kids aren't stupid these days. They know where the cameras are. Especially if they're up to no good.'

'All the same, can you follow up on the bullying angle, Chris? See if we can come up with some names. The teachers must have an idea who it might be.'

'Right, boss.'

'Who's next – Quinn?'

Quinn gets up and comes to the front. 'Barry Mason claims he was late home that day because of an emergency at one of his sites. One in Watlington. Well, I've checked, and he only has one job there, and work's been halted for three weeks. The owner told me she paid Mason ten grand a month ago and hasn't seen him since. Keeps saying he's coming and never turns up. She knows of at least three other people in the same position. Builders, eh? What a wanker.'

'Don't get me started,' I mutter blackly. 'So, if Mason wasn't in Watlington where he was supposed to be, where the hell was he? Quinn, can you see what you can find?'

'Won't be easy without access to his credit cards and phone records. But I can see if number-plate recognition has picked him up anywhere.'

'OK, everyone, one last thing. As at now, we have no grounds to arrest either of the Masons, so the family will be going home. In the full glare of the watching media. It's going to get pretty tough for them the next few days, but whatever the press and the Twitter trolls throw their way, we can't afford to be blinkered. There could still be other explanations for Daisy's disappearance that don't involve the family at all. As the lawyer the Masons will no doubt soon be hiring will be the first to tell me.'

Gislingham makes a face. 'What I wouldn't give to be a fly on the wall in that house tonight. Or a bug in the blender.'

I see Anna Phillips smile at that. 'Bug as in insect, or bug as in device?'

Gislingham grins. He has a good grin. 'Either would do.'

'So,' I say, bringing it to a close. 'Has anyone got

anything else? No? In that case meet again first thing tomorrow. Thanks, everyone.'

As I make my way back to the door, Everett swings alongside me. I could tell she had something else on her mind, but she obviously didn't want to raise it in public. She does that a lot; I wish she'd have the courage to back her own instincts, because she's rarely far wrong. And it would do Quinn good to be challenged once in a while. By someone other than Gislingham.

'What is it, Ev?'

'In Daisy's classroom they had a board up with drawings the children did of their fairy tales.'

I wait. Ev's not a time-waster. There'll be a point to this.

'Before we realized Daisy's story was missing, I had a look at the picture she did of it.' She gets out her phone and opens up a photo. 'See?'

It's not that easy to make out, but I think there's a little girl at the bottom of the picture wearing a tiara and a pink tutu, and towering over her a much taller female figure with a broomstick and an outsize handbag. There's a rather strange creature with foliage growing around its head like ivy, holding a bundle under one arm, and on the right a young male figure with yellow hair is fending off a monster with a huge snout and a curled tail. 'So you think –'

'That the little girl is Daisy? Definitely. All little girls want to be princesses. Or ballerinas.'

I smile. 'Or both, it would seem, judging from this.'

124

'And Daisy's father was always calling her his princess.'

My turn to make a face. 'Pass the sick bag.'

'I know, boss, but if you're eight –'

I shake my head. 'I'm not disagreeing. Just nauseated.'

But Ev's not finished. 'What really struck me is the woman behind the little girl. See the shoes? Those strap things at the front? And talk about killer heels.'

And now I see what she means. 'They're just like the ones Sharon Mason was wearing this morning. Is *still* wearing, for all we know.'

Ev nods, then points to the monster. 'Nanxi Chen told me Daisy had a new name for her dad. She'd started calling him the He Pig.'

I glance at her quickly and she nods. 'I know, and I'm trying very hard not to jump to the obvious conclusion. Trouble is, these days we see child abuse everywhere. It may not be that at all – it could just be she'd had a row with her father and she was letting off steam. Something completely innocent. Like not getting the latest Cabbage Patch doll.'

I smile. No prizes for guessing Everett has no kids. 'I don't think they're quite the thing any more, Officer.'

She grins. 'Showing my age. But you get what I mean. We all know how kids overreact sometimes. Everything seems enormous when you're that age.'

She flushes a little then, but I don't let it register. 'When did this start – the pig name?'

'Not sure exactly, only a few weeks ago? But that would make it about the same time they were doing those stories.'

'So you think we should check the CCTV to see if Barry's been in that classroom in the last week or so?'

She nods. 'I asked the head and as far as she's aware Barry hasn't been in any of the school buildings for months. There was a parents' evening last week, but Sharon went on her own. I'm going to drop by the house on my way home and ask if they know where the story is. It might answer the other big question, too.'

I frown. 'Which is?'

'Whether Daisy's school bag is in the house.'

I stare at her. How the fuck did I miss that? Call myself a sodding detective.

'She had it when she left the school – we saw that on the CCTV,' continues Everett, apparently oblivious to my sudden attack of self-doubt. 'So if it's in the house, that would mean she must have made it home after all, like the parents said. But if it's *not* there –'

'– it's much more likely she went missing somewhere between the school and the estate. Which could put the Masons out of the running.'

'You saw the room that night, didn't you, boss? Do you remember seeing the bag? It was one of those Disney Princess things. Pink.'

I think back. I wouldn't say I had a photographic memory, but I don't miss much. And surely the bag would have leapt at me – the only thing in all that glut of floral tat that didn't have a daisy stuck to it somewhere.

'No,' I say at last. 'I don't think it was there. But it doesn't necessarily prove anything. She could have put it away in a cupboard or something. Or Sharon could. The whole place was like a bloody show home.'

'Well, there's nothing to stop me asking.'

She's about to go, when I call her back. 'Barry Mason may give you a hard time – I doubt we're their favourite people right now.'

'I know. But I think it's worth a try. I'll back off if it gets rough.'

And it may not be a bad idea for the media mob to see a police officer at the door, either.

I take a deep breath. 'OK, go ahead. Wear your uniform, will you, so the hacks know who you are?'

She makes a face, but she knows what I'm getting at.

'And have a discreet chat with that neighbour first –'

She frowns. 'Fiona Webster?'

'That's the one. She strikes me as pretty sharp. You never know what might come out if you ask a few leading questions. And talk to the family doctor as well – see if they had any suspicions of abuse.'

'He's on holiday, I checked. But I'll email him.'

'Did the teacher say how Daisy had been lately?'

'Quieter than normal, but she was at pains to stress it was a very minor change. That it might mean nothing. To be honest, they were more concerned about Leo.'

'They're the only ones who were, then.'

'I know. Poor little sod.'

Everett takes another look at the photo on her phone. 'Even without the yellow hair, one thing I do know is that the prince in this picture is most definitely *not* Leo Mason. Can't see him saying boo to a goose, never mind fighting a monster.'

'You and me both. But if it's not Leo, then who the bloody hell is it?'

* * *

22 June 2016, 3.29 p.m.
27 days before the disappearance
5 Barge Close, upstairs bedroom

'You're not supposed to be in here.'

It's Leo, standing at the entrance to his parents' bedroom. Both the wardrobe doors are open, and Daisy is sitting at her mother's dressing table, putting mascara on her lashes. She's surprisingly adept at it. She smiles into the mirror. There's bright pink lipstick on her mouth and blue shadow on her eyelids.

'You're not supposed to be in here,' Leo repeats, frowning. 'She's downstairs. She'll know.'

'No she won't,' says Daisy carelessly, not looking at him. 'She never does.'

She slithers off the stool and goes over to the long cheval mirror. She's wearing a blue bikini and a pair of little glittery mini-me shoes with high heels. She takes up position, then walks towards the mirror, stops, drops her hip and strikes a catwalk pose. Then she turns away and looks back, blowing a kiss at her own reflection.

Leo wanders across to one of the wardrobes and sits down, pulling things out randomly and looking at them without any real interest. A pair of trainers, a musty towel, a hoodie. There's something solid and rectangular in the sweat pocket which thuds out on to the carpet. Daisy glances over. 'You're not supposed to know about that.'

Leo picks it up and stares at it. 'Whose phone is this?'

'I told you. It's a secret.'

* * *

The phone operators get the call at 5.30. It's then checked, rechecked and further details taken, before it eventually gets through to me at around 6.15. I'm in my office at St Aldate's, and Quinn is telling me we can't find any trace of Barry Mason on Tuesday afternoon or even confirm what time he got back to Canal Manor.

'Trouble is, he often came back during the day,' says Quinn. 'Dropping in between site visits presumably. So people would have got used to seeing his pick-up at odd times. It wouldn't have stood out. And in any case, most of the time it was Sharon's car on the drive, not his.'

I go to the window and look down at the street. Outside the Tesco opposite, a little boy is playing with a small grey dog, swinging a tennis ball round and round on a piece of string. I sigh; the dog is not the only one going in circles right now.

'Look,' says Quinn eventually, 'I hope you don't mind me saying this, but do you think there's a chance that we've got this all wrong?'

I wait. Then, 'How, exactly?'

'You said it yourself earlier – Daisy could have left the house while Sharon was out and Leo probably wouldn't even have noticed. Is it possible the poor little cow just ran away? With that family, you couldn't blame her.'

I sigh. 'I wondered that too. But it's two days now. With the number of people we have looking, and her face all over the media – we'd have found her. One way or the other.'

'Knock knock.' It's Gislingham at the door, with a sheaf of papers under his arm. 'We just had a call from a woman who recognized Barry Mason on the TV appeal –'

'Yeah, and?' says Quinn sardonically. 'Must be hundreds of people out there who recognize him. Most of whom he's ripped off. Frankly, I'm surprised it's not him that's gone missing – enough people must fantasize about doing him in.'

Which is in questionable taste, but I understand the sentiment.

Gislingham makes a face at the back of Quinn's head. 'If you'd let me finish. This woman – Amy

Cathcart – says his name isn't Barry Mason at all. It's Aidan Miles.'

Quinn and I exchange glances. 'And who the hell is Aidan Miles?'

Gislingham flips open his notepad. 'Thirty-something divorcee, flat in Canary Wharf, job in investment banking. No kids but open to suggestions. Likes keeping fit, travel, the theatre, French cooking and all the good things in life.'

'What the fuck –?'

'It's his profile. On FindMeAHotDate.com.'

We must be gaping, because he grins. 'No, really, I'm not making this up.'

He puts some papers on my desk. 'This woman, Amy Cathcart, has been texting and emailing him for weeks. She sent me the whole lot – look.'

He shoots a side glance at Quinn; DC one, DS nil.

Quinn, meanwhile, is racing through the printouts. 'No wonder Mason didn't want his face on the news. Has this woman actually met him?'

'Not yet. But look at the profile pic – it's obviously him. Though if you go on the site now, you won't find it. He deleted every trace the morning after Daisy disappeared.'

I sit back in my chair. 'So no prizes for guessing what he was really up to when he claims he was underwater in Watlington.'

'Will it be enough for a warrant?'

'For the house, possibly not. But it may get us his phone and credit cards. I'll get on it.'

* * *

Interview with Fiona Webster, conducted at
11 Barge Close, Oxford
21 July 2016, 5.45 p.m.
In attendance, DC V. Everett

VE: Thank you for seeing me again, Mrs Webster. I know this must be a difficult time for everyone.

FW: Do you know how long the press are going to be here? They're turning the place into a pigsty. Litter everywhere, beer cans, and as for the parking –

VE: I think you said your daughter, Megan, is in the same class as Daisy?

FW: Yes, that's right. Though how any of us didn't notice it wasn't her at the party, I'll never know. Apparently all the kids knew the two girls had swapped costumes, but didn't think to divulge the fact to their benighted parents.

VE: I believe one of this term's projects was to write a fairy story?

FW: Oh yes, they had a lot of fun with that. Even the boys.

VE: What did Megan write about?

FW: Oh, the usual, princesses and dwarves and wicked stepmothers. *Rapunzel* meets *Cinderella* with a dollop of *Frozen* thrown in for good measure.

VE: Funny how the stepmothers are always wicked. It would make me think twice marrying a man with young kids – seems you're on a hiding to nothing whatever you do.

FW: Oh, don't let that put you off. In my experience mothers *in general* are on a hiding to nothing when they get to this age. You can't do anything right. In fact I wouldn't be at all surprised if the wicked witch in Megan's story is based entirely on me.

VE: Funny you say that. The picture Daisy drew has a woman with shoes just like her mother's.

FW: Shaz's stilettos? Oh how funny – did they have the red soles too? Sharon claims they're genuine Louboutins but personally I think it's just nail varnish. I'm afraid they've become rather her trademark round here – she wears them everywhere regardless of the weather. Or the occasion. I saw her once half stuck in mud on the touchline when Leo was playing football. She did nothing but moan all afternoon. I don't think she's been to a match since.

VE: Does Barry Mason go - to the football, I mean?

FW: Sometimes. Not often. He and Leo aren't exactly close.

VE: But I remember you saying Barry definitely was close to Daisy - the 'dads and daughters thing'. Something about him carrying her around all the time?

FW: Well, yes. But I haven't seen him doing that so much lately.

VE: But they're close?

[*pause*]

FW: What are you getting at? Are you asking me if Barry could have been abusing his own daughter?

VE: Well, could he?

[*pause*]

FW: To be honest, it's not the first time I've asked myself that since she disappeared, but I really can't put my finger on anything one way or the other. He was all over her a year or so ago when they first moved here, but the last few times I've seen them together she's definitely been holding back. But honestly, you could say the same about my husband and Alice. A lot changes between six and eight. Girls just start to get shy, even with their own dads.

VE: And is there anything else – something that may not have struck you at the time, but now –
[*pause*]

FW: Actually, there was. I'd completely forgotten, but Barry came to pick Daisy up from school about three weeks ago. He doesn't do it very often but I think Leo had a doctor's appointment or something so Barry collected Daisy. I wasn't close enough to hear what happened but she suddenly started screaming and crying. Which is not like her at all. She's usually very calm, very 'composed'. Anyway, Barry played the dippy dad card – the whole lost and clueless what-do-I-do-now look, you know the sort of thing. Which at the time I just dismissed as another ploy to get the attention of the yummy mummys. But it was a bit odd, now I think about it.

VE: And what's he like – more generally? With you, say?

FW: Do you mean, has he come on to me? Then yes, he is a bit on the 'handy' side – you know the type, always touching your arm, the small of your back. Not safe in taxis, as my old boss used to say. He's always very careful to stay the right side of banter, but I know what would happen if you gave him the right signals. The sort of bloke who's always on the lookout, presumably on the basis that if you try often enough the odds are you'll strike lucky eventually.

VE: And what does Sharon think about that?

FW: Oh Lord, he doesn't do it around her! She's the jealous type. Full-on green-eyed monster. I saw her look daggers at Julia Connor once, just because Barry said something about her looking like she'd lost weight. That's always a sensitive subject where Sharon's concerned.

VE: There's a monster in Daisy's fairy tale too. One with a snout and a curly tail like a pig.

FW: Well, makes a change from dragons, I suppose.

VE: You haven't heard anything else about pigs, by any chance?

FW: *Pigs?*

VE: It came up when we talked to Nanxi Chen.

FW: No, sorry. Rings no bells with me.

VE: I see. Thank you. One final thing, Mrs Webster. Barry's flirting - is Daisy aware of it, do you think?

FW: Interesting question. She's very clever.
      Very observant. It wouldn't surprise me. It
      wouldn't surprise me at all.

* * *

Sent: 21/07/2016, 17.58
From: Richard.Donnelly@
            poplaravenuemedicalcentre.nhs.net
To: DCVerityEverett@ThamesValley.police.uk
CC: DIAdamFawley@ThamesValley.police.uk

Subject: Daisy Mason

Thank you for your email. You will understand there are
issues here in relation to patient confidentiality, but I can
appreciate the gravity and urgency of the situation. My
first duty is to the interests of the child, and that being
the case, I don't see any problem in confirming to you
that nothing I saw of Daisy Mason would suggest she
was being abused. I would, of course, have taken
appropriate action had any such suspicion ever arisen.
She was rather agitated when I last saw her (about three
weeks ago), but not in any way that would suggest
abuse. At the time I put it down to overexcitement.

   You did not ask about Leo Mason. He came in for his
check-up about two weeks ago, just before I left for my
holiday, and I noticed he had some fairly severe grazes
and cuts, which Mrs Mason said were the result of some

'rough and tumble' in the playground. I spoke briefly to Leo's school nurse about this just before I left and I will be following up with her next week. I therefore feel able to share this information with you as well.

If I can be of any further help, let me know, but please be aware that I will not be able to provide any further details about either of the children, or Mr and Mrs Mason, without the appropriate authorization.

* * *

At 6.35 Verity Everett rings the bell at 5 Barge Close. As she waits she smooths her uniform. It was still in the removals box in the spare room and smells more than a little musty after all these months. She shunts the belt down a bit, then back up – whatever she does, it never seems to sit right. She wonders in passing how Erica Somer manages to carry hers off so well. Not sexy, exactly, but at least she doesn't look like a sack of potatoes. She can hear the press pack buzzing behind her, held back at the end of the drive, and she pulls her cap down a bit further over her eyes. But her face is still going to be all over the late-evening news. At least her dad will enjoy that – she must remember to ring and tell him. Not that he's likely to miss it: ever since her mother died he's had the telly on all day. *Jeremy Kyle*, *Loose Women*, teleshopping. Anything to force back the silence.

And then the door opens. It's Leo. Which wrong-foots her for a moment.

'Hello, Leo. I'm Detective Constable Everett. Verity Everett. Is your mum or dad in?'

She knows they're in – of course they are. They're under siege. But what else could she say?

Leo turns. 'Mum! It's the police again.'

And then he disappears, leaving her standing at the step, acutely aware of the flashing cameras behind her as the photographers try to get a glimpse of the inside. The killer shot. In both senses. Then Sharon Mason appears. She pulls her cardigan round her. 'What do you want?' she says tetchily. 'I'm not inviting you in.'

'It won't take long, Mrs Mason. I think Daisy was writing a fairy tale at school recently?'

Sharon blinks, then looks past Everett to the cameras. If she's calculating whether it would be better for her public image to be seen talking to the police or slamming the door in their face, she apparently decides on the former. 'So?'

'We were just wondering if you have it? Her teacher can't find it.'

Sharon makes a face; she's clearly no great fan of Kate Madigan. 'I can't think what you want that stupid thing for.'

'She did a lovely drawing to go with it. There was a princess and a prince and a monster that looked like a pig –'

'Oh, don't talk to me about pigs. She's been drawing nothing but pigs for weeks. Pigs going shopping, pigs driving cars, pigs getting married.'

'How strange. Did she say why?'

Sharon shrugs. 'Who knows. Children never do things for logical reasons. Like who's friends with who. One minute it's Millie Connor then all of a sudden that's off and it's all Portia and that Chen girl. I try to ignore it most of the time.'

'So have you seen the story?'

'I saw it a couple of weeks ago. She was just finishing it. I checked it through to make sure there weren't any mistakes.'

'You don't remember what it was about?'

'Oh, the usual silly sort of thing. It was all a lot of nonsense.'

'I see. Could you have a look for it for me? It might be in her school bag.'

'I don't think Barry would –'

'It's not here.'

The voice is Leo's. He's at the foot of the stairs, swinging on the bottom banister. 'Her school bag. It's not here.'

Sharon frowns at him. 'Are you sure? I'm sure I saw it in her room.'

She turns and bustles past him up the stairs. Leo is still swinging on the banister. They can hear Sharon moving things about upstairs.

'Portia wasn't.'

Verity blinks at him. 'Sorry? Portia wasn't what?'

'Portia wasn't Daisy's best friend. Portia didn't like her.'

Verity opens her mouth to say something but then

there's a clatter of heels on the stairs and Sharon has come back.

'He's right, for once. It's not there, but how –'

But then, behind her, Everett hears the sound of a car drawing up and a clamour of cameras and questions. She turns to see Adam Fawley and Gareth Quinn striding up the path towards her.

'Where's your husband, Mrs Mason?'

Sharon's eyes narrow. 'Why? What do you want him for?'

'We can do this here,' says Fawley, 'in front of the media, or inside – it's really up to you.'

Sharon turns her head slightly, but her eyes never leave Fawley's face. '*Barry!*'

When he emerges, he has a can of lager in one hand and a tabloid newspaper in the other. 'This had better be bloody good.'

'A call was passed through to our incident room this evening, Mr Mason,' says Fawley. 'From a Miss Amy Cathcart. It seems you and she have been corresponding by email for the past three weeks.'

Sharon grips him by the arm. 'What are they talking about – who the bloody hell is *she*?'

'No one,' says Barry, shaking her off. But his face is white. 'I've never met anyone called Amy Cathcart.'

'That's true, Mrs Mason. Strictly speaking your husband has never actually *met* Miss Cathcart. But that's clearly what he had planned. I mean, why else join a dating site?'

'A *dating site*?' Sharon is incandescent. 'You've been on a bloody *dating site*?'

'I'm afraid so, Mrs Mason. Using a false name and a pay-as-you-go mobile phone I suspect you know nothing about. Am I right?'

Quinn only just intervenes in time as Sharon hurls herself at her husband's face. Christ, thinks Everett, feeling the flashes at her back, the press must be absolutely beside themselves.

'It occurs to me, Mr Mason,' says Fawley as Quinn pulls Sharon back into the house, 'that you might prefer to continue this conversation at the station.'

Barry throws Fawley a look of pure hatred. There's a scratch below his left eye. Then he squares his shoulders and thrusts the can and the paper into Everett's hands before turning to Fawley. 'Let's get this over with.'

* * *

7 June 2016, 10.53 a.m.
42 days before the disappearance
The Pitt Rivers Ethnographic Museum, Oxford

It's a bright summer day and three teachers from Bishop Christopher's are attempting to shepherd an unruly line of pupils into something resembling a queue. One of them is Kate Madigan, another Melanie Harris, and the third is Grania Townsend, who's wearing an eclectic mixture of clothes ranging from a pair of Doc Martens to a floral cardigan with a lace collar. The older children look bored already, having no idea what 'ethnographic' means and clearly sceptical about anything that calls itself a 'museum'. 'Just bear with me, OK,' says Grania. 'This is nothing like any museum you've ever been in before – I promise. There's a toad stuck with pins, and voodoo dolls, and a witch in a bottle, and a totem pole. A proper, big totem pole. You remember, like we saw in that book about the Native Americans?'

There's a flicker of interest at that. One of the smaller boys squints up at her. 'Is there *really* a witch in the bottle? How did they get her in?'

Grania grins. 'I don't think anyone knows. The bottle was given to the museum about a hundred years ago by a very old lady who warned there'd be no end of trouble if they ever opened it.'

'So they never did?'

'No, Jack, they never did. Best to be on the safe side, eh?'

Up ahead the queue begins to move and Kate Madigan starts to guide the younger children through into the main gallery, where they stand in a group looking up into the dim cavern of a room. There are African shields and Inuit skins hanging under the ceiling and the floor before them is a maze of glass display cases, crammed with every conceivable type of human artefact – *Musical Instruments, Masks, Featherwork and Beadwork, Funerary*

Boats, Weapons and Armour, Pottery, Coiled Baskets. So far, so organized, but inside each case is a glorious chaos of dates and places of origin, with Samurai jumbled with Surinam, and Melanesia with Mesopotamia. Some items still have their original labels – minuscule Victorian handwriting on yellowing paper attached with string. It's as if time stopped in 1895. And in some ways, it did. At least in here.

Kate Madigan comes up to Grania. 'Mel just had to take Jonah Ashby to the Ladies. He's got a nosebleed, poor little man – I think all this excitement was a bit too much for him. But I know what he means. This place is amazing.'

Grania smiles. There are children everywhere now, pointing and gasping and racing from one case to the next. 'I know. I love bringing classes here. The weirder the stuff is, the more the kids seem to like it.'

'No surprises there then.'

Grania nods towards one display where at least a dozen children are thronged round. 'That's the *tsantas*. Never fails to draw a crowd.'

'*Tsantas?*'

'Shrunken heads.'

Kate makes a face. 'Rather you than me.'

Grania grins. 'It is an acquired taste, I'll give you that.'

She makes her way over to the display, to find Nanxi Chen reading out the sign on the case with obvious relish, while a crowd of boys stares inside. There are a dozen heads in the case, most the size of a fist, but some much smaller. Several have rings through their noses and their original hair, out of all proportion to the tiny blackened elongated faces.

'*Shrunken heads were made by taking the skin off, and removing the skull and brain,*' Nanxi is saying. '*The eyes and mouth were sewn up to prevent the spirit of the dead coming back to haunt its killer. Then the skin was boiled in hot water, which caused it to shrink.* Wow, that's seriously disgusting.'

Grania Webster smiles. 'They're very old and they come from South America. Back then the tribespeople thought that taking your enemy's head would capture their soul and give you their power. They'd wear the heads round their necks at ritual ceremonies.'

One of the boys stares at her. 'Really? That's *awesome*.'

On the other side of the case, under *Treatment of Enemies*, Leo Mason is looking in at a collection of decorated skulls. Some are studded with shells, others have animal horns impaled on their foreheads. The one that's engrossing Leo is so small it must be from a child. There are metal skewers piercing the eye sockets, and the bone is bound tight with leather thongs. One of the curators wanders over. 'Bit scary, aren't they?' he says pleasantly.

Leo stares. 'Why does it have those pointed things stuck through its eyes?'

'Now that's a great question. It could have been for revenge. Or the sorcerer of the tribe might have done it to destroy an evil spirit.'

One of the other boys peers round the side of the case at Leo and lifts his hands, spectre-like. 'Whooooo!' Leo starts and leaps backwards, gripping the curator's jacket. The man puts his hand on the boy's shoulder.

'Are you OK? Do you want me to fetch your teacher?'

Leo shakes his head, but he hasn't let go his grip.

'How about going on a treasure hunt instead, then? There are fourteen wooden mice hidden somewhere in these cases. Some of your classmates are off looking for them, and your teacher says there's a prize for anyone who finds all of them. What do you think?'

Leo shakes his head again. 'I like the skulls,' he says eventually.

On the far side of the ground floor Kate Madigan is with a group of girls looking at *Amulets, Fetishes and Curses*. Portia Dawson is diligently copying down the names of the different types of talisman in a little notebook, while Daisy Mason is enchanted by a collection of silver filigree ornaments mounted on black velvet.

'They're like on a charm bracelet,' she says, glancing up at her teacher.

Kate smiles. 'They are, aren't they? I've seen them before. In Italy. People used to hang them over a baby's cradle, to protect them from harm and keep bad spirits away while they were sleeping.'

'Like the evil fairy in *Sleeping Beauty*?' asks Portia.

'Yes, a bit like that.' Kate moves closer and points through the glass. 'They're supposed to look like branches hanging upside down. Like mistletoe, at Christmas?'

Portia looks up and peers through the glass at the label, then writes CIMARUTA in careful capitals and starts to draw a picture of one of the charms.

'They all have different good luck symbols on them,' continues Kate. 'Can you see, Daisy? There's a moon and a key and a flower and a dolphin.'

Daisy is silent a moment. Then, 'Are they *really* magic, Miss Madigan? Can they really keep bad things away at night?'

Kate's face is serious. 'Some people think so. Where I come from, lots of the older people still believe in things like that.'

Daisy is still looking at the silver trinkets. 'I wish it was real,' she says wistfully. 'I'd like to get a charm like that.' She looks up at Kate Madigan, and then across at her brother. A group of older boys are pointing at a badly chipped carving of a lion in one of the cases, and gesticulating at Leo, laughing and sticking their fingers in their mouths.

'Nuka the puker! Nuka the puker!'

Daisy's voice drops to a whisper. 'I'd get one for Leo too.'

* * *

When Everett first transferred to Oxford she had the choice of a two-up two-down Victorian cottage off the

Botley Road that needed a lot of work or a refurbed flat above a dry cleaner's in Summertown. The flat won out, but only after she'd made sure it had a fire escape with access down to the street. It wasn't for her, it was for the cat. Not that her large lazy tabby uses it much. When she closes the door behind her at 9.15 that night, Hector is on his usual armchair, blinking at her in the sudden light. She throws her uniform cap on the settee and sits down, scratching Hector absent-mindedly behind the ears. He looks a lot like Portia Dawson's cat. And that in turn reminds her of what's been nagging at her ever since she left the Masons' house.

Portia.

She'd wondered briefly, at the school, why Portia, alone of Daisy's friends, had been so upset her parents had to keep her at home, and now that idle curiosity has snapped into sharp relief. Everyone said they were best friends – the teachers, Sharon, Portia herself. But not Leo. Not Leo. And what did Fawley call him? – a 'watching sort of a kid'. Could he have seen something no one else did? What if they've been missing something all along? She thinks of that last CCTV footage of Daisy and replays it in her mind. Daisy and Nanxi were talking, but Portia was hanging back, and as far as she can remember, Portia was still standing there, watching, when Daisy followed Leo towards Canal Manor. If they were best friends, you wouldn't think anything of it. But what if they weren't? What if Portia actually disliked Daisy – how would you interpret that scene then? Everett picks up her mobile and calls Gislingham.

'Sorry it's so late. I just had a quick question about the footage from the school.'

She can hear the TV in the background, and Janet asking who's on the phone.

'Sorry, Ev – can't hear for *Corrie*. OK, I'm in the kitchen now. Shoot – what is it?'

'When you were looking at the CCTV to see if any of the boys followed Leo, do you remember noticing Portia Dawson? Do you remember what she did after Daisy and Leo disappeared out of view?'

'Phew, now you're asking. I'm pretty sure she went off the same way a few minutes later, but don't quote me on that. Why, is it important?'

Everett takes a deep breath. 'I think it could be. I need to call Baxter and ask him to check. Because if you're right – if Portia really did follow Daisy that day – she wasn't going home. The Dawsons' house is in the *opposite direction.*'

* * *

'Well, Mr Mason, we really must stop meeting like this.' It's cheap, I know, but irresistible.

He's in Interview Room One. No comfy chairs here, and spare me the Spanish Inquisition jokes because I've heard them all before. Paintwork some dead colour you wouldn't paint a khazi and windows so high you can't see out. And in the middle, four plastic chairs and one of those black tables with a wooden edge that I swear they only make for police stations. The architecture of intimidation, Anna Phillips called it. Personally, I'm wary of attributing anything like intelligent design to the criminal justice system, but even if it's accidental, I can't deny it works. Just one more element of the same attrition creep. Kettle, nettle, unsettle. Barry Mason, though, seems determined not to let the dismal surroundings get to him. It's probably all that time he spends on half-finished building sites. I haven't had a great experience with builders, but you've probably gathered that.

Quinn closes the door behind us. The air is rancid with the sweat of lies. Barry smells of beer and cheap aftershave. I'm not sure which is worse.

'So, Mr Mason,' I begin, 'now we all know where we stand, perhaps you could tell us where you really were on Tuesday afternoon. Because it clearly wasn't Watlington, was it?'

'All right, I wasn't there. But I wasn't in Oxford killing my daughter either.'

I raise my eyebrows, mock-shocked. 'Who said anything about killing your daughter? Did you, DS Quinn?'

'Not me, boss.'

'I know what you're thinking. I'm not stupid,' says Mason, turning away.

'So tell us where you actually were. From 3.30, say.'

He shoots me a look, then starts to chew the side of

his thumbnail. 'In Witney. In a bar. Waiting for some tart who didn't turn up.'

I smile in what I hope is a particularly irritating manner. 'Must have got a better offer, eh? Can't say I'm surprised. You're not much of a catch. Big mortgage, two kids. Oh, but I forgot, you tell them you don't actually *have* any kids, don't you?'

He refuses to rise to that one.

'Did you pay by credit card, Mr Mason?' asks Quinn.

'Do I look stupid?' he snaps. 'My bloody wife goes through my pockets.'

'So you can't actually prove you were there?'

'Sorry, didn't know I'd need a bloody alibi, did I?'

'And what about afterwards?'

'After what?'

'Well, I can't believe you sat there all afternoon like some sad stood-up teenager. How long did you give it before you gave up?'

He shifts in his chair. 'Dunno. Half an hour, maybe.'

'And then you left.'

He hesitates, then nods.

'What time was that?' says Quinn.

'Around four. Four fifteen maybe.'

'So why didn't you go home then?'

He glowers at me. 'Because I'd already rung Sharon to say I was going to be late and I didn't want to get roped into all the pissing about for the bloody party. All right? Satisfied? That makes me a lazy git, not a murderer. There's no law against that.'

I wait. 'So what did you do? Where'd you go?'

He shrugs. 'Just drove about a bit.'

Another pause. Then we get to our feet and he looks from one to the other. 'You mean, that's it? I can go home?'

'Yes, you can go home. Though I'm surprised you want to, given the reception you're likely to get.'

He makes a face. 'It was a figure of speech. There are plenty of hotels in this sodding town. In case you hadn't noticed.'

'On which subject, don't go anywhere without telling us first. We still need to check your whereabouts that afternoon.'

'I've already told you, I can't prove it.'

'CCTV doesn't lie, Mr Mason. Rather like DNA.'

Am I imagining it or does something flicker across his face at that?

'I want a lawyer,' he says sullenly. 'I'm entitled to see a lawyer.'

'You can see whoever you like. Be sure to tell them you've not been arrested.'

At the door I pause and turn towards him. 'What did Daisy call you?'

He blinks. '*Sorry?*'

'It's a simple enough question. What did Daisy call you?'

I use the past tense deliberately, intrigued to see if he challenges it. But he doesn't seem to notice.

'*Daddy?*' he says, sarcastic. 'Perhaps the odd *Dad* on

occasion. Sorry, but we don't go in for *Pater* where I come from. What the fuck difference does it make?'

I smile. 'Perhaps none. I was just curious.'

* * *

At 10.35 a.m. the following morning Everett knocks again at the door of the Dawsons' house. She can see the cat perched on the back of a chair in the front room, eyeing her suspiciously through the geraniums in the window box. The door opens to a tired but distinguished-looking man with greying hair.

'Yes?' he says with a frown. He has a strong Ulster accent. 'We don't buy at the door.'

Everett raises an eyebrow and her warrant card. 'Neither do I. Detective Constable Everett, Thames Valley CID. May I come in?'

He has the grace to blush, then stands back and gestures for her to pass. She walks through the passage down into the big white and ash kitchen on the lower ground floor, where Eleanor Dawson is pouring coffee.

'Oh, Detective!' she says gaily. 'I didn't realize you were coming back.'

'I wasn't expecting to, Dr Dawson. I came to see Portia. Is she here?'

Patrick Dawson glances at his wife. 'She's upstairs. What is this about? I thought she'd already told you everything she knows.'

'I just have a few more questions. Could you call her down?'

There's an awkward few moments as the three of them wait in silence for Portia to appear. Which she does, eventually. And warily.

'What does she want, Mum?' she says, her eyes wide. She sounds very young – she *is* very young.

Eleanor Dawson goes to her daughter and puts her arm round her. 'There's nothing to worry about, darling. I'm sure it's just routine.'

Everett takes a step towards her. 'I just wanted to ask you again about the day Daisy disappeared. You see, my colleague looked at the TV footage from the school gate and it looks like you followed Daisy. Even though that's not your way home. Is that right?'

Portia looks up at her mother. 'I didn't do anything, Mum,' she says in a small voice.

'I know you didn't, darling. Just explain what happened to Constable Everett and everything will be fine.'

'So did you follow Daisy, Portia?' says Everett.

There's a pause, then a nod. 'Just for a little way. Then I had to come back so Mum could take me to my maths class.'

Eleanor Dawson intervenes. 'That's absolutely correct, Constable. The class starts at 4.30 so Portia must have been back here by 4.15 or we'd have been late. Feel free to confirm that with them. It's the Kumon Study Centre on the Banbury Road.'

Everett hasn't taken her eyes from Portia. 'I'm still curious why you followed Daisy that day.'

'I just wanted to talk to her.'

'Because you two were best friends – that's what you told us, isn't it?'

Portia seems to have realized where this is tending, because she just stares. Tears start to well in her eyes.

'You see, Portia,' says Everett gently, moving towards her, 'we've been told you'd fallen out with Daisy. And when DC Baxter looked at the CCTV for the week before the party, we saw the two of you having a big argument – you hit her and pulled her hair and shouted at her. There's no sound, but it's easy to see what you were saying. You're saying you hate Daisy and you wish she was dead.'

Portia hangs her head and the tears roll down her face. 'She was mean to me. She said my dad didn't think I was clever enough to be a doctor like him and being good at drawing wouldn't get me anywhere –'

'Oh, *darling*,' says Eleanor Dawson, reaching out and wiping the tears from her daughter's cheek. 'You mustn't believe everything Daisy told you. She was always making things up.'

Portia is shaking her head. 'But I know this was true because she sounded just like Daddy – she did his voice and everything –'

Eleanor Dawson shoots an angry look at her husband, then crouches down and whispers, 'It's all right, Portia. No one thinks you did any harm to Daisy.'

Portia is still shaking her head. 'But you don't under*stand* – I made one of those voodoo curse things like we saw in the museum and I stuck pins in it and wished she was dead, and now she is and it's all my fault . . .'

Patrick Dawson steps firmly between Everett and his family. 'I think that's enough, Constable. You can see you're distressing my daughter. And you can't seriously suspect her of having anything to do with that child's death. She's only eight years old, for heaven's sake.'

Everett looks at the sobbing girl and then back at her father. 'We don't yet know that Daisy Mason is dead, sir. And you might consider all this is just trivial playground squabbling, but children take that sort of stuff deadly seriously. As your daughter obviously did. And you'd be surprised what kids can be capable of, if pushed. Even if they are only eight.'

* * *

On my way to the station I find myself redirected by roadworks and realize I'm only five minutes from Port Meadow. I'm not sure quite why I do it, but I pull down the side road and park up near Walton Well, then get out and walk for a while. Ahead, the old village of Binsey is just visible amid the trees; behind me the towers of the city; to the north, much further away, a smudge of brown that marks Wolvercote. And to the right, closer than any of them, the roofs of Canal Manor, one or two windows catching the sun. Out on the meadow, the mist is still clinging in the hollows and the cattle are moving slowly through the tufts of grass, their ears flicking at unseen midges. And above it all, a huge sky billowed with pinkish clouds. I loved clouds as a kid. I knew all their names – mackerel skies, cirrus, cumulonimbus. We lived in such a shitty little suburb I made my landscape from the one over my head – mountains and castles with ramparts and warring armies. I don't think kids do that any more. They do that sort of thing on Xbox or *Clash of Clans* instead. No imagination required. I always hoped I could share my clouds with Jake, but he just wanted an Xbox too. Like his mates. Perhaps he was just too young.

And later, after we lost him, I used to come here to walk, pounding my grief into the dirt. An hour out, an hour back. The same monotonous grinding pace, day after day, month after month. Rain, snow, ice, fog. I remember suddenly that Sharon Mason used to run here too. Perhaps I saw her. Perhaps she even smiled at me. Perhaps all this was building, even then.

When I get to the station I realize the cost of my detour. I haven't been able to get a proper coffee and have to resort to the machine in the corridor. I'm standing at it, trying to decide on the lesser of its various evils, when Gislingham comes slamming through the swing doors towards me. I can see at once that something's happened.

'It's Sharon,' he says, out of breath. 'She wants to see you. I've put her in Interview Room Two.'

'What's it about?'

He shrugs. 'No idea. You're the only one she'll speak to.'

'And where's Leo? Surely she didn't leave him on his own in the house with that pack of vultures outside?'

'Don't worry, he's with Mo Jones in the family room.'

'Right, well, that's something. Can you go back and sit with him until I finish with Sharon —'

'Me? Isn't that what Mo's for?'

'Trust me, it'll be the best fun you have all day — in fact, it'll probably be the first time you've ever had an audience that actually enjoys listening to you crapping on about football. Find Quinn, can you, and get him to join me.'

* * *

---

* * *

Interview Two is, if anything, even ranker than Interview One. But looking at Sharon Mason's face, 'rancour' might be the better description right now. She can scarcely contain her fury. Woman scorned doesn't even come close.

I pull out the chair. She looks at Quinn and then at me. 'I said I wanted to speak to you. Not him.'

'DS Quinn is just here to satisfy procedure, Mrs Mason. It's in your interests as well as ours.'

She makes a little huffy movement, and I gesture to Quinn to wait by the door.

'So, Mrs Mason, how can I help you?'

'You said my husband had been on a dating site. But that he hadn't actually met that woman, what's-her-name.'

'Amy Cathcart. No, he hadn't met her.'

'But she wasn't the only one.'

'We're still waiting for full records from FindMeAHotDate —'

She winces as the knife twists, but I don't care.

'— though it looks like he's been using it for months. He tried to delete his profile on Wednesday morning. The day after Daisy disappeared.'

I wanted to see how she took that, but she has other things on her mind.

'So he's been seeing other women all that time — seeing them and — and — *sleeping with them*?'

I shrug. 'I have no proof of that, Mrs Mason. But I suppose we must assume so. It's possible more of them will come forward. Then we'll know more.'

Her face is so red I can almost feel the heat off her. 'And what does she look like, this *Amy Cathcart*?'

This, I confess, does wrong-foot me. But as soon as she's said it, I know why. I turn round to Quinn. 'I haven't seen a picture of her. Have you, Sergeant?'

He twigs what I'm doing straight away. 'Only her profile pic, boss. Blonde hair. On the slender side, but very nice curves, if you get what I mean. Very nice-looking, actually.'

Sharon is struggling to contain herself now. Her shoulders are trembling with the effort.

'I brought you something,' she says eventually. 'Two things.'

She reaches down and puts a Morrisons carrier bag on the table. The thing inside glints lazily in the low light. Blue and green. Overlapping like the scales on a fish tail –

I feel my heart jerk. 'Where did you find that, Mrs Mason?'

'In *his* wardrobe. When I was packing up his crap so he can bloody well move out. It was hidden under his dirty gym kit.'

I hear Quinn's intake of breath, and then the sound of the door opening, and a few moments later he's back in the room wearing plastic gloves. He takes the carrier bag and puts the whole thing carefully into an evidence bag.

'You do know,' I continue, 'that we will now have to take a DNA sample from you, Mrs Mason?'

'Why?' she bridles. 'What have I done? It's not me you should be looking at –'

'It's purely for elimination,' I say, placatory. 'I assume you weren't wearing gloves when you found this costume in the wardrobe?'

She hesitates, then shakes her head. 'No.'

'Then your DNA will inevitably be on it. And we'll need to eliminate that from the investigation.'

I'm not sure she'd thought that all the way through, but it's too late now.

'There was something else?'

She says nothing, and I try again. 'Mrs Mason? You said you had two things?'

'Oh. Yes. There's this. It was in the wardrobe as well.'

She opens her handbag – the fake one – and takes

out a piece of paper. A4 originally but folded in two, like a birthday card. There are creases where someone has screwed it up and then flattened it out again. She pushes it towards me, and I see it is, in fact, an actual birthday card. A handmade one, from Daisy to her father. She's written the words on the front so that they form the outline of a birthday cake with a candle. Something as precise as that, for an eight-year-old, it must have taken her hours. I find myself seeing her – the real child, the living laughing child – more vividly than I ever have. And I am more than ever convinced that she is dead.

H
appy
Birthd
ay
Da
ddy

You are the best Daddy in the world. You always look after me and kiss it better when I fall over. We have fun when I swing in your lap and in the swimming pool. When I am big and I am rich I will buy you all your favrite things

I'm feeling slightly sick. The lap, the swimming – it could all have a perfectly innocent explanation. But if it did, Sharon wouldn't be sitting here right now. I look up and meet her eye and I don't like what I see. She's been wronged, I know that, but Christ, the woman is hard even to pity.

'Turn the page,' she says.

And so I do.

The inside is stuck thick with pictures. Mostly colour, one or two from newspapers. All her father's favourite things. Fish and chips and mushy peas. A can of lager. A bodybuilder with dumb-bells. A sports car. But these are dwarfed by the image in the centre, and not just in terms of size. It's a pair of breasts with huge red nipples. They're cut out in close-up so they look disembodied, almost anatomical. But there's nothing scientific about the impact this picture has.

'She must have got that from one of his dirty mags,' says Sharon.

My first thought is to wonder, if that's true, what else she must have seen. I have a horrible image of a clever, intent little girl, carefully scrutinizing each sordid page, looking for what her daddy likes.

'When's your husband's birthday?' My throat feels dry.

A pause this time. 'April the second.'

'Didn't you see it then – when she gave it to him?'

Her eyes narrow. 'No, of course I didn't. What do you take me for? It was *their little secret*. Don't you get it?'

'Oh, I get it, Mrs Mason.' I push back my chair. 'Thank you for bringing this to our attention. Could I ask you to remain here for a little while, in case we have other questions? DS Quinn will get you some tea.'

'I don't want your tea. I told you before. I don't like it.'

'Cold drink?' says Quinn. 'Diet Coke?'

She throws him a venomous look. 'I'll have fizzy water.'

Outside, in the corridor, I lean heavily against the wall.

'You OK, boss?'

'I knew that bloke was a wanker, but Christ almighty.'

'Look on the bright side: it might get us our warrant – access to his computer. Even if it's not enough for an arrest.'

But I'm not so sanguine. 'I suspect we'll need more than the card for that. But there's no harm asking. Let's hope we get a magistrate with an eight-year-old daughter.'

'OK, I'm on it.'

He's about to go when I call him back. 'Tell me, if Mason had gone straight home from Witney, rather than "driving around" as he claims, how long do you think it would have taken him to get there?'

Quinn considers. 'That time of day – half an hour, forty minutes tops.'

'So it's possible he got home at exactly the moment Sharon Mason was out.'

Quinn frowns. 'I guess so. Doesn't leave much time, though. To kill the girl, get rid of the body and be gone before his wife gets back.'

'But what if that's not what happened? What if Sharon came back and found them together – found him actually doing something to Daisy? There's a huge row, and somewhere, in the middle of it, Daisy gets killed. Accident or rage, the result's the same.'

'So either one of them could have actually killed her?'

'If that's really the scenario, then yes.'

'But it's Barry who got rid of the body?'

I nod. 'I'm guessing so. Can't see Sharon doing it, can you? Not in those bloody shoes of hers, anyway.'

'So all this happened between 5.30 when Mason got home and – what? – six-ish?'

'Half six at the latest, since they were expecting people by then. The question is how far he could have driven and still got back in time for that. Somewhere he could have buried the body or hidden it well enough that no one's found it yet. But remember, he's a builder – he has his own sites, and he'd know about others – jobs he'd bid for. Empty building plots with big holes in the ground just waiting to be filled.'

Quinn's still processing all this. 'But if what you say is right, why didn't they just claim the girl had been abducted on her way home from school? Why go through all that pantomime with the party?'

'Because they couldn't be sure someone hadn't seen Daisy on the estate that afternoon. We know now that didn't happen. But neither of the Masons knew that – she could have talked to a neighbour, stopped to pet a dog –'

'But it was a complete fluke no one realized she was missing hours earlier – right at the start of the party. The whole thing was the most colossal risk.'

'Murder always is,' I say drily. 'Especially when it isn't planned. And what other choice did they have?'

'But in that case, why did she shop him now? It would have been much harder to break them if they'd stuck to the same story. Even Sharon Mason must have realized that.'

'I think we have Amy Cathcart to thank for that. She was the last straw. Think about it from Sharon's point of view – she's been telling lie after lie to cover up for Barry and now she finds out he's been cheating on her for months. Right now, revenge is all that matters. I don't think she realizes how much danger she's put herself in.'

'So do we arrest her?'

'No, we can't, not yet. All we have is guesswork. Let's give her some rope – make her think she's succeeded in throwing all the blame on Barry. I'm betting she'll make more mistakes.'

'I'll get on to the search team – see if there's anywhere we could have missed that's within an hour's range of the house. Though with a car, and that much time, we're talking a pretty big area.'

'I know. But that's where we are. And when you've done that, get everyone in the incident room in an hour.'

'Where will you be?'

'Talking to Leo. If anyone knows what happened that day, he does.'

* * *

In the family room, Gislingham is as happy as a pig in shit. Though to be fair, Leo appears to be enjoying himself too – when I push open the door they're watching goals from Chelsea's 2015 winning season on the DC's iPhone.

'Did you see that pass?' says Gislingham excitedly as tinny cheering comes from the mobile. 'Fàbregas was brilliant in that game.'

He looks up and sees me. 'Oh, sorry, didn't realize you were there, boss.'

'How are you, Leo?' I say, pulling out a chair and sitting down. 'DC Gislingham been keeping you entertained?'

Leo blushes and looks down. Then he nods.

'You want to show me – that goal you were both just looking at?'

Leo comes over and stands next to me. It takes him a moment or two to reset the video, but then we go through the goal again. The pass, the back heel, the pass.

'Do you remember,' I say casually, 'when you were here last time, and you told me what happened the day Daisy disappeared?'

He nods, his thumbs speeding over the touchscreen. He clearly has a knack for these things – it took me weeks to master mine. It was Jake who set it up for me in the end. Smiling and giving me that why-are-parents-so-useless look. I didn't mind being useless with phones; I just wish I hadn't been so useless in the ways that really mattered.

I take a deep breath. 'You said that you got home and went up to your room. Did you see your dad that afternoon?'

He slides a glance at me. 'No. He came in later.'

'And if he'd come in before that, you'd have known? You'd definitely have heard if someone came in the house?'

A shrug.

'Did you hear your mum go out?'

He shakes his head. 'I had my headphones on.'

'But you're sure Daisy was in her bedroom?'

It's hot in here and he pushes up his sleeves, almost without thinking. 'The music was on.'

'So just to be sure I'm clear, you were in your own room all the time till the party, with your headphones on. And you didn't hear your mum go out, or anyone come in, or any other loud noises?'

'I was annoyed with Daisy. She ran away.'

'Yes, I remember. OK, Leo, I'll leave you to talk some more with DC Gislingham. Your mum is helping us with some things, so it may be a while before she can come and get you. Are you all right staying here a bit longer?'

But I'm not sure he even hears me. He's on to the next goal.

Gislingham follows me out and pulls the door to.

'Boss,' he says, keeping his voice low, 'I've been watching him for half an hour now and I have to tell you, I'm not sure that kid's all there. I think he might be, you know, autistic or something.'

'I don't think it's that,' I say slowly. 'But I agree with you. From what I just saw, something's very wrong.'

* * *

At Bishop Christopher's the corridors ring with the emptiness of the end of term. One or two teachers are still on-site, tidying and taking posters down ready for a new start in September, but otherwise the building is eerily empty. In the caretaker's office at the back, Andrew Baxter has set up a rackety fan, and is sitting in front of the computer screen still scrolling through the footage from the school gate. His shirt is sticking to the back of the chair and he's already had two texts from his wife asking when he's going to be home. But he keeps telling himself, just one more file, just one more file. And sometimes, that sort of diligence is more than its own reward. He sits forward suddenly. Replays. Replays again. Then gets out his mobile and makes a call.

'Boss? I'm at the school. I think you should see this. I think the goalposts may just have moved. Again.'

* * *

Scott Sullivan @SnapHappyWarrior   14.06
Just saw the news and want to say to all the prats out there – you were wrong, even the fuckwit police suspect the parents now #DaisyMason

Annabel White @TherealAnnabelWyte   14.08
Add a ✿ to your avatar to show your support
and fight back against the trolls #DaisyChain
#FindDaisy

Amanda May @BuskinforBritain   14.09
I can't believe it – someone just said that
#DaisyMason's father had been grooming young
girls on a website? Is that true? #disgusted

MtN @Nuckleduster1989   14.10
Those #Mason shits deserve to rot in jail – I reckon
they were in it together – he was abusing the
kid + the mother covered it up #sick

MickyF @TheGameBlader666   14.11
@Nuckleduster1989 I hope they get cancer. I hope
they die a vile & horrible death #Masons

Anon Anon @Rottweiller_1982   14.11
@Nuckleduster1989 @TheGameBlader666 Jail's too
good for them – they should burn in hell for what
they did #DaisyMason #guilty

MickyF @TheGameBlader666   14.14
@Rottweiller_1982 @Nuckleduster1989 Perhaps
someone should help them on their way. Police
r so shit theyll never prove nothing

Beat Pete @dontgivemethatshit   14.15
Wd be doing the world a favour to kill those
bastards – wish theyd fuck off and die
@TheGameBlader666 @Rottweiller_1982
@Nuckleduster1989

Anon Anon @Rottweiller_1982   14.15
Can't be hard to find out exactly where they live???
@TheGameBlader666 @dontgivemethatshit
@Nuckleduster1989

UK Social Media News @UKSocialMediaNews 14.15
So who do you think is guilty? Barry Mason or
Sharon Mason? Tweet us and join in our poll
#DaisyMason

Emma Gemma @TiredandEmotional   14.15
❀❀❀❀❀❀❀❀❀❀❀❀❀ #DaisyChain #FindDaisy

Ellery B @InTheKookoosNest   14.16
@UKSocialMediaNews I think it was the mother –
looks like an utter utter cold-hearted bitch
#DaisyMason

Anne Merrivale @Annie_Merrivale_   14.16
I really want to believe the Masons are innocent,
but how can you? You just need to take one look at
the way they were on TV #DaisyMason ❀

MickyF @TheGameBlader666   14.17
Those Mason scum are going to get away with murder someone ought to go round there

Ellery B @InTheKookoosNest   14.18
Police shd give them a lie detector bet they wd fail #liars #DaisyMason

Linda Neal @Losingmyreligion   14.18
I truly do not know how those parents can live with themselves #DaisyMason

Angela Betterton @AngelaGBetterton   14.19
@Losingmyreligion You have it *so* wrong – they're a nice normal family – I know them, you don't. #DaisyMason ✾

Janey Doe @VictoriaSandwich   14.20
I bet the body will never be found. It'll be just like all those other missing children. #DaisyMason #RIP ✾✾✾

Seb Keynes @CastingAspersions   14.20
@UKSocialMediaNews I think the wife did it too – just look at that TV appeal #DaisyMason

Ellery B @InTheKookoosNest   14.21
Here r the Qs I wd ask 1) how did an intruder supposedly get into yr garden when all those ppl was there? #DaisyMason

Ellery B @InTheKookoosNest   14.22
2) And Y R the police now asking about the time
B4 the party? #DaisyMason

Linda Neal @Losingmyreligion   14.24
Is that tweet I just saw true? Do the police think she
was dead before the party even started?
#DaisyMason #appalled

Janey Doe @VictoriaSandwich   14.26
I think theyre in it together – father killed her & the
mother covered it up. Just shows u never know what
goes on in private #DaisyMason

Bethany Grier @BonnieGirlie9009   14.29
A friend of mine says she's sure she's
seen the father's face on FindMeAHotDate.com
– the cheating bastard
#DaisyMason

Holly Harrison @HollieLolliepops   14.32
OMG I just found out I was only emailing the
father of that poor little #DaisyMason – he was on
a dating site under another name . . .

Holly Harrison @HollieLolliepops   14.35
. . . he's deleted his profile but I downloaded
it – you can see it <u>here</u> #cheat #liar
#DaisyMason

Linda Neal @Losingmyreligion   14.37
Well if the father can #cheat then perhaps he can
kill as well – clearly had a lot of nasty secrets
#DaisyMason

ITV News @ITVLiveandBreaking   14.55
BREAKING Reports coming in that the father of
#DaisyMason has been leading a double life under a
false name and frequenting dating sites.

ITV News @ITVLiveandBreaking   14.56
More to come on this story as soon as we get it.
#DaisyMason

*   *   *

Outside Bishop Christopher's, I park up and call the station. Apparently the magistrate isn't playing ball. Wants
to talk to the Super first, and since he's out today we're
going to have to wait till tomorrow morning. I swear.
First at Quinn and then, after I end the call, at the universe in general. Then I sit for a moment before turning
off the engine. A few yards away, two young women are
talking by one of those two-seater Nissan Figaros. One
of the women has long dark red hair in a ponytail and a
hessian bag with raffia flowers around the top, the other's standing by her bicycle. Her bleached hair has bright
pink ends, and she has a stud in her nose and a pair of
camouflage cargo pants. It strikes me suddenly that

174

she's the only real human being I've seen since this investigation began. All those people leading their plastic Stepford lives. Not a hair or a blade of grass out of place. I get out and lock the car, and as I walk to the door I'm aware the two women are talking about me.

When I find the caretaker's office, there's a woman there with Baxter. She gets up at once and comes towards me, hand outstretched. She's nervous, edgy.

'Alison Stevens, I'm the head. DC Baxter asked me to pop over and look at the footage he's found, but I'm not sure I can be of much help.'

I pull out a chair and sit down next to Baxter. 'What have you got?'

'The quality's not great,' he says. 'No sound and it's only black and white, but it's better than sod all. The first one is early April. After the Easter break. This is lunchtime on the twelfth.'

The image is of the school gates, which are closed, and the chicken-wire fence either side. There are kids running in and out of shot in the playground. Balls bouncing, two girls doing some immensely complex clapping game. Three skipping. Then I see her. Daisy. She's alone, but she doesn't seem bothered by her lack of company. She stoops to look at something on a leaf, then watches as it flies up and away. A butterfly, perhaps. It's strange, watching her like this – this girl I have thought about every minute of every day since she disappeared, and yet know so little about. She couldn't possibly have known anyone would look at this footage. She might not even have known the camera was there. It feels curiously intrusive and I realize suddenly that this is what paedophiles do. It's not a good thought.

And then a figure appears on the pavement opposite. He must be fourteen or fifteen. Tall, blond. He comes up to the gate and calls Daisy over. She's clearly intrigued, but wary, and she stays a good foot shy of the gate. They talk a while – or rather he talks and she listens – and then the bell must go because the kids start to drift towards the school door, and the boy disappears out of shot, leaving Daisy gazing after him.

'The next one is a couple of days later,' says Baxter. 'Pretty much the same thing, only Daisy's keener to talk that time, it seems. And then there's April nineteenth. At 12.05 there's a delivery and the van blocks the view for five minutes or so, then it moves away and this is what we see.'

Daisy is alone on the pavement. She keeps looking around, presumably to check if any of the supervisors in the playground have noticed she's outside the gate. A few moments later, the boy arrives. Daisy seems really happy to see him. They talk briefly, and once or twice the boy looks over his shoulder, as if at someone just out of view. Then the two of them head off together towards his unseen companion.

I turn to Alison Stevens.

'I want to say at once,' she says quickly, 'that what you just saw is absolutely against all our operating procedures. Playground supervisors are required to monitor any traffic coming on to school premises and ensure all the children are inside the gates –'

'Right now, I'm not interested in what should or shouldn't have happened. All I want to know is if you have any idea who that boy is.'

She swallows. 'I wish I did. I didn't come to Kit's until last year, so he'd have left here by then if he was one of ours. I've just sent a still from the footage to the local secondary heads, but no one's come back to me yet. I'm afraid some might already have gone on holiday.'

'Baxter, what time does the camera show Daisy getting back to school that day?'

'On the nineteenth? She comes back into view about five to one. The bell is going so she just mingles with the other kids as they go back in. None of the supervisors seems to have noticed. And after that, there's just one more sighting. You said check breaks and lunchtimes, but I thought it worth scanning home-time as well, just in case.'

He clicks on another file and the same corner of the street appears again. The same, but different, because you can tell summer is coming. There are flowers on the honeysuckle and the grass is lush. It reminds me of an old *Columbo* episode where he cracked the whole case by noticing that one CCTV shot showed a cut hedge and another, supposedly later the same day, an uncut one. If only it were always that easy.

The screen says 3.39 on 9 May. Daisy comes into

view, talking to Nanxi Chen. Then Nanxi's mother appears and there's some discussion between them.

'Looks to me like Mrs Chen was due to pick both girls up after school but Daisy's persuaded her otherwise,' says Baxter, as Nanxi's mother leads her away, glancing back once at Daisy before moving her daughter towards their car.

'We'll need to check that with Mrs Chen.'

'Easily done.'

The film continues and three minutes later Daisy is suddenly alert. She can see something – or someone – just out of range.

'If it's the boy, looks like he's staying deliberately out of the way this time,' says Baxter. 'Either he's just realized the camera's there –'

'– or he suddenly has a reason to be a lot more careful.'

I see the anxiety flood Alison Stevens's face. 'Oh no, surely not – he can't be more than fifteen!'

On the screen, Daisy looks both ways, then hurries across the road. Baxter freezes the frame just before she disappears out of shot. She has a huge smile on her face.

'That's as far as I got,' he says, sitting back and looking at me. 'But didn't Everett say Daisy was really upset after she'd had her secret meeting?'

'Not upset. Angry.'

'She doesn't look angry there.'

'No,' I say slowly, 'she doesn't, does she? Wind it forward – do it in slow-mo.'

We watch, all three of us. Mothers and sons, mothers and daughters. Even the odd dad looking awkward and out of place. One man wobbles off by bike with two little children pulled behind in a canvas trailer and another drifting along out of sight behind him on a tricycle.

'Do you offer cycling proficiency tests?' I say askance.

Alison Stevens blinks, nonplussed. 'The children are a bit young –'

'I don't mean for the kids. For the fathers.'

A couple of cars go by. Big four-by-fours, a people carrier, even a Porsche. And then an old Ford Escort. It has a bent bumper and a smashed back light, and a dirty rag hanging out of the boot that – deliberately or not – is concealing almost all of the number plate. It's impossible to see who's driving, but there's clearly someone in the back seat.

'There – freeze there.'

Even at that distance, there's no doubt at all.

It's Daisy.

*   *   *

25 May 2016, 11.16 a.m.
55 days before the disappearance
Bishop Christopher's Primary School, Oxford

'Can I have some quiet, please? Settle down and pay attention. Tabitha, Matty, can you go back to your desks? That's grand.'

Kate Madigan smiles at her class, and when she's sure she has their attention, she turns to the whiteboard and writes a word in large capital letters.

FRIENDS

She snaps the top back on the pen and turns to the children. 'We're going to spend some time now talking about *friendship*. What makes a good friend, how to be a good friend, and other things, like what to do if you have an argument with your friend and want to make it up. So who wants to go first – what do you think makes a good friend?'

A hand goes up. It's a little boy at the front, with curly brown hair and thick glasses.

'Yes, Jonny, what do you think a friend should be?'

'Someone who lets you play with their toys,' he says softly.

Kate nods encouragingly. 'Yes, that's a very good start. Someone who will share their toys. Because sharing is very important, isn't it? We talked about that before. And sharing is an important way to make friends. Anyone else have some ideas?'

A little girl with dark hair in an Alice band puts up her hand.

'Yes, Megan, what do you think?'

'A friend is nice to you if you're sad.'

'Very good, Megan. That's important too, isn't it? If you're someone's friend you try to cheer them up if they're unhappy.' The little girl nods shyly and puts her finger in her mouth.

'Anyone else?'

Daisy stands up.

One of the boys at the back makes a face and mutters, 'Teacher's pet.'

'*I* think,' says Daisy, 'that a friend is someone who will help you if bad things happen, and someone you can tell your secrets.'

Kate smiles. 'That's very good, Daisy. And do you have a friend like that?'

Daisy nods vigorously, her eyes shining, and sits down.

Later, in the playground, Portia and Nanxi are sitting on the bench while Daisy plays hopscotch. Millie Connor is hovering nearby, desperate to be invited to join in, but the others are pretending not to notice her. Over by the wire fence some of the older boys are kicking a football, and a small boy with red hair is tugging the sleeve of the teacher on duty, saying, 'Look, look! My tooth came out!'

On the bench, Nanxi is texting on her mobile phone, but Portia is watching Daisy.

'You know what you said to Miss Madigan about your friend,' says Portia, 'who did you mean?'

Daisy gets to the end of the hopscotch grid, then turns and puts her finger to her lips. 'That's a secret,' she says.

Nanxi glances up, unimpressed. 'You *always* say that.'

'Well, it's true.'

'So you didn't mean me or Nanxi?' persists Portia.

'Might have,' says Daisy, avoiding her eye. 'I'm not telling.'

'I don't know why we have to talk about stupid things like that anyway,' says Portia, peevish now.

'It's called Sex and Relationships Education,' says Nanxi, not looking up. 'My mom said. She had to sign something saying it was OK.'

'What's sex?' says Millie, edging closer. The others stare at her and Nanxi rolls her eyes.

'You know,' says Daisy, as if talking to an idiot, 'when a boy sticks his thing in you down there and stuff comes out.'

Millie opens her mouth in horror. 'What, in your *knickers*? Ergh, that's disgusting!'

Daisy shrugs. 'It's what grown-ups do. It's supposed to be nice.'

Nanxi stops texting for a moment and looks up. 'I'm with Millie. I think it sounds disgusting. And any case, how come you know so much about it?'

Daisy throws her stone on to the hopscotch squares and watches it roll to a halt before starting back down the course.

'I just do,' she says.

* * *

At 1.30 I give up trying to sleep and get up. As the weight in the bed shifts, Alex murmurs, then turns over. This time of year, the sky never seems to get fully dark. I go out on to the landing and into Jake's room, the dark blue silence ringing in my ears. The window is slightly open and the pennant on the wall trembles in a current of air. I go over to close it and see next-door's cat prowling across the grass. Jake loved that cat. He was always on at us to get a kitten, but I always said no. That's only one of the many things I regret not doing now.

In his room, nothing has been changed, nothing moved. We'll have to do that eventually, but neither of us can face it yet. We have a cleaner come in once a week, but it's Alex who cleans in here. She does it when I'm out. She doesn't want me to see how careful she is that everything goes back exactly where it was. I sit down on the bed and think about Leo, and how we're going to have to talk to his GP. Because if I can see there's something wrong, then his doctor sure as hell has. I lie down on the bed and then turn slowly to bury my face in Jake's pillow. His smell is still there, but it's going, and I panic for a moment, knowing that it won't be long before I've lost that too.

I close my eyes and breathe him in.

'Adam! *Adam!*'

I lurch upright, my heart pounding. Alex is standing there. I have no idea how long I've been asleep but it's not yet light.

'It's ringing,' she says in hollow tones, holding out

my mobile. 'And given that it's two o'clock in the morning, I doubt it's good news, do you?'

I swing my legs down on to the floor. The screen says it's Gislingham.

'What is it?'

The noise on the line is incredible. I can hear at least two sirens.

'I'm at the house,' he yells, over the din.

'Did we get the warrant?'

'Look – I think you'd better come.'

*   *   *

It's like bloody *Rebecca*. I can see the lurid glow above the estate all the way along the ring road, and the smoke hits me long before I turn into the close. There are three squad cars, an ambulance and two fire engines. A couple of firemen are up a telescopic ladder, hosing down the flames at the upstairs windows. There's ugly black soot spreading across the red brick. As I draw up, Gislingham detaches himself from the crowd and comes towards me.

'What the fuck happened?'

'Looks like arson. You can smell the petrol. There was a small group of troublemakers here earlier, apparently, shouting threats and making a lot of noise, but uniform came out and dealt with that. One yob chucked a brick, but he was too far away to do any damage. The fire officer I spoke to thinks whoever did this probably came along the towpath and lobbed something over the fence. Some sort of do-it-yourself Molotov cocktail.'

'Where's Sharon and the boy? Are they OK?'

I should have asked that first. I do know that.

Gislingham nods. 'Everett's with them in the car. They're a bit shaken. Specially the boy. He's gulped down a lot of smoke.'

I look over to the squad car. The passenger door is open and I can see Sharon with a blanket round her shoulders. I can't see Leo.

'We're bloody lucky there were no other casualties. The family one side are away and the other lot got out when Sharon went and banged on the door. Media's loving it, of course. The Sky lot were camped out in their van overnight. They can't believe their luck – they got to film the whole bloody thing.'

'Please tell me that was *after* they dialled 999.'

'They said Sharon had already done it.'

'OK, I want that footage. *Before* they broadcast it. And find the senior fire officer on site. I want to see him in the morning – as soon as the house is declared safe.'

I glance across at the hacks, pushed back further behind a cordon, but straining at it like attack dogs. There must be half a dozen outside-broadcast vans here now, gathered like sharks on blood. 'The Super's going to have my head on a pole for this. And the bloody IPCC will get their oar in too, I shouldn't wonder.'

'You couldn't have known this would happen, boss.'

'No, but I could have moved the family as soon as it got out they were being questioned. That's no doubt the line the ACC will take. Well, we're going to have to do it now. Have you got somewhere lined up?'

'There's that B&B we've used before off the Cowley Road. Thought it best to get them out of the immediate area. Just in case anyone's still hanging around. We're waiting for the paramedic to check the boy over, then Everett will take them. Sharon's in no fit state, and in any case, her car's a write-off – it was in the garage.'

'Good work.'

He doesn't look that happy. 'I mean it. You've done well.'

'It's not that, boss. I was going to leave it to the morning, but since you're here –'

I take a deep breath. 'More bad news? Not sure how much worse it can get, but spit it out.'

'That pay-as-you-go mobile Mason has been using to text his lady loves? I ran it through the PNC and it came up. It's on the CEOP database of phone numbers that downloaded material from a porn site hosted in Azerbaijan. It's hard-core stuff, boss. Kiddies. Babies, some of them.'

He swallows and I remember. He's having his first.

I reach out and touch him lightly on the arm. 'I think Barry Mason had better get himself that lawyer. He's going to bloody well need one.'

*

186

As I walk towards the squad car, Everett comes towards me. 'I've checked and there are two spare rooms at the B&B. If you're OK, I'll get uniform to drop them off and then grab some stuff from home and camp out over there. At least for a couple of days.'

'Good idea. I can't see anyone tracking them down that far away, but you never know. And in any case, we need to keep tabs on Sharon. Without making it obvious that's what we're doing.'

'Right, boss.'

She turns to go but I hold her back. I get out my phone.

'Once he's had the all-clear, can you show this to Leo? See if he recognizes him.'

She looks at me with a question. 'Is this who I think it is?'

'Got it in one. Daisy's mysterious handsome prince. I just hope the real story doesn't turn out to be Beauty and the Beast.'

I explain what we saw on the CCTV.

Everett frowns. 'But if the last time she saw him was May the ninth I don't see how –'

'The last time we *know* she saw him. We can't be absolutely sure she didn't meet him the afternoon she disappeared – he could even have gone to the house when Sharon Mason was on her quest for mayonnaise, and Daisy could have let him in. In fact, he's the only person we know about who she might have gone off with willingly.'

She nods. 'OK. But I think we should wait till the morning. Leo's pretty distressed right now. We don't want anyone saying we questioned him when he wasn't in a fit state. Reasonable Doubt and all that.'

'Fair enough. I'll email you the picture. Ring me tomorrow.'

I watch her walk back towards the car. In the front seat, Sharon has her handbag out and is checking her face in a small mirror.

*   *   *

When Everett pulls up outside the B&B at 3 a.m., there's no sign of life. Unlike on the Cowley Road a hundred yards away, where what the authorities euphemistically call the 'night-time economy' is still in full swing. Its rather scruffy state aside, the B&B doesn't look much different to the house the Dawsons live in, but the resemblance stops at the architecture. This end of town has always gone its own way and the Victorian developers who tried to turn it into a lucrative mini model of its grand northerly neighbour quickly found it wouldn't take, and the experiment fizzled out. Some of the houses are still there, but most are student digs, or offices, or B&Bs. Like this one. Carved into the lintel above the door the name Ponsonby Villa is still just about legible; the current owner – perhaps advisedly – has changed it to The Comfy Inn.

Everett gets out and locks the car carefully (she

knows better than most what the crime levels are like round here), then opens the back seat and hauls out a canvas holdall. She's packed some clothes Sharon can borrow, as well as a couple of toothbrushes and some basics. Should be enough until the shops open in the morning. She makes a mental note to call her neighbour to feed Hector, then lumbers the heavy bag up the path to the front door. It's a good five minutes before the owner appears, in a rather unsavoury vest and some stained pyjama bottoms that Everett doesn't dare inspect too closely. Upstairs, in their room, Sharon is sitting on the bed, still wrapped in the blanket the ambulance crew gave her. All she has underneath is a nightdress. Leo is huddled against her, coughing now and again, his face smeared with soot. Everett starts to unpack the bag. A sweatshirt, some jeans, a couple of T-shirts. Sharon looks at them with distaste.

'I don't like wearing other people's things.'

Everett glances at her. 'Well, I'm afraid you don't have many other options, do you? And everything's perfectly clean. It's straight out of the washing machine.'

Sharon shudders. 'That stuff is at least three sizes too big for me. I wouldn't be seen dead in it.'

Everett feels like telling her she's lucky not to be dead, full stop, but stifles her anger by telling herself the woman's probably still in shock.

'Well, like I said,' she says evenly, 'you don't have much choice. You can go out first thing and get some more. After all, you managed to save your handbag, didn't you? Most people in your position don't even have credit cards.'

Sharon looks at her narrowly, then reaches for the pink towel laid out folded on the bed.

'I'm going to have a shower,' she says.

* * *

law. 'This behaviour is a form of modern terrorism. Those responsible will be traced, and they will be charged.'

Twitter has issued an official statement condemning the violence, and offering the police their full cooperation in tracking down those responsible.

Anyone with any information about Daisy should contact Thames Valley CID incident room on 01865 0966552.

* * *

'Mind where you're treading. The top layer is cooling, but it's still burning underneath in places.'

It's 8.05 on Saturday morning, and I've already had far too much coffee, which does nothing to help the slightly hallucinogenic feeling induced by what's left of the Masons' sitting room. The senior fire officer comes slowly towards me over the cheap acrylic carpet. Most of it has melted into evil-smelling sludge, and there are patches where you can see the concrete underneath. They're still hosing outside and the exterior walls are running with blackened water, but most of the internal ones are down. Just plasterboard, most of them; they didn't stand a chance.

'As it happens,' I say, indicating my boots, 'I've done this sort of thing before.'

'So how can I help you, Inspector?'

'I'm assuming arson is a given?'

'No question. You can still smell the accelerant upstairs. We're picking through the glass now – if we're lucky, we could find some fragments of the bottle it was in.'

'Any idea how it started – precisely?'

He turns and points up through the gaping hole that was once a staircase. 'We're currently working on the theory that someone chucked it in through the upstairs window at the back.'

'The daughter's bedroom?'

'If you say so – to be honest, you couldn't tell whose it is from the state it's in.'

'You think someone could really throw a bottle like that from the towpath? It's what, thirty feet away, even thirty-five?'

He considers. 'It could definitely be done, but you'd need to get some height on the throw, so it was either an adult or a pretty hefty kid. That may be why only one shot actually made its target – there's two or three blackened craters in the back garden where the others must have landed. We're collecting the glass fragments inside the house and we've taken samples on the path, but unless we're lucky and we get some fingerprints we're unlikely to be able to identify the culprits. Hundreds of people traipse up and down at the back there so footprints are worse than useless.'

It's a blow, even if it's one I expected. 'How come the fire spread so fast? I mean, look at this place. There's nothing left.'

'I wondered about that too – we only took eight minutes to get here, but it was already completely engulfed. These modern houses look nice but they've no guts. One of those big Victorian ones beyond the canal – they'd take a lot more burning.'

'You said "some of it".'

'Well, the accelerant wouldn't have helped. And all the man-made fibres in here – they'd go up like the fourth of July. But all the same, I'm surprised it got such a hold in so short a time.'

'Right,' I say thoughtfully. 'Thanks. Let me know if anything else comes up.'

'Will do.'

Out in the back garden, Challow is squatting down with his case open and a pile of evidence bags in front of him. Some clothes, mostly coats and jackets as far as I can see, a few shoes, what looks like a duffel bag. A lot is black and charred. Some of it is barely recognizable.

'Is there anything – anything at all?'

He straightens up, his paper suit creaking. 'Not much, to be honest, and only from downstairs. I might get something from the shoes, but it'll be touch and go with the amount of fire damage. Upstairs is a write-off. If you were hoping for something from the girl's bedroom, forget it. She could have bled out up there and I doubt we'd find it now. And you and I both know that room had been scrubbed down to the atoms. We were only ever going to get trace.'

'I should have pushed harder for that bloody search warrant.'

'Don't blame yourself. You did what you could – the Super will have to take the heat on that one.' He stops. 'Sorry. Crass choice of words.'

There's a silence. Challow shakes his head then bends to get a bottle of water out of his case. He takes a swig and pulls a face. 'Warm.'

'Anything else?'

'The fire crew brought down the father's computer, but I suspect the hard drive's gone.'

'Bring it in anyway. I hope we'll have evidence on the phone, but the PC may have more.'

'And there is this rather sad item.'

He holds up an evidence bag. Whatever's in it, once had fur.

'Jesus, Alan, what the hell is that – the family rabbit?'

He smiles wryly. 'The Masons didn't appear to go in for pets. They no doubt produce far too much mess for the über-tidy Mrs M. No, this fur is definitely of the fake variety.' He hands it to me. 'One lion costume, badly torn. I suspect young Leo was rather underwhelmed by the prospect of fancy dress.'

I see him again. Telling me how the boys pick on him because of his name. How they turn it into a weapon to use against him. No wonder the poor little sod didn't want to dress up as the king of the bloody jungle.

'And the school bag?'

'No sign.'

'Shit.'

'It doesn't mean it wasn't here – it could easily have gone in the fire, given it was almost certainly plastic. Or they could have got rid of it. They've had the best part of a week, after all.'

'Got rid of it like they got rid of her.'

Challow takes another swig of water. 'Sounds like you need cheering up. There is *one* element of your theory that survived the flames. Mason's pick-up. It's round the corner in Waterview Crescent. I've got a tow truck coming.'

'In full view of the press. Bloody marvellous.'

'Not much I can do about that, I'm afraid. Tow trucks don't really do discreet.'

'But you know what's going to happen, don't you? Yet more fodder for the feeding frenzy.'

'Perhaps they've learned their lesson.' He gestures around him. 'All this carnage. Someone could have got killed. Thanks to sodding Twitter.'

'Learned their lesson? I'm not banking on it.'

* * *

MtN @Nuckleduster1989   09.09
LMFAO Someone with some balls took out those fucking #Masons last night – hope they all died

MickyF @TheGameBlader666   09.10
@Nuckleduster1989 Just heard on the news – cant
believe it – creds to whoever had the nuts – #Masons

PeedoHunter @Peedofiletracker   09.11
@Nuckleduster1989 @TheGameBlader666 HAHAHA –
u shd have seen it go up – fuckin awesum!!!!

PeedoHunter @Peedofiletracker   09.12
@Nuckleduster1989 @TheGameBlader666 didn't
think it took but suddenly BOOOOM!!! Thatll teach
the peedo bastards

MickyF @TheGameBlader666   09.17
@Peedofiletracker 👊👊👊👊 Wish I lived close – wd
have joined in! Hope the pigs don't catch on to you
@Nuckleduster1989

PeedoHunter @Peedofiletracker   09.19
@TheGameBlader666 No sweat on that – pigs round
here don't know there arses from there knobs #twats

Zoe Henley @ZenyatterRegatta   09.20
As far as I can tell the father wasn't in the house
when it caught fire. Just the mother and brother
#DaisyMason

J Riddell @1234JimmyR1ddell   09.21
If anyone's guilty in the #DaisyMason case it's the

mother. Hard-faced cow – no wonder hubby was forced to go elsewhere

J Johnstone @JaneJohnstone4555   09.21
@1234JimmyR1ddell That's a pretty sexist view, if you don't mind me saying so

J Riddell @1234JimmyR1ddell   09.21
@JaneJohnstone4555 Might not be a popular POV, but everyone I've spoken to thinks she's the guilty one #Masons

UK Social Media News @UKSocialMediaNews 09.22
Our poll is still open, as it stands 67% think Sharon Mason is guilty, 33% say Barry. 23,778 votes in so far #DaisyMason

Lilian Chamberlain @LilianChamberlain   09.23
Does anyone know how Leo Mason is? He breaks my heart, poor little kid. Stuck in the middle of all this

Lilian Chamberlain @LilianChamberlain   09.23
And now he's lost his home and all his possessions into the bargain #DaisyMason 😞😞

Angela Betterton @AngelaGBetterton   09.29
@LilianChamberlain I know what you mean. But they've moved the family now – I saw them driving away in a police car last night

Lilian Chamberlain @LilianChamberlain 09.29
@AngelaGBetterton Thank God for that – he's
the one innocent in all this tragic mess
#DaisyMason 🏵🏵

Kathryn Forney @StarSignCapricorn 09.32
@LilianChamberlain Funny you say that, I was
reading about a US case where a mother was
convicted of killing her baby daughter . . .
@AngelaGBetterton

Kathryn Forney @StarSignCapricorn 09.33
. . . then years later DNA proved it wasn't her.
She'd been covering up for her other kid the
whole time . . . @LilianChamberlain
@AngelaGBetterton

Kathryn Forney @StarSignCapricorn 09.34
. . . It was the 10yo brother who'd done it. It was the
brother who was the killer @LilianChamberlain
@AngelaGBetterton #DaisyMason

* * *

In the first-floor front bedroom of the Comfy Inn, Leo
is standing looking out of the window. Sharon is out
shopping and Everett – who cursed herself for forget-
ting to bring a book – has resorted to playing four-suit
solitaire on her mobile phone. Someone told her the

odds of it coming out are over 300 to one. So far she's done it 176 times. It hasn't come out.

Every now and again she glances up to check on Leo, but for the last half hour the boy hasn't moved. Two pigeons are walking up and down on the window-sill outside. Every now and again they clatter against each other, beating their wings.

'I heard them screaming,' he says, tracing his finger on the glass.

Everett jolts alert. 'Sorry, Leo, what did you say?'

'I heard them screaming.'

Everett puts the phone down and comes to the window. She forces herself to stand and watch the pigeons for a few moments before saying, 'Who was screaming, Leo?'

He's still staring at the birds. 'It was in the night.'

'When was this?'

He shrugs. 'Dunno.'

'Was it Daisy?'

There's a long pause, and then he says, 'It was the birds.'

'The birds?'

'On Port Meadow. There are seagulls there. I went once. There are lots of them. They make a really bad noise.'

Everett finds herself breathing again. 'I see. And they make that noise even in the dark?'

Leo nods. 'I think they must be unhappy.'

Everett makes to reach for him, hesitates, but then bends quickly down and puts her arms round him.

He turns his face into her shoulder and whispers, 'It's all my fault. It's all my fault.'

* * *

Back at the station, my one consolation is that Barry Mason will be feeling even worse than I do. He certainly smells a whole lot worse, and I wonder for a moment where he was last night. Wherever it was, they clearly don't run to much by way of complimentary toiletries. His lawyer, by contrast, is as crisp as a new-cut lawn. She reminds me of Anna Phillips, actually. Tall, white shirt, pale grey skirt, matte leather ballerina pumps. I wonder if Mason knew her before, or she'd just drawn the short straw. And straws don't get much shorter than this. She has no idea of the shit about to come her way.

Quinn takes a seat and puts down his newspaper. He just so happens to have left it turned to the picture of Barry being shunted into the squad car. Quinn is holding the car door open and has his hand on Barry's head. Classic demeaning demeanour. And quite probably the reason why Barry looks so furious – not to mention about as far from forlorn father as you're ever likely to get. Quinn looks good though, very suave; I imagine that's a cut-out-and-keeper. I see the lawyer looking at it and Quinn clocking that she does.

'Why have you asked to see my client again, Inspector?' she says as we sit down. 'This is veering perilously close to harassment. As far as I am aware he has cooperated fully in your enquiries and you have no grounds for suspecting him of any involvement whatsoever in his daughter's disappearance.'

Barry Mason stares at me. 'If you put half the effort into finding *her* as you are persecuting *me*, you might actually have found Daisy by now. Because she's out there. Do you hear me? She's out there somewhere, alone and frightened and wanting her mum and dad, and all you fucking morons can do is try to frame me. I'm her *father*. I *love her*.'

I turn to the lawyer. 'As and when we have an arrest to make in connection with the disappearance of Daisy Mason, we will do so. For the moment, I wish to question your client on another matter.' I reach for the machine. 'For the tape, present in the interview, Detective Inspector Adam Fawley, Acting DS Gareth Quinn, Miss Emma Carwood and Mr Barry Mason.'

I open the brown cardboard folder in front of me and take out the birthday card. It's opened out, in a plastic evidence bag. I show them the front, with the words, and then turn it over and leave it there. I keep my eyes on Emma Carwood and I see a tiny flicker of disgust as her shiny professionalism falters, just for a moment.

'Have you seen this before, Mr Mason?'

'Where did you get that?' he says, wary.

'For the tape, this is a birthday card made by Daisy Mason for her father. It consists of a number of images cut from magazines and pasted on to the paper. It also makes reference to activities they enjoy together. Including swimming and what she describes as "swinging in his lap" –'

'You have got to be fucking kidding me –'

'When did she give you this, Mr Mason?'

He makes a face. 'For my *birthday*, genius.'

Miss Carwood intervenes. 'You won't help yourself by taking that tone, Mr Mason.'

'Which birthday? This year? Last year?'

'This year.'

'So this April. Three months ago.'

He doesn't answer.

'This image,' I say, pointing to the breasts. 'Where did she get that from – some sort of adult magazine? Are you in the habit of leaving material like that where a child of eight can find it?'

Mason stares at me, then takes the card and looks at it closely through the plastic. 'I think you'll find,' he says eventually, 'that that picture is from the *Sunday Sport*. So all right, it's not very PC, but hardly top-shelf. It's just a bloody red top. We're not talking *porn* here.'

'Really?' I say, placing the card to one side. I take out another sheet of paper and put it in front of him.

'Can you confirm that this is the number of the mobile you use to contact women you meet on the dating site – the phone your wife didn't know you had?'

He glances at it. 'Yeah, looks like it. So what? I don't use it that much.'

'You did use it, however, on the sixteenth of April

this year. This number is logged on the database of the Child Exploitation and Online Protection Centre as having accessed an Azerbaijani website hosting several thousand images of children. And there, Mr Mason, we most certainly *are* talking porn. Porn of the most depraved and illegal kind.'

Mason is gaping at me. 'That's a lie – I never went near anything like that. I'm not into *kids*, for fuck's sake. That's disgusting – perverted –'

'Barry Mason, I am arresting you on suspicion of the illegal possession of indecent images of children, contrary to Section 160 of the Criminal Justice Act 1988. You do not have to say anything, but it may harm your defence if you do not mention when questioned something which you later rely on in court. Anything you do say may be given in evidence. You will be required to surrender the phone in question, so that it can be examined by forensics officers –'

'Well, I can tell you now you won't bloody well find anything – I've never even used the bloody camera –'

'You will now be taken to the cells. Interview terminated at 11.17.'

Quinn and I get up and turn to go.

'It was Sharon, wasn't it?' he says. There's panic in his voice now. 'She gave you that sodding birthday card. She had to. The rest of the bloody house burned down, thanks to you.' He slams his fist on the table. 'Aren't you supposed to protect us from psychos like that? Isn't that your *job*?'

'You can rest assured that the Police Complaints Commission will ascertain exactly what happened.'

'Can't you see what she's doing? She's trying to frame me. She found out about the dating thing and she's flipped her bloody lid.'

'Are you suggesting she downloaded porn on your phone, too?'

He opens his mouth and then closes it again.

'I'll take that as a "no".'

I turn again, but he's not finished.

'I'm not joking – that woman's mental – she's got a screw loose somewhere. I'm not just talking about her temper – she's even jealous of her own fucking daughter – can you believe that? It's bloody unnatural, that's what it is.'

Actually, I can believe it, all too easily. I sense Quinn glance at me, and I know why. The man's playing us our own scenario. Just without him in it.

'What are you saying, Mr Mason?' I say evenly.

'I'm *saying* that if anyone did anything to Daisy, it was *her*, not me. I mean – it happened before, didn't it?'

He looks from me to Quinn, at our blank, uncomprehending faces.

'You do *know* about her, right?'

* * *

'My boss is going to have my hide for giving you this.'

It's an hour later, and inside the cramped Sky news

204

van, Paul Beaton is sitting in front of a bank of screens. At his side is Acting Detective Sergeant Gareth Quinn.

'I'm sure you've been at this game long enough,' says Quinn, 'to know that cooperating with the police is always the best policy. Especially in a murder inquiry.'

Beaton looks at him. 'Is that what it is? I didn't think you had a body?'

'We don't. But we don't need one – not necessarily. You didn't hear it from me, but it's only a matter of time.'

'Any chance of a heads-up before you go public with that? For being so helpful and cooperative?'

Quinn smiles. 'Let's see what you've got first.'

Beaton taps the keyboard. 'Something tells me you're not going to be disappointed.'

The footage appears on the screen. It's clearly a hand-held camera – the image lurches wildly before settling on the Mason house in darkness. The time-code at the bottom says 01.47.

'I was woken up by this huge bang,' says Beaton. 'Got my camera on before my kecks. That's what ten years on this job and three tours of the Middle East does to you.'

'Tell me about it,' says Quinn, who's not been any further than Magaluf.

At 01.49 the door to the house bangs open and Sharon Mason comes out. She's wearing a white lace negligee and has her handbag in one hand. She stares around, blinking and swaying unsteadily, then starts to totter across the gravel towards the house next door, where she rings the bell several times. It's 01.52 before the door is answered.

'At this stage I still had no idea what had happened. As you can see, she gets the neighbours out of the house, and then you see the fire for the first time.'

The shot veers skywards to show flames rising from the roof. Then the camera is on the move – the floor, the cameraman's feet, the door of the van, then a wild swing up to the house again. A man in pyjama bottoms is disappearing into the front door. Sharon Mason is sitting on the wall, her head between her knees. There are two little girls with her and a woman. The cameraman says something to Sharon, but it's too muffled to make out.

'That's when I asked her if she'd called 999.'

The shot swings again to the Masons' front door, which is open. And then up above, to where the first-floor windows are glowing a furious orange. The curtains are already alight.

Quinn sits forward. 'Where's Leo – where the fuck's her kid?'

'I wondered when you'd ask that. Keep watching.'

The shot tilts back to the front door, just in time to see the neighbour career out of the house, pushing Leo ahead of him. Both are smeared with soot and they're only yards from the doorway when the first-floor windows explode in a shower of sparks and glass that rains down on the drive. Man and boy are hurled to the ground. The time-code on the screen says 02.05.

Quinn gets to his feet. 'Thanks, mate.'

'You'll be in touch? Let me know if there's going to be an arrest? I mean, if we aired this stuff, Jesus, it'd be dynamite.'

'Don't worry. You'll be the first to know.'

Outside in the close, Quinn gets out his phone. 'Gislingham? It's Quinn. Can you get someone to find out what time that 999 call got logged? And while they're at it, get them to check if there were any other calls just before that – any attempts that might have got cut off. Thanks, mate.'

*　*　*

At the other end of the line Gislingham puts down the phone and turns back to his computer screen. Janet's been on his back about working at the weekend, and while half of him really would rather be at home, the other half is copper first, expectant dad second, and this is one of those cases that won't leave you alone. It's not just that it's a kiddie, it's the knottedness of it. It doesn't feel right calling it a puzzle – not when there's a little girl still missing – but that's what it is. That's why he's here, that's why he's been sat at this desk since mid-morning, in a room with no air conditioning, going through possible local matches for the number plate of the car Daisy was seen in outside the school. He'd told Janet it'd only take ten minutes, half an hour at the most – after all, how many bloody Escorts can still be out there? – but with only two letters to go on and no idea of the colour of the car, the list seems to be never-ending.

Seems to be, but suddenly isn't. Because there it is – a 2001 model, Toreador red, registered to an address in East Oxford. Gislingham punches the air, then abruptly sits forward. He navigates quickly to a different section of the Police National Computer, and types in a name.

'Shit,' he says. 'Shit shit shit.'

* * *

'How the hell did we not know this?'

I'm in my office, standing at Anna Phillips's shoulder, staring down at her laptop screen. She glances up at me. 'To be fair, it took a lot of digging up – the newspaper archive is online but it's all just PDFs. It would never have come up on an ordinary search.'

'We do have other ways to find things out. Aside from sodding Google.'

The door opens and Bryan Gow comes in, looking slightly overheated and more than a little irritated at being dragged in on a summer weekend. 'So what's so important I had to miss *Oliver Cromwell* at Didcot?'

I raise an eyebrow. 'You into Sealed Knot now, too?'

He looks at me witheringly. 'It's a locomotive, you philistine. A Britannia standard class seven, to be precise. One of the last steam locos British Rail ever ran.'

I shrug. 'I was never one of those kids who wanted to be a train driver.' I point at the screen. 'In any case, this is rather more urgent.'

The Croydon Evening Echo
3rd August 1991

TRAGEDY STRIKES FOR HOLIDAY FAMILY

A Croydon family are returning home from Lanzarote tomorrow, after tragedy struck what was supposed to be the holiday of a lifetime.

Gerald Wiley, 52, and his wife Sadie, 46, jetted off to the holiday island a week ago, with their two daughters Sharon, 14, and Jessica, 2. Mr Wiley had recently been laid off after 30 years with London Underground, and decided to use his redundancy money to take the family on a holiday to remember.

The family were enjoying a beach party organised by the hotel where they were staying, when the catastrophe occurred. Witnesses say that the weather was good and the sea calm. Jessica and her sister had earlier been playing on a small inflatable dinghy, and shortly after 4 p.m. hotel staff realised that the girls were missing. It was Mr Wiley who saw the dinghy some way out to sea, and he then raised the alarm. Hotel staff immediately called for help and Mr Wiley attempted to swim out to the girls. Several other holidaymakers also tried to offer assistance,

continued

209

but by the time the girls could be reached the dinghy had capsized, and both were in the water.

Paramedics attempted resuscitation, but Jessica Wiley was pronounced dead at the scene. Mr Wiley, who suffers from angina, had to be treated at the local hospital. Sharon Wiley, who attends the Colbourne School, was treated for cuts and bruises.

Pauline Pober, 42, from Wokingham, saw the whole incident. 'It's just heart-breaking. We were all enjoying the party – the kids were having a lovely time and everyone was just relaxed and enjoying themselves. Jessica was such a beautiful, happy child – the apple of her parents' eye. What an awful thing to happen. My heart goes out to poor Sharon. She was distraught when they brought her back to the beach.'

Local people confirmed that the tides on that stretch of beach can be treacherous. There have been three drownings in the area since 1989.

Mr Wiley said yesterday, 'My wife and I are devastated. Jessie was our gift from God. Our lives will be empty without her – we will never get over it.'

'So,' I say, 'what do you think?'

Bryan takes off his glasses and cleans them on a rumpled handkerchief. There are shiny red patches either side of his nose. 'You mean, do I think it really was an accident?'

'We can start with that.'

'There's not a hell of a lot to go on –'

'I know. But in theory – what could we be looking at?'

'Well, if we're only looking at what's *possible*, rather than an actual *profile* –'

'Fine. That's all I need right now.'

'Then I'd say that even if Sharon had nothing to do with Jessica's death, it's quite conceivable that some part of her – conscious or unconscious – wanted it to happen. Do the math, to coin a phrase. Sharon would have been twelve when her sister was born, and judging by the parents' ages, I'm guessing the pregnancy came as a surprise to all of them. Hard to know where to start on the cocktail of destructive emotions that could have ignited. Sharon's just entering puberty, and she's suddenly confronted by the reality of her parents' sex life. Awkward, as I believe the young people say. Add to that being deprived of her only-child status, out of the blue, after twelve years assuming that's the way the world was. "*When they said he was their only son, he thought he was the only one.*"'

He's lost me now. '*He?*'

He smiles wryly. 'Sorry – it's that seventies song. It came up in the quiz last week. You remember. About the kid who has to cope with suddenly finding he's got a baby sister. That's never easy, however well-balanced the kid is, and however sensitively the parents handle it. Only in Sharon's case it looks like all the parents' love and attention transferred wholesale to the new baby, and Sharon found herself, without warning, a very inferior second best.' He shakes his head, then gestures at the screen with his glasses. 'I'm guessing they never forgave Sharon for being the one who survived. They may even have told her outright she was to blame. And if she wasn't – if it really *was* just an accident – well, I can't think of anything much shittier than that.'

'Is that a technical term?'

'It serves. When dealing with the untrained.'

I see Anna suppress a smile.

'OK,' I say. 'Now wind forward twenty-five years. Second time around?'

'Pretty much, judging by what I've seen of Sharon. Which again isn't much, but enough to see she's socially insecure, personally vain and almost certainly extremely jealous where that errant husband of hers is concerned. And all that being the case, Daisy is just Jessica all over again. Only far, far worse. Because this time the attention Sharon's competing for is not her parents' but her husband's – someone who should put *her* first. Or at least that's how she'd see it. Crueller still, the younger interloper is her *own fault* – she brought that kid into the world, she presumably made all sorts of sacrifices as a mother, and this is how she's repaid. All the resentment she felt against Jessica transfers wholesale to Daisy, only magnified many times over. And it'd be all the more toxic because she almost certainly buried her feelings after Jessica died.'

'So you think she would be capable of killing her own daughter?'

He nods. 'In theory. If the triggers were powerful enough. If, say, she caught Daisy and her husband together in a situation that suggested anything remotely sexual – in a moment like that, when the red mist came down – I don't think she'd have seen the husband as being the one to blame. I don't even think she'd be capable of seeing Daisy as her daughter. All she'd see was a rival.'

He sits back. 'What you also need to remember is that if Sharon *was* complicit in some way with the sister's death – even if only by failing to do anything to save her – then she's long since come up with a narrative that shifts the blame on to everyone else. The parents, the bystanders, even Jessica herself. And if she really *did* do something to Daisy, the same thing will be happening now. It will be all the husband's fault, or even the daughter's. Textbook denial, fathoms deep. You won't be able to get her to admit she was in any way involved without tearing down psychological defences she's taken years to build. Don't underestimate how hard that will be. I'm prepared to bet this woman never apologizes for anything, however trivial.'

I turn to Anna. 'That woman – Pauline Pober – any chance of tracking her down?'

'I could try. It's an unusual name. And Wokingham isn't a big town.'

'And the parents – do we know if they're still alive?'

'I checked. Gerald Wiley died in 2014. Heart attack. Sadie is in a care home in Carshalton. Sounds like she has fairly advanced Alzheimer's. So I suppose you could say Sharon's the only one left.'

'It explains a lot about Sharon.'

She glances up at me. 'The story?'

'Not just that. The picture.'

'*The Wiley family in happier times*', the caption says. It shows Gerald with Jessica on his knee and Sadie beside him, her hand on his shoulder. Jessica's wearing a white dress with a sash and her hair is in long ringlets tied with ribbons. She looks eerily like the pictures I've seen of Daisy Mason. As for Sharon, I would hardly have recognized her. A heavy, awkward child, standing on the edge of the picture as if she's been Photoshopped into her own life. Her mousey hair hangs in dull strands. No ribbons for her, it seems. I wonder what it was like living in that house, after Jessica was gone.

It's the first time I've actually felt sorry for her.

* * *

When I look up, they're both standing there. Quinn and Gislingham. Together.

I look from one to the other, not bothering to hide my surprise. 'What is this – are you two declaring a ceasefire? Have we called the UN?'

Gislingham has the grace to look sheepish. 'Not exactly, boss. It's Mason's phone. Forensics have confirmed there are indecent images on it. Videos, to be exact, and it's really hardcore stuff. They were deep down on the memory card, but they're definitely there.'

I sit back. 'So he was lying.'

'And that's not the only thing,' says Quinn. 'It's the car. The one Daisy was seen in. We know who owns it.'

He pauses. 'Azeem Rahija.'

It's a hot day, but I'm suddenly icy cold. 'Bloody hell, not —'

He nods. 'Younger brother of Yasir Rahija, and cousin of Sunni Rahija.'

He doesn't need to say any more. Yasir and Sunni Rahija were at the heart of one of the rings of particularly vicious sex abusers who targeted vulnerable white girls in East Oxford. And it took this police force far too long to nail them. It wasn't my case, but we've all been scarred. We all feel guilty.

'Azeem is only seventeen,' says Quinn, 'and there's nothing to suggest he was involved in the grooming or the gang rapes, but in the circumstances —'

I put my head in my hands. I've been so sure — so *sure* — that Daisy was killed by someone close to home, but what if I'm wrong? What if, all this time, she's been in some filthy cellar on the Cowley Road, subjected to the most disgusting —

'And there's something else.'

Gislingham this time.

'Everett just called. She says she showed Leo the picture of the boy on the CCTV, like you asked. He said he didn't know his name. He also said he'd never seen him with Daisy –'

I sigh. 'I guess it was too much to hope he'd seen him before.'

'But that's just it, he *had* seen him before. But not with Daisy – with *Barry*.'

I stare at him. 'I don't get it – what possible connection could there conceivably be –'

But Gislingham has had more time to think about that than me.

'It could add up, boss. I've been asking myself for days now what happens to Mason's money. He's ripping people off right, left and centre, taking thousands of pounds for work he never actually does, and yet everyone says the family are hard up. But all that money has to be going somewhere. And he must be getting people to pay him in cash, too, because as far as I can see, there's nothing like enough in his bank account, compared to the size of jobs he's doing.'

'Could be going on gambling? Drugs?'

But Gislingham's shaking his head. 'We've not found any evidence suggesting that. But what we *do* know is that he got hold of kiddie porn on that website. A habit like that – it gets expensive. And the more illegal it is, the more it costs.'

'So you think it's more than just staring at videos? He's actually paying for sex with children – with under-age girls like the ones the Rahijas were abusing?'

Gislingham shrugs. 'Like I said. It adds up.'

'And this boy on the CCTV that Leo saw him with – he's Mason's contact with the paedophile ring?'

Quinn intervenes. 'Just because most of them are in jail, doesn't mean we managed to close it all down. Azeem may have picked up where his brother and cousin left off.'

'So what was this boy doing talking to Daisy?'

They look at each other. 'Perhaps Mason owed them money,' says Gislingham eventually. 'Perhaps they were using Daisy to put pressure on him. Threatening her as a way of showing him what they were capable of if he didn't cough up.'

'Let's hope so. Because the alternative doesn't bear thinking about. There's no healthy explanation for a boy that age being interested in a child like Daisy. Especially a boy who has paedophiles for friends.'

But even as I'm saying it I'm remembering that her friends said she was angry after she met that boy. Not upset, not distraught. Angry. But it's only what we were told – I don't know it for sure. And that's one reason why the Rahija gang got away with it for so long – people like me saw what we wanted to see and heard what we wanted to hear. I can't afford to let us make the same mistake again.

'OK, round up some uniforms and warn the community team and the press office, so they know what to say when the phones start ringing. I'll clear it with the Super. I'm sure he'll be absolutely bloody ecstatic.'

I get to my feet. Given the state of community

relations in East Oxford, this is one operation I can't delegate.

* * *

12 May 2016, 7.47 a.m.
68 days before the disappearance
5 Barge Close, kitchen

Barry Mason is at the breakfast table and Sharon is by the window, feeding chunks of fruit into the juicer. Leo and Daisy are in school uniform and Daisy has a pink cardigan over the back of her chair.

'I think we should have a party,' says Sharon. 'For the end of term.'

Barry looks up from his bowl of cereal. 'A party? Why?'

'Well, we never did have a housewarming, and I know people would like to see the place.'

On the other side of the table, the boy looks up and the girl looks down. Barry picks up his spoon again. 'Wouldn't something like that be a lot of work?'

Sharon glances back at him. 'We could do a barbecue. With salads and sandwiches and jacket potatoes. You'd hardly have to do anything.'

Barry opens his mouth to say something, then closes it again. The children exchange glances as their mother starts to chop up more fruit, knifing it with far more effort than appears required by the task.

'What if it rains?' Barry says eventually. 'We couldn't fit everyone in here.'

'Fiona Webster says we can borrow their gazebo. And I'm sure Owen wouldn't mind helping you put it up.'

Barry shrugs. 'OK, if you're sure. What d'you think, kids?'

'It will be great for them,' says Sharon. 'A chance to meet some of the children on the close – the ones who don't go to Bishop Christopher's.' She turns back to the juicer and turns it on again. The mixture starts to jump and spin, turning into a greenish mucus that slides stickily down the plastic when she flips off the switch.

'What time will you be back tonight?'

Barry hesitates. 'Could be a late one. I'm at a site meeting in Guildford this afternoon. It may run on. What about you, princess?' he says, turning to his daughter. 'You get that English test result today, right? Bet it'll be top marks again. Nothing else is good enough for my special girl.'

Daisy smiles briefly at her father before returning to her cereal. 'Leo was picked for the football team.'

Barry raises his eyebrows. 'Is that so? Why didn't you say so, son?'

Leo shrugs. 'It's only the reserves.'

Barry's face falls. 'Oh well, just shows you need to try a bit harder. Like I said.'

Sharon is still absorbed in the intricacies of the juicer, which appears reluctant to be dismantled. 'OK.

219

I'll leave you something cold for when you get back. Don't forget, my aerobics is at eight.'

Barry smiles broadly at Daisy. 'Make sure you bring that test result home so I can see it, eh, Dais?'

Sharon glances round. 'I do wish you'd use her proper name, Barry. How can we stop her friends calling her that, if they hear her father doing the same?'

Barry reaches across and tousles his daughter's hair. 'You don't mind, do you, Dais?'

'And remember to give that make-up bag back to Mrs Chen when you see her at school today, Daisy. Tell her thank you, but we can afford to buy our own things.'

'I'm sure they didn't mean it that way,' says Barry. 'They just had two the same, and thought Dais would like one.'

'I don't care. Make-up isn't appropriate. Not for a girl her age. It just looks common.'

'Oh, come on, it's just a bit of fun. You know what girls are like – dressing up and stuff.'

'I told you, it's not appropriate. And in any case, we don't need their charity.'

Barry tries to catch his daughter's eye but Daisy appears intent on her cereal. Then he pushes back his stool and gets up. 'Don't go to too much trouble tonight,' he says to Sharon. 'A sandwich will do. Tuna or something.' He picks up his briefcase and keys, and unhitches his high-viz jacket from the back of a chair. 'I'm off then. Bye, kids.'

When the kitchen door closes, Daisy puts down her

spoon and carefully smooths her hair back down with both hands. Leo edges off his stool and goes up to his mother. 'Who will you be inviting to the party?'

'Oh, you know, the neighbours, your classmates,' she says, pouring the smoothie into a glass.

'What about that boy Dad knows?' says Leo.

'What boy?' says Sharon distractedly. By the time she has rinsed the juicer and turned back to her children, Leo has gone.

* * *

The Rahija home is identical to a thousand others in that part of East Oxford. Pebbledashed thirties semi with a bay window at ground and first floor. There's a garage door at the side with most of the paint peeled off, apart from the abuse someone's spray-canned across it. Someone who can't spell 'paedophile'. One first-floor window is boarded up, and there are six wheelie bins in the front garden, two of them tipped over, with trash and rotting food spilling over the concrete.

I have a team blocking off the alley at the back, and there are a dozen of us at the front. One of them has a battering ram. I nod to him and he hammers on the door.

'Police, open up!'

There are sounds inside at once – women screaming and a male voice shouting in a language that's not English. A baby starts to wail.

'I said Police – open the door or we'll break it down!'

A minute passes, perhaps two, then there's a scrabbling noise on the woodwork and the door opens a couple of inches. It's a woman in a headscarf. She can't be more than twenty.

'What do you want? Can't you leave us alone? We haven't done anything.'

I step forward. 'I am Detective Inspector Adam Fawley of Thames Valley CID. We have a warrant to search these premises. Please open the door. It will be much better for everyone if we can carry this out in a civilized manner.'

'*Civilized?* You come here, beating down the door, terrifying my mother and my children, and you claim to be *civilized*?'

A crowd is gathering in the street now, most of them young Asian men, some in kufis. I see Quinn reach to his truncheon. The mood is getting ugly. I don't want a riot on my hands.

'Look, we can do this the hard way or the easy way. Let us in and I give you my word we will make every effort to do what we have to as quickly and with as little disruption as possible. But be in no doubt, if I have to break down the door, I will, and that'll mean your name in the papers and all the abuse you got last year starting up all over again. I can't believe you want that any more than I do. But you need to decide, and decide now.'

The grip on the door loosens. I make eye

contact – force her to look at me – and, eventually, she nods. I can scarcely breathe for the pounding in my chest. I turn and gesture the uniform team to back off to the pavement.

Then I beckon Brenda, the Community Liaison Officer. 'Can you make sure the women and children aren't unduly frightened. Quinn – you and Gislingham come with me.'

Even in this weather, the front room smells of damp. Discoloured wallpaper is hanging off the walls and there's an old gas fire in the hearth that has deathtrap written all over it. Even without the four of us, the room is crowded. There are two older women in black sitting on the sagging sofa and keening backwards and forwards, and three younger mothers, their arms round their children. The kids are looking at us with huge wary eyes. I smile at one of them and she smiles back, before burying her face in her mother's niqab. There are no men.

Behind me, I hear Quinn direct Gislingham through into the back room and the kitchen, and Quinn himself takes the stairs, two at a time. Then I hear him on the floorboards above.

'Boss?' he calls. 'Up here.'

The cigarette smoke should warn me, and at some subliminal level, it does. I reach the landing and round the corner. There are two sets of bunk beds in a room barely big enough for a single, and Azeem Rahija is sitting cross-legged on one of the lower ones. I know it's him because I've seen his brother, but there's something less hardened about this kid, something that gives me a flicker of hope that he hasn't yet gone the same way. But then I look in the face of the other person in the room. Sitting on the top bunk, smoking, his legs swinging as if he was still a little boy.

'Afternoon, ocifers,' he says, his voice slurring slightly. There's a four-pack of Strongbow lying beside him. He's not as attractive as he appeared on the footage. Distance makes the hair look blonder, clearly. And he has a scatter of acne about his chin and cheeks. But it's his manner that unmakes him – the devious, narrowed eyes, the self-satisfaction. The crotch of his jeans is hanging near his knees, and he has one of those earrings that make a hole the size of your finger. They always make me feel slightly ill.

He takes a draw on his fag and blows smoke at me.

'I don't believe we've been introduced,' I say, echoing his tone. 'I'm Detective Inspector Adam Fawley. And you are?'

He grins unpleasantly and points at me, not quite managing to keep his finger steady. 'That's for me to know and you to find out.'

'DS Quinn, take this child out to the car. And if he's still refusing to divulge his name, get a social worker organized. There's no way this *boy* is sixteen.'

There's a rather unseemly scuffle, but Quinn has a foot and several stone on his side. The kid's already yelping about 'brutality' as I follow the two of them back to the landing and call Gislingham up.

'Start the search in there. There's at least one laptop hidden in the bedclothes.'

When I turn to look back at Azeem I think it's quite possible he's shat himself.

* * *

Interview with Barry Mason, conducted at
St Aldate's Police Station, Oxford
23 July 2016, 12.42 p.m.
In attendance, DI A. Fawley, Acting DS G. Quinn,
Miss E. Carwood (solicitor)

EC: Are we to take it that you are ready to
    press charges?

AF: We still have some questions to ask your
    client, Miss Carwood.

EC: In relation to the pornography allegations?

AF: For the moment, yes.

EC: Very well. But may I remind you, the clock
    is ticking.

AF: Mr Mason, are you in contact with an
    individual by the name of Azeem Rahija?

BM: I haven't a bloody clue who you're talking
    about.

EC: Are we talking about the same family as
    Yasir and Sunni Rahija?

BM: What, those Asian paedophiles who were in the papers? Of course I bloody well don't know them. Jesus Christ.

AF: Azeem Rahija is the younger brother of Yasir Rahija. He's seventeen.

BM: So?

AF: So you have never had any contact with him, or any of his family? You've never accessed pornography from them –

BM: How many more bloody times. I don't buy porn. Not from them, or anyone else. I've bought the odd girlie mag, but that's it. End of. Go on - check my phone - check my bloody PC - you won't find any of that shit on it.

AF: Unfortunately the hard drive on your computer was destroyed in the fire. We have no way of knowing what was on it. Or what might have been erased. We have to tell you, however, that we've found two videos on your mobile phone. Videos which contain extreme and sexually explicit images of young children –

BM: No way – *no fucking way*. Do you hear me? I did *not* download anything like that. It must be a virus or something – that happens, right? Or someone hacked it –

EC: [*intervening*]
    What evidence do you have that my client

knew the Rahijas? Do you have phone
records? An email trail?

BM: They don't have any of that because I *never
bloody well spoke to them.*

AF: For the tape, I am showing Mr Mason a still
taken by a CCTV camera. Mr Mason, we
believe you made contact with the Rahijas
through this youth. We have a witness who
saw you together.

BM: [*looking at the picture and then at the
officers*]
Where the fuck did you get this?

* * *

11 May 2016, 7.09 p.m.
69 days before the disappearance
The Chen home, 11 Lanchester Road, Oxford

Jerry Chen comes into the kitchen, where his wife is
stacking the dishwasher. The sun is declining and the
golden light glimmers through the leaves of two silver
birches, which hang like curtains either side of the large
and mature garden.

Jerry puts down his bag on the kitchen island, and
his wife pours him a glass of wine.

'How did the lecture go?'

'Professor Helston was there. He's asked me to give
it again at the LSE in the fall.'

'High praise, coming from him. Will you be back from Stanford by then?'

He takes a sip of the wine and checks the label. 'This is pretty good. And yes, should be fine – Stanford's in September. This would be November sometime. Where's Nanxi?'

'In the sitting room. She's teaching Daisy to play chess.'

Jerry smiles. 'It's about time Nanxi had a decent opponent her own age. I can't keep letting her win.'

'You shouldn't do that. She knows when you're faking it. She's not stupid.'

'You're probably right. You usually are.'

Joyce's turn to smile. 'As far as I could tell, Daisy had never even seen a chessboard before.'

'Well, *that* doesn't surprise me. If she didn't look so much like her mother, I'd swear that child was a change-ling. I daren't even imagine the debility of the Mason gene pool.'

He makes a face and his wife laughs as she closes the dishwasher door and straightens up. 'What was it Eric Hoffer said? Even if most of the human race are pigs, every now and again a He pig marries a She pig and a Leonardo is born. Something like that.'

She glances at her watch. 'Lord, is that the time? I need to run Daisy home. Can you call her?'

Jerry goes up the steps towards the living room, but the little girl is already standing there.

'Oh, Daisy,' he says, slightly discomfited. 'I didn't notice you. How long have you been standing there?'

'I wanted to thank you for the make-up bag. I love it.' She's swinging it now, by its little strap. It's striped black and white, with a neon pink splash in the centre saying *Girly Crap* in large wobbly letters.

Joyce Chen looks up. 'You're very welcome, Daisy. Isn't it irritating when two people send exactly the same present? We could hardly return it, and Nanxi thought you might like to have the same one as her. Did the two of you have a nice time this afternoon?'

'Oh yes,' says Daisy, smiling. 'It's been the *best* day.'

* * *

'You can't smoke in here.'

'Yeah, right.'

The boy's lying full stretch on the sofa in the family room, his feet up on the seat. There's a paper plate on the floor with a dozen fag ends in it already. Maureen Jones is sitting as far away from him as the space will allow, and the social worker is standing by the door. It's Derek Ross, the same bloke who came in for Leo. We exchange a silent acknowledgement and I ask him if he has any idea what the kid's name is.

'Mickey Mouse,' the boy says, leering at me. 'George Clooney. The Dalai Lama. Queen Vic-fucking-toria. Take your pick, pig.'

'That's not going to help,' says Ross. He sounds exhausted and he's barely been here an hour.

'Right,' I say. 'As I'm sure you know, members of your friend Azeem's family have recently been convicted of sexual assaults on children. We are currently going through material seized at the house to ascertain whether further offences have been committed.'

'Can't scare me, pig. I don't know nothin' about any of that shit.'

He starts coughing and sits up. 'I'm outta here. You can't stop me.'

'If you insist on leaving I will have no choice but to arrest you.'

'It's really best if you cooperate,' Derek says to the kid. 'Seriously.'

The boy and I stare at each other for a long moment, but he blinks first.

'So where's my fuckin' lawyer?'

'Like I said, you're not under arrest. And Mr Ross is here to protect your interests.'

'I want to make a complaint – that git hit me. The cocky one.'

I'm tempted to ask if he's playing the role of pot or kettle on that score. 'If you want to make a complaint, you'll have to tell us your name.'

He grins at me nastily and taps the side of his nose. 'You'll have to do better than that, pig. No flies on me, see.'

I reach for one of the hard-back chairs and swing it

alongside him. Then I sit down and open my cardboard folder and show him one of the CCTV images. The one of him and Daisy on 19 April.

'Do you know who this is?'

He takes a deep drag and blows the smoke in my face. 'What if I do?'

'This girl is Daisy Mason. Her face has been all over the press and the web for the best part of a week. I can't believe you haven't noticed.'

He narrows his eyes, but says nothing.

'She's missing. She may even be dead. And a few weeks before she disappeared she was seen talking with you.'

'I talk to lots of people. Sociable bloke, me.'

'I'm sure you're quite the life and soul. Only that wasn't the first time you'd spoken to her, was it?'

I get out more pictures. 'April twelfth, April fourteenth, April nineteenth. And here, on May ninth, is Daisy Mason in the back of a car registered to Azeem Rahija. With you presumably in the front seat.'

More silence. More smoke. I can see his brain working in his eyes. He doesn't know how much I know.

'Why were you stalking her?'

'*Stalking?* Fuck off. That's not stalking.'

'So what's a boy your age doing hitting on an eight-year-old girl if it's not stalking? We have you with her on camera, four separate times. On the last occasion she's seen in a car with you and the brother of a convicted child rapist, and a few weeks later she disappears. You think a jury won't draw the obvious conclusion?'

'I wasn't *hitting on* her –'

'So what was it then? Why else would you bother with a kid like that? Getting in touch with your feminine side, were you? Or did you develop a sudden over-whelming interest in My Little Pony? Or perhaps Barbie is your doll of choice? I mean, it's 2016 – boys can play with girls' toys, right?'

He swings his legs down and plants his feet on the floor. He won't look at me, but the hand that holds the fag is shaking.

'You were grooming her, weren't you – getting her to trust you so you could abuse her –'

'I did *not* abuse her –'

'Did you give her to those sickos the Rahijas used to deal with? I bet they'd pay a fortune to rape a girl like that. Or did you want her for yourself? Is that what happened that day? You go round to the house, all smiles, all Prince Charming. And her mother's not there so she goes out to play with you and for a while it's nicey nicey. Only by the time you have your fist in her knickers –'

'Inspector,' pleads Ross, 'is that really necessary?'

'– she realizes what you really want and she's scream-ing and you have to shut her up but she's struggling and you have your hand over her mouth –'

'You're *disgusting*,' yells the boy, lurching to his feet. 'I didn't lay a fuckin' *finger* on her. You're fuckin' sick, that's what you are – only some sort of weirdo pervert would do that to their own *sister* –'

I take a deep breath, count to five. 'Your sister.'

He swallows. 'Yeah. Barry Mason is my dad.'

He sits back down, heavily. 'The sodding bastard.'

* * *

Back in my office, I call Alex.

'Where the hell are you, Adam? I thought we were supposed to be going to your parents' for lunch.'

Shit. I'd forgotten all about it.

'I'm sorry. Things have rather –'

'Got away from you. I know. This is me, remember?'

I sigh. 'Am I really that predictable?'

'During a big case? That would be a yes.'

'I'm sorry. I'll call my mother. I promise. Look, I wanted to ask you a favour. I know your firm isn't big on Legal Aid, but we've got this kid in here who was seen talking to Daisy outside the school. Turns out he's Barry Mason's son by a first marriage.'

'Shit. Sounds like someone slipped up.'

'I know, but to be fair we had no reason to go looking. Not till now anyway. The problem is we can't find either his mother or his stepfather. Neither's answering their phone and the next-door neighbour thinks they could be away for the weekend. The duty solicitor is stuck on another case and we haven't yet found anyone who can get here much before this evening. So I was wondering –'

'– if I'd find someone for you?'

I bite my lip. 'I'm sorry. It always seems to be me asking the favours these days.'

'And me doing them.' There's a long intake of breath, then, 'OK, leave it with me. I may be able to lean on a junior who's got more ambition than social life. What's your kid's name?'

'Jamie Northam.'

I can hear the surprise. 'Not Northam as in Marcus Northam?'

'I've no idea. Why – should I have heard of him?'

'Put it this way, we'll be charging him the full rate. Plus expenses. I'll make a couple of calls and ring you back.'

'Thanks, Alex, I really –'

But the line has gone dead.

* * *

Continuation of interview with Barry Mason,
conducted at St Aldate's Police Station, Oxford
23 July 2016, 3.09 p.m.
In attendance, DI A. Fawley, Acting DS G. Quinn,
Miss E. Carwood (solicitor)

AF: I'd like to ask you some questions about
     your son, Jamie Northam. When did you last
     see him?

BM: He was waiting outside one day when I left
the office. Sitting on the wall.

AF: Do you know how he found you?

BM: He said it took him about five minutes to
find the firm on the internet. I didn't
realize they were living so near here. I
haven't seen Moira in years.

AF: And was that the only time you've seen him
recently?

BM: No. I didn't have time to talk to him that
night so I said I'd see him in a coffee shop
on the Banbury Road a couple of days later.
The Starbucks. I had Leo in the car so I
only had ten minutes. To be honest, I was
hoping he wouldn't turn up - I was hoping
he'd have forgotten the whole thing.

AF: But he didn't.

BM: No.

AF: So what did he want?

BM: He said he'd like to see me - a couple of
times a month or something. I gathered he
was having a pretty shitty time at home.
Moira's always been a cold bitch, and that
stepfather of his is clearly a self-
important tosser.

AF: So he was hoping for some support from
you, as his biological father? Someone to
give him the affection he wasn't getting
at home?

BM: You're twisting it - it wasn't like that -

AF: So what was it like?

BM: What he wanted - it would have been a
    nightmare. Sharon's never even let me tell
    the kids about Jamie, never mind let me see
    him. I'd have had to make up all sorts of
    lies about where I was going -

GQ: I dunno, you seem pretty good at that
    to me.

BM: - and when she did find out she'd have blown
    her bloody top. It was just all too sodding
    difficult.

AF: So what did you say? When you blew your son
    off?

EC: There's no need to take that tone,
    Inspector.

AF: Well, Mr Mason?

BM: I told him we were having some family
    trouble. That I'd think about it again when
    things had quietened down.

AF: What sort of trouble?

BM: What difference does it make?

AF: What sort of trouble, Mr Mason?

BM: Well, if you must know, I told him Daisy
    was having problems at school.

AF: What kind of problems?

BM: You know, that she was falling behind with
    her work - that the school was really

236

competitive and we were having to help her because she was struggling to keep up.

AF: Was that true?

BM: No, of course it wasn't true. Daisy's way smarter than any of those stuck-up kids in her class.

AF: So it was a lie. Instead of taking responsibility for your own decisions, like a man, you put all the blame on your eight-year-old daughter.

BM: For fuck's sake, it was just a white lie –

AF: I think you'll find kids aren't very good at telling the difference, Mr Mason. A lie's just a lie, in their book.

BM: Whatever. Like I said, what difference does it make?

AF: Did you stop to think for a moment what damage it might do? That Jamie might resent your daughter after what you told him? That he'd see her as the reason why he couldn't have a relationship with you – that it was all *her* fault? He already had a criminal record. He's an angry and unstable young man, and now he has a grievance. Did you think for a moment what might happen, if they met?

BM: They weren't *going* to meet –

AF: I know that's what you assumed, but it's not
        what happened, is it? He tracked her down,
        just like he tracked you down. And this is
        the result.
        [*shows still from CCTV*]
        That's your daughter, Mr Mason. In the back
        of a car owned by the brother of a known
        paedophile.
BM: [*looking at picture*]
        Jesus Christ - are you telling me *Jamie* did
        something to her - that *he's* the one who
        took her?
AF: I have no idea, Mr Mason. Because, right
        now, none of us knows where she is.
        Do we?

Out in the corridor, Quinn turns to me. 'You know,
despite everything, I'm more and more convinced he
didn't do it. The porn, yes; the abuse, perhaps. But not
the rest of it – not killing her. I saw his face just now,
when you told him about her being in Azeem's car. I
don't think anyone could fake that.'

'So like 67 per cent of the shits on Twitter, you think
she did it.'

'If it has to be one of those two, then yes. But right
now, my money's on Jamie Northam. For what it's
worth.'

* * *

* * *

I stand for ten minutes, watching Jamie Northam on the video feed from Interview Room Two. He must know we're watching him, but he doesn't seem bothered. In fact, I'm prepared to bet he's putting on a show for my special benefit. Derek Ross has been replaced, to his obvious relief, by someone from Alex's firm. Though he looks scarcely out of university, and has spent the whole time I've been standing here boning up on the Police and Criminal Evidence Act. Gislingham comes up behind me. 'Anything interesting?'

'So far I've seen him scratch his arse, pick his nose and dig crap out of his ears. All I'm missing is him squeezing his zits and I'll have a full house. Any news from the search at the Rahijas'?'

'No sign of Daisy. They don't have a cellar or anywhere they could have kept her. Challow's lot are going over it now, just to be sure, but the house looks clean as far as we can tell.'

'Anything on Azeem's laptop? He looked shit scared of something.'

'Well, that something wasn't porn. Looks like he's been running a nice little earner dealing ketamine and skunk. Probably to students – always a ready market there.'

'And he was idiot enough to leave the evidence on his laptop?'

'Seems he's doing Business Studies at the furthur education college. He was practising his double-entry accounting.' He sees my face. 'No, seriously, I'm not joking.'

I shake my head. 'Jesus wept.'

'Anyway, we're charging him. His mother's coming in.'

'OK. So that just leaves us Jamie Northam. Whose mother certainly isn't coming in. She's still not answering her phone.'

'You want me to sit in?'

'No, I'd rather you made a start on the paperwork. See if you can find Quinn.'

"Right, boss.'

* * *

I push open the door and go into the room. The lawyer pings upright as if he's on elastic, then pushes his glasses up his nose. 'Right, er, Sergeant –'

'Detective Inspector. For the record.'

The door swings open and Quinn comes in and joins me. He's had a shower – I can smell his Molton Brown bodywash. I wish I'd thought to do that. Too late now.

'So, Jamie –'

'Jimmy,' he says sullenly. 'My name is Jimmy.'

'Fair enough. So, *Jimmy*, you are not at present under arrest. Mr Gregory is here to make sure that everything's done according to the regulations. We all clear on that?'

No answer.

'OK, I'm going to start by asking you some questions about Barry Mason. He says you found out where he worked and came to his office.'

He shrugs, but says nothing.

'Why did you want to talk to him, Jimmy?'

Another shrug. 'Just wanted to see what he was like. Mum's always saying I'm like him.'

Something tells me Moira Northam only says that to her son when he's pissed her off.

'Do you get on with your stepdad?'

He looks up at me, then back at his bitten finger-nails. 'He doesn't like me much. He says I'm fuckless.'

'Feckless.'

'Whatever.'

There's a silence. I looked up Marcus Northam after I spoke to Alex – his big house on the river, his thriving property business, his extensive connections and his son at medical school. Hard to see him regarding this kid as anything other than a royal pain in the arse, and I'm sure he makes his feelings on the subject abundantly clear. And even if Jamie's every bit the delinquent his stepfather considers him, the question is which came first, the acting-up or the disdain? Either way, it's no surprise Jamie thought he might have more in common with Barry than either of the parents he's forced to live with – no wonder he thought he might get a more sympathetic hearing from the man who actually fathered him.

'So how did it go, when you met Barry?'

'He said we couldn't meet up. That it wasn't a good idea.'

'Did he say why it wasn't a good idea?'

He looks away.

'It was because of Daisy, wasn't it? He said she was having problems at school. Is that why you tracked her down? Is that why you wanted to talk to her – to see if it was true?'

There's a silence. He looks suddenly defeated. White about the eyes.

'When he mentioned her I remembered. I'd forgotten, but then I remembered there was this little kid. She had blonde hair. We met her once at the zoo, me and my mum. She gave me a piece of her chocolate.'

'She was nice to you.'

'My dad was there too. I wanted to talk to him but he went away.'

I sit back again. 'So you recognized your father – you remembered him. Even though you were only four when he left.'

He looks away. 'I remember him boxing with me when I was little. In the garden. Mum didn't like it.'

'You were quite young, weren't you? For boxing?'

'Dad said I needed to be able to look after myself. When I went to school. So no one would bully me.'

'He taught you how to fight to be nobody's fool.'

The lawyer gives me an odd look.

'Sorry – it's from a song. It's been in my head all day.'

The lawyer obviously thinks he's scored some sort of point. 'I'm not sure where all this is going, Inspector.'

'We're getting to that. So, Jimmy, you managed to work out which school Daisy went to.'

'Piece of piss. Just sat outside a couple of schools at home-time until I saw her.'

'Then you went back there later and spoke to her. It must have been a real shock for her – finding out she had a half-brother.'

'Nah. She already knew.'

Now he really does have me wrong-footed. 'Are you absolutely sure? Her parents didn't want her to know about you. How did she find out?'

'Don't ask me. All I know is that she knew my name and everything. I think she thought it was cool to meet me. I think she liked having a secret from her mum.'

'She didn't get on with her mum? Do you know why?'

He shakes his head.

'So what happened, Jimmy? You meet up, and she's clearly happy to see you. She tells her mates she's got a new friend and you see each other a couple more times, and suddenly she's telling her friends she doesn't want to talk about it any more. She's angry and she won't say why. What the hell happened?'

He shrugs.

I force myself to have some patience. It's never been my strong suit.

But it pays off this time. Eventually.

'She wanted to go to the circus on Wolvercote Common,' he says at last, 'so I got Azeem to take us. That's why we were in the car. But it was crap. Kids' stuff.'

I know the circus he means. We went, once. It was magical. One of the best days. I remember Alex lifting

Jake so he could stroke the nose of a white pony they'd got up like a unicorn with a twisted golden horn. He talked about nothing but unicorns for days afterwards. I bought him a book about them. It's still there, in his room.

Quinn's voice dispels the memory. 'Wasn't the funfair there that weekend as well?'

Jamie nods. 'But her mum won't let her go to things like that. She'd never even seen candyfloss before. She didn't know you were supposed to eat it.'

I have a sudden sad image of the two of them just being kids. Having a tiny afternoon of the ordinary childhood they might have had.

'Sounds like a nice day,' I say. 'So what happened?'

He flushes. 'Azeem said she'd get over it.'

'Get over what, precisely? What *exactly* did you do to her, Jimmy?'

* * *

9 May 2016, 7.29 p.m.
71 days before the disappearance
The Grays Family Circus, Wolvercote Common

The big white tent has an arena of sand in the middle, and flags and bunting hung round the edge. Daisy is sitting on the front row of one of the banks of seats. She is alone, but the benches either side of her are so crowded with parents and kids that no one notices. The air is noisy with expectation, and soon the gypsy band strikes up and the master of ceremonies appears. A big round man, half clown, half hobgoblin, with a painted face and a serial flatulence problem that has the children squealing with laughter every time he appears. As the story gradually unfolds, fairies swing from a feathered trapeze, jugglers throw showers of fire and strange creatures in glittery bodysuits dance on the backs of spotted horses. Doves fly out of enchanted caskets, a mouse the size of a man salsas on a golden ball and a tame goose wanders in and out, seemingly unperturbed by all the hullabaloo. There is music, there are masks and there is magic, and Daisy is entranced, her little mouth open in an enormous wondering O.

When the show has finished and the cheering is over, Daisy makes her way outside, where Jamie Northam is waiting. Smoking. One or two of the passing parents glance circumspectly at him as they go by.

'Jesus,' he says, chucking away his fag. 'It went on a bit, didn't it? Azeem has to get back.'

He turns to go and Daisy runs to catch up, then skips along beside him.

'It was a-mazing. There was this little girl who was stolen as a baby and imprisoned by a witch in a magic garden. But the animals helped her escape and she went on a huge journey over the mountains to a beautiful castle on a hill and it turned out she was a princess after all. And she lived happily ever after with her real mummy.'

'Sounds like bullshit to me.'

Daisy frowns. 'No it's not. Don't say that!'

'It's just a stupid fairy tale. That's not how things are.'

'They are! Sometimes they are!'

He stops and turns to her. 'Look, kid. People don't get stolen as babies and find out they're bleeding royalty. That's just kids' stuff. Fairy tales. I know your parents are crap, but you're stuck with them. Sorry – that's just how it is.'

She's close to tears now. 'They're *not* my parents,' she says. 'Whatever *you* say. *I know*.'

Jamie lights another fag. 'What are you on about?'

She's sullen now. 'I heard them. My dad was saying how they almost didn't get me and how it had been really difficult but my mum had done it. See – she stole me. When I was a baby. It's a secret. I'm not supposed to know.'

'He actually said that? That she *stole* you?'

She shakes her head, a little reluctantly. 'Not *exactly*. But that's what he meant. I know that's what he meant. He said they had to pay for an ivy thief.'

'You what? What the fuck's an ivy thief?'

Daisy looks at her feet. 'I don't know,' she says softly, her cheeks red.

Jamie starts laughing, spluttering into his fag. 'You got it all wrong, kid. It's not an ivy thief. It's *IVF*. It's something they do in hospital. For people who want babies. Sorry, but there ain't nothin' you can do about it – you're their kid all right.'

She stares at him, her mouth open, but in anger this time, not delight. Then she shouts, *'I hate you! I hate you!'* as loudly as she can and runs away towards the trees.

He stands gaping after her. 'What the fuck? Oi – come back here!'

But she doesn't turn, perhaps she doesn't even hear him. After a moment he tosses his fag into the undergrowth, hunches his shoulders and starts after her.

'Daisy? Where are you?' he calls as he pushes through the trees. He's getting pissed off now; first it was that stupid bloody circus and now she thinks she's a sodding princess. 'You can't hide from me. I'm going to find you. You know that, don't you, Daisy. *I'm going to find you.'*

* * *

Quinn buys us a coffee in the café across the road and comes over to the table where I'm sitting by the window. I take a mouthful. It's too hot. But it beats the station stuff hands down. 'So, having heard all that, do you still think Jamie did it?'

Quinn opens a sachet of sweetener and tips it into his cup. 'I don't think he abused her, if that's what you're asking. Not sexually, anyway. He seems genuinely repelled by that idea. As for killing her? Possibly. But if he did, I don't think it was planned. He's not that methodical. It would have been rage – something that flared up. And I suspect that happens on a pretty regular basis, because let's face it, he's one angry kid. An angry kid who also doesn't have an alibi. Or, at least, not one he's prepared to share with the likes of us.'

'So if he'd done it, we'd have found her by now?'

'Probably. I can't see him covering his tracks that well.'

I nod. 'Did you believe the story about the circus?'

He's more equivocal now. 'If it did happen like he says, I find it hard to believe Daisy reacted so badly. OK, she might not get on with her parents, and she might have that fantasy a lot of kids do about being adopted. All the same, it's a bit of an extreme reaction, isn't it? But, hey, I'm hardly the one to ask. I don't know how eight-year-olds think.'

But I do. '*Everything seems enormous when you're that age.*'

'Sorry?'

'It was something Everett said. A couple of days ago. And she's right. Kids that young get things out of proportion. Especially bad things. They can't put them in perspective, and they can't see beyond how bad they feel right now. If children under twelve commit suicide, that's usually the reason why.'

I stick my spoon in my coffee and stir it. I can feel Quinn looking at me. Wondering how to react. It's more than I've ever said to him before. More than I've said to pretty much anyone.

The café door swings open and I see Gislingham coming briskly towards us. On a mission, clearly. 'Challow just called,' he says as he gets to the table. 'He's tested the mermaid costume.'

'And?'

'There's a rip in it, at the neck, but given it was being worn by kids week in, week out, it could just be normal wear and tear. There wasn't any blood, but there was DNA. Four different individuals. Sharon Mason, who we know handled it; Daisy Mason, likewise; and another unknown female, presumably Millie Connor.'

'And the fourth?'

'Male. A pubic hair, to be precise.'

There's a rock in my chest. 'Barry Mason?'

'Yup, in one.'

Quinn makes a face. 'The same Barry Mason who claims not to know the costumes were switched – who claims not to know there even *was* a mermaid costume.'

'Ah, but that's where it gets complicated,' says Gislingham. 'Sharon says she found it under his gym kit, so if it came to court his defence is bound to argue that his DNA got on the costume that way.'

'But if Barry was the one who hid it, that in itself would be proof enough –'

'We can't prove that,' says Gislingham, not letting Quinn finish. 'It could have been Sharon, trying to frame him. He's going to say that, isn't he, even if it's bollocks? And there's one more thing.' He turns to Quinn. 'We checked the time of the 999 call to the fire service, like you asked.'

Quinn sits back. 'And?'

'You were right. The call came through at 2.10. That's

nearly ten minutes *after* Sharon got out of her burning house, leaving her son inside.'

'OK,' I say, 'give Ev a call and get her to ask Sharon what the hell she thinks she was doing. Not in those exact words, of course.'

Quinn collects the empty cups and we're getting up to go when I catch sight of the desk sergeant gesturing to us from the doorway. It must be something important to get him off his ample behind. And then I see: he has a young woman with him. Mid height, long auburn hair. She has a raffia bag over one shoulder and that's when I realize I've seen her before – at the school. Right now, half the men in the place are staring at her. I sense Quinn straighten his shoulders, but it's not him she's come to see. Or so it seems. She scans the room anxiously then alights on Gislingham and comes quickly towards him. I see Gislingham slide Quinn a glance, and I have to admit, the look on Quinn's face is priceless. DC two, DS nil.

'DC Gislingham,' she says, slightly breathless. 'I'm so glad I caught you. I asked for your colleague – the woman – I forgot her name –'

'DC Everett –'

'– only they said she wasn't here so I thought I should talk to you instead.'

Gislingham turns to me. 'This is Daisy's teacher, boss. Miss Madigan.' He introduces Quinn too, but I can see she's too distracted to register who either of us are. Which Quinn clearly finds peculiarly devastating.

'It's the fairy story,' she says, turning to Gislingham again. 'Daisy's fairy story. I was packing up the flat and found it behind the desk. It must have slipped down there when I was marking them. I'm so sorry – it's all my fault.'

Gislingham smiles. 'No worries, Miss Madigan. Thanks for bringing it in.'

'No,' she says, 'you don't understand. That's why I'm so worried. At least now I look at it again.' She stops, then puts a hand to her forehead. 'I'm not expressing this very well, am I? What I meant to say is that reading the story now, all these weeks later, after what –' She takes a deep breath. 'I think there's something in it that I missed at the time. Something awful.'

She turns to the bag and pulls out the sheet of paper. When she passes it to Gislingham I can see her hands are trembling. He reads it, serious now, then hands it to me. The woman's cheeks have gone red and she's biting her lip.

'I'm so sorry,' she says softly, her eyes filling with tears. 'I will never forgive myself if something's happened and I could have prevented it. What she says about the monster – how could I not have seen –'

Her voice falters and Gislingham moves a step closer. 'You couldn't have known. Not just from this. No one could. But you did the right thing, bringing it in.' He takes her gently by the elbow. 'Come on, let's get you a nice cup of tea.'

As they walk away towards the counter I hand the story to Quinn. He scans it and looks up at me.

I know exactly what he's thinking.

The Sad Princess

By Daisy Mason, age 8

Once upon a time there was a little girl who lived in a hut. It was horribelhorrible. She did not know why she had to live there. It made her sad. She wanted to isscape escape but a wicked witch wood would not let her. The wicked witch had a monster that looked like a pig. The little girl wanted to run away and she tried to be brave but every time she tried the monster came into her room and held her down. It really hurt. Then the little girl found out she was reely really a princess in dizgise disguise. But she could only go and live in the castle like a real princess if someone killed the wicked witch and the monster. Then a prince came in a red charrit chariot and she thoght thought he would take her away. But he diddent didn't. He was mean. The little girl cried a lot. She was never going to be a princess. She did not live happily ever after.

The end

* * *

Back in my office I open the window as wide as it will go and have a fag, standing there. The venetian blinds are thick with dust. I've always hated those bloody things. I wonder for a moment about calling Alex, but

I don't know what I would say. Silence has become an easy lie. For both of us. There's a father and son waiting at the crossing. It looks like they're on their way to Christchurch Meadow – the boy is carrying a bag of sliced bread to feed the ducks. They may even see swans, if they're lucky. I think about Jake, who loved swans too, allowing myself a thin ration of memory from the tiny hoard my heart marks safe. I think about Daisy, and the father who turned into a monster. And I think about Leo. The lonely boy. The ghost in his own life. Missing in subtraction. Because where, in everything I've heard today, was Leo?

* * *

Half an hour later, Quinn swings by.

'Everett just called. Apparently Sharon claims she was confused. She took two sleeping pills and was completely disorientated. And she does look pretty spaced out in that video. I thought she was pissed, first time I saw it. She got pretty arsey when Everett pushed her, but she eventually agreed to us speaking to her doctor to confirm she has a prescription. She also insists she called out to Leo before she went down the stairs but got no answer, and when she saw the back door was open she thought he'd already got out. It was the neighbour who realized Leo was still up in his room and went in to get him. Jesus, if he hadn't been there, we'd have two dead kids on our hands, not one.'

'I know.'

'So do we believe her?'

I turn to the window and close it, then back to face him. 'Do you think she could have set the fire herself?'

His eyes widen. 'Seriously?'

'Think about it. The one person who benefits from that fire is her. She's already given us some pretty nasty evidence against Barry and anything in the house that might have incriminated her has now gone up in smoke. Literally. And that includes the car, which as far as I can work out, never usually got put in the garage. Which means that without a confession or some evidence on the body –'

'If we ever find it.'

'– we're going to find it bloody hard to convict her.'

'Assuming she did it.'

'Assuming, of course, that she did it. But if she was capable of killing Daisy, perhaps she's capable of leaving Leo in a burning house. Think about it – she could walk away from this whole mess scot-free, and start a new life somewhere else. With only the insurance money for company.'

Quinn whistles. 'Jesus.'

There's a knock at the door. One of the PCs who's been putting in all hours on the search. She looks exhausted.

'Yes?'

'The guys on duty at the house asked me to collect this for you on my way in, sir. It's the Masons' post. Most of it is bills and crap, but there's one you need to see. And before you ask, it wasn't me that opened it – the flap must have come unstuck in the post. When I picked it up, the contents fell out and I saw what it was.'

The padded envelope is about six inches square. Addressed to Sharon and postmarked Carshalton. On the back, the sender's address is given as the Haven-view Care Home. And inside, a DVD. As soon as I look at it, I know why the PC brought it in.

I look up at her. 'Good work – sorry, I don't know your name.'

'Somer, sir. Erica Somer.'

'Good work, Somer.'

I stand up and stretch my aching back. 'I'm going to go home for a couple of hours. Give me a call if Jamie's parents get in touch.'

'That's the other thing,' says Somer. 'The desk sergeant asked me to tell you. It's Mrs Northam.'

I sit back down, heavily. 'At last. OK, show her up.'

Somer looks embarrassed. 'Actually, she wants you to go there. To her house. Sorry. If it had been me I'd have told her –'

I wave a hand. 'Don't worry,' I say wearily. 'It's not that far out of my way.'

* * *

1 May 2016, 2.39 p.m.
79 days before the disappearance
5 Barge Close

Daisy is sitting on the swing at the bottom of the garden, twisting it desultorily from side to side. Behind her is the piece of fence her parents don't know is loose. She went out through it a few minutes ago, lifting the greenish panel carefully in both hands so as not to mark her dress. If someone had seen her she'd have said she wanted to look at the ducks on the canal. But that wasn't the real reason. And in any case, nobody saw. Not her mother in the kitchen, not the people on the path. No one noticed. No one ever notices.

She kicks her legs out and starts to move, backwards and forwards, higher and higher into the air. With each swing the metal frame wrenches slightly out of the ground where her father didn't fix it firmly enough. Her mother is always moaning about it, on and on about how you'd have thought a builder could fix a simple thing like a child's swing. Daisy lifts her face into the sun. If she closes her eyes she can almost believe she's flying, gliding above the big billowy clouds that look like beautiful snowy mountains or fairy castles where princes and princesses live. It must be amazing to fly right through the clouds like a bird or an aeroplane. She went in a plane once but it was a long time ago and she can't remember what it was like. She wishes she could. She wishes she could look down right now at

257

the houses and the roads and the canal, and her own self, very small and very far away.

There's a tap, then, on the kitchen window. Finger-nails on the glass. Rap rap rap.

Sharon opens the window. 'Daisy,' she calls, 'how many times have I told you about swinging too high? It's dangerous, the state that thing is in.'

Sharon stands at the window until Daisy slows the swing down. As it comes to a halt there's a sudden high-pitched buzzing, like a mosquito. Sharon can't hear it because the frequency is too high. But Daisy can. She watches until her mother closes the window and disappears back into the kitchen before reaching into her pocket and taking out a small pink mobile phone.

There's a new text on the screen.

I like your dress

Daisy looks round, her eyes wide. The phone buzzes again.

I'm always here

And then

Don't forget

Daisy drops off the swing and goes back to the fence, and slips quickly through it. She looks up and down the towpath. At the families walking with their dogs and pushchairs, the group of teenagers smoking on the bench, the ice-cream van, and the cars parked on the other side of the bridge. She puts the phone back in her pocket and climbs back through the panel.

She is smiling.

* * *

When I pull up on the Northams' semicircular drive it's alongside a Bentley and a bright red Carrera. Like Canal Manor, this is new-build masquerading as heritage, but that's where the resemblance ends. Because everything here is on an infinitely grander scale. A three-storey mock Georgian in cream stucco sitting in its own grounds, with an orangery one side, a separate garage block got up to look like stables, emerald lawns sweeping down to the river and a gleaming white and chrome gin-palace moored off a jetty, bobbing gently up and down. It's like finding yourself inside a colour supplement.

I'm not surprised to find the door is opened by a housekeeper in a black dress and apron – in fact, the only thing that surprises me is that they haven't gone the whole hog and got themselves a bloody butler.

The woman shows me into the cavernous sitting room and Moira Northam rises from a white leather sofa to meet me. The first thing that comes to my mind is that Barry Mason has a type. The blonde hair, the heels, the jewellery, the rather artificial way of dressing. The only difference is that Sharon is ten years younger, and getting her animal-print miniskirts from Primark.

'I hear Jamie has got himself into bother again,' says Moira, gesturing me to sit down. She has a large glass of gin and tonic by her side. She doesn't offer me one.

'I think this is a little more serious than "bother", Mrs Northam.'

She waves a hand airily and her gold bangles clatter. 'But he hasn't actually *done* anything, as far as I'm aware?'

'He's been associating with members of a family who were involved in an East Oxford sex-grooming ring. We have still to establish how far he might be implicated.'

'Oh, I doubt you'll be able to prove anything against Jamie. He's all talk. He likes to strut it about, but when it comes down to it, he's a bit of a coward. He takes after his father.'

She may look superficial, this woman, but she has Barry Mason bang to rights.

'Did you know he'd been seeing Daisy?'

She raises an eyebrow. An eyebrow that's been painted on. 'My dear Inspector, I didn't even know he'd been seeing *Barry*. We don't exactly keep in touch. I move in very different circles these days. Barry pays maintenance for Jamie, of course, my lawyer saw to that. He puts it into an account in my name. In cash.'

I look around. At the mirrors, the vast flat-screen TV, the swanky metal light fittings, the view of the river. So this is where Barry's money has been going. Siphoned off to this house, month after month, for at least the last ten years. I wonder what Sharon thinks about that. Meanwhile Moira is watching me. 'I know what you're thinking, Inspector, but it's a question of principle. Barry left me, and Jamie is his child. He can't expect Marcus to fork out for him.'

I suspect that's very much Marcus's view as well, and for the second time today, I feel a tiny flicker of sympathy for Sharon Mason.

'Barry has the standard access rights. Not that he's ever exercised them.'

I'm incredulous. 'Not at all? How old was Jamie when you split up?'

'Just turned four.'

So Barry Mason walked away from a four-year-old child who up till then had called him Daddy. A child he'd read to, tucked in, piggy-backed, pushed on a swing.

Moira is still eyeing me.

'To be fair to my less-than-estimable ex-husband, it was Sharon's idea,' she says. 'The whole "fresh start" thing. Though I did bump into her and Barry once – it was London Zoo, of all places.'

'I know. Jamie said. He recognized his father.'

That stumbles her for a moment. 'Really? Frankly, you stagger me. He hadn't seen Barry for years.'

'You'd be surprised, Mrs Northam. How much children can hold on to things like that.'

She gathers herself once more. 'Well, anyway, Jamie

had dragged me to see the spider house, horrible child, and out of the blue there was Sharon, with this tiny pretty little girl. Desperately awkward, can you imagine? We just stood there staring at each other for about five minutes, trying to think of something to say. And then Barry appeared and she rushed him away like we'd just sprouted leprosy. I got a note from Sharon after that, clarifying – *that* was her word – that she and Barry wanted no further contact, and that it was best for the children too.

'To be honest,' continues Moira, 'I think the real reason for all that fresh start baloney was that she didn't want Barry coming round here, even to see Jamie. She wanted him all to herself. Not very keen on sharing, our Sharon. Unfortunately for her, Barry is *very* keen on sharing. Likes to spread himself around in liberal quantities. If you catch my drift.'

'Do you know how they met?'

'Oh, she was his secretary, back in the day. That building firm of his? I used to work there too, until I had Jamie, at which point he hired her. I turned up one afternoon with the baby in the stroller to find this bimbo in stilettos and a short skirt and earrings the size of hubcaps. I said to Barry, she'd be quite pretty if she didn't try so damned hard. She was supposed to be engaged to someone back then. A mechanic – Terry or Darren or some such. But he clearly wasn't going to deliver the lifestyle she was after, and I think she set her sights on Barry the minute she clapped eyes on him. It was Barry this, Barry that – in fact, we used to joke about it. But she must have got him into bed eventually because the next thing I know she's claiming to be pregnant and Barry's being led by his you-know-what straight into the divorce courts. I made him pay though. For the company, I mean. He'd put it all in my name in case he ever went bust, and I forced him to buy me out at the top of the market. He had to take out the most enormous loan.'

And what with that and the child support, no wonder money is tight. I make a note to myself and then look up at her again. I'm sure the tan is fake. The tits certainly are.

I gesture round the room. 'You seem to have moved on very successfully.'

She laughs, a little self-consciously. 'Oh, Marcus is much better husband material than Barry ever was. He's not that interested in sex.'

She smooths her skirt over her rather too visible thighs, and eyes me, an unspoken question hanging in the air. But I have a type too, and believe me, Moira Northam's not even close.

She stares at her manicure, and then at me. 'And Marcus already had the requisite son and heir so I didn't need to ruin my figure having any more.'

I smile. It seems called for. 'You said "claimed".'

'I'm sorry?'

'Just now, you said Sharon "claimed" to be pregnant. Wasn't she?'

She opens her hands and the bangles jangle again. 'Who knows? It's the oldest trick in the book, after all, and men never seem to know any different. Lord, you'd think they'd have learned to keep it in their pants by now. All I do know is, nine months later, no baby. And they had to have IVF to have Daisy. Or at least that's what someone told me.'

And that probably cost them, too.

'And as far as you know, Daisy didn't know she had a half-brother – she didn't know about Jamie?'

'Not unless Sharon or Barry told her, and I think that's *highly* unlikely. As far as Sharon's concerned, Barry's life before her has been entirely – what's that word? *Redacted*. That's it. Even to the extent of claiming that she only started seeing him after we divorced, which is obviously *completely* untrue.'

'And did Jamie know about Daisy?'

She flushes, just a little, under the tan. 'I can assure you *I* never mentioned her. I have no idea how Jamie can possibly have found out. I'm afraid you will have to ask him.'

'I'll do that. I will also be asking him – again – about where he was when Daisy Mason disappeared. Because until we can confirm his whereabouts I'm afraid we can't eliminate him from our enquiries.'

She smiles. 'That's exactly what I wanted to talk to you about. I don't know why Jamie is being so stubborn – perhaps he thinks a spell in the cells will do wonders for his street cred with those insalubrious associates of his. Anyway, the point is this: I know precisely where he was on Tuesday afternoon. He was with me.'

'That's easy to say, Mrs Northam –'

'Very possibly. But I happen to have proof. Marcus's niece is getting married next week, and we were at my ghastly sister-in-law's for the rehearsal. There are even pictures, though Jamie won't thank me for showing them to you. He doesn't like to be seen in proper trousers. Lord knows how I'm ever going to shoe-horn him into morning dress.'

She takes out her phone, finds the photos and passes the handset over to me. I notice, in passing, how easily her hands give her away. Her face is botox-bland but her hands are veining and blotching with age. She reaches for a tissue in her handbag and I see it's exactly the same as Sharon's. Only I'm prepared to bet this is one thing about her that's the genuine article.

'So,' she says, giving me the full force of her smile, 'can you release Jamie now?'

I pass her back the phone and get to my feet. 'I need to ask him a few final questions. I imagine you'd want to be there for that. I can give you a lift back now or you can meet me at the station. And after that we can release him into your charge. You can have him back here tonight.'

She glances at her watch – more gold. 'We have the

Andersons coming this evening. I can't cancel that – Nicholas Anderson is our local councillor. Perhaps you could get that social worker person to step in again?'

Like I said, Barry Mason has a type.

* * *

When I eventually get home, Alex has already gone to bed. The bottle of sleeping pills is open on the bedside table. I pick it up – mechanically – to check the weight. Alex has always been the strong one of the two of us. Or at least I always thought so. I remember my best man calling her my rock, and everyone at the reception smiling and nodding, recognizing the Alex they knew. It was the Alex I knew too, even though I hated the cliché. It's only in the last few months that I've realized how terrifyingly apt it can be. Because rocks aren't flexible, rocks don't give. Alex's sort of strength, faced with the unbearable – it just splinters. That's why I check her sleeping pills. And why I make sure she never sees me do it. I can't let her think I see a connection. I can't let her think she's to blame. She feels responsible enough already, without that.

Downstairs, I pour myself a large glass of Merlot and take the DVD into the sitting room. The image on the case is of Daisy. Daisy in a swimming pool, smiling up into the camera. It's a DVD sent to her mother, and it should – for that reason alone – be completely innocent. But all I can think of is that chilling fairy story. And

266

that birthday card. As the machine loads, I read the note that came with it.

Havenview Care Home
Yeading Road
Carshalton
20th July 2016

Dear Mrs Mason,

    Thank you for sending your contribution to Sadie's 'treasure chest'. Collecting items that have a special memory attached to them, or which recall times gone by, is proving to be a very effective way to stimulate our residents with Alzheimer's, and help them keep a connection with their past.

    Sadly, I'm afraid this particular item has not been as successful as we had hoped. We showed Sadie the film, and at first there was very little reaction, but when we got to the section featuring your little girl she became extremely distressed and started to talk about someone called 'Jessica'. She was so upset that we decided, with regret, the film was doing more harm than good. I am very sorry. I am returning the DVD in case you have another use for it.

    Yours sincerely,

    Monica Hapgood (Care Manager)

So Sharon Mason hasn't told her mother's carers she had two daughters, not one.

I pick up the remote and press Play. There's a blank blue screen, and then a title: *To Mum, From Sharon, Barry, Leo and Daisy.* Then

~ *Chapter one: Barry and Sharon's wedding* ~

There's no soundtrack, just a saccharine panpipe instrumental, which lasts about three minutes before I have to put it on mute. The film starts with a still of Barry wearing a tuxedo with a red rose in his button-hole and Sharon in a strapless tight-fitting satin dress and a diamanté tiara, holding a bunch of red roses. Then the camera shows Sharon walking up the aisle in a hotel function room. There are about thirty people in the audience and red bows tied round the backs of the chairs. A banner on the wall behind says HAPPY CHRISTMAS 2005, and there are garlands of holly and ivy, and a Christmas tree. Gerald Wiley is much heftier than he was in the newspaper photo, and escorts his daughter with difficulty, breathing heavily. His face is purplish. Sadie, by contrast, is thinner, and fidgets all the time – with her handbag, her hat, her corsage. I wonder whether she was already in the early stages of dementia. There are shots of the vows, then some of the reception. Barry making his speech, the two of them cutting the cake. Gerald Wiley can be seen in the background. He's not smiling.

~ *Chapter two: Leo's first birthday* ~

Leo is sitting in a blue high chair in a kitchen – it's not the room at Barge Close. He's holding a yellow plastic spoon in one hand and banging on the chair tray. He has some sort of puree across his chin. The camera moves back and shows a pregnant Sharon holding a birthday cake with one candle on it. The cake is in the shape of a lion. She puts it down in front of Leo and he stares at it and reaches for the flame. She grasps his fist and holds it back. She looks tired. Someone – presumably Barry – blows out the candle. Leo starts to cry.

❧ *Chapter three: Daisy's christening* ❧

The weather is wintry. The group standing awkwardly outside the church are huddled against the wind. Sharon is shown holding a baby heavily wrapped up in a shawl. Sadie is wearing the same coat that she had on at the wedding. Gerald is leaning on a stick. There are two other older people who are presumably Barry's parents. Barry has Leo by one hand. The little boy is in a suit and tie, with his hair smoothed down, but he's pulling away from his father, and appears to be screaming. Sharon looks annoyed, but then smiles quickly when the camera focuses in on her and the baby. She lifts the baby's head so we can see her.

❧ *Chapter four: Summer holidays and another birthday* ❧

This sequence was taken abroad somewhere. The Algarve perhaps, or somewhere in Spain. We see Sharon, in a bikini and high-heel shoes, walking up and down the side of the hotel pool, pausing occasionally and dropping her hip like a beauty queen. She has a tattoo behind her left ankle, and I find myself starting when I realize it's a daisy. At one point she stops with her back to us and looks over her shoulder, winking at the camera and blowing a kiss, Marilyn-fashion. She's in great shape, and looks as if she could even have done that sort of thing professionally. Her skin is tanned and she's smiling. She's happy. The camera cuts to Daisy, who's in a little flowered dress and a pink floppy sun-hat, and is clapping her chubby hands. She can't be more than two. Then we see Barry with Daisy in the pool. He's holding her by her waist above his head and then aeroplaning her low over the water. Up and down, up and down. She's screaming with delight. Then Sha-ron in a white cotton dress and a pair of dangly earrings, sitting in a deckchair opening birthday presents. The section ends with Daisy toddling towards the camera, smiling, and holding up a placard that says '*I love you Mummy*'.

❧ Chapter five: Christmas ❧

A shot of a tree (artificial) with the fairy lights on. Judging by the gloom, it's early on Christmas morning. The door opens and Daisy comes in. She must be about four years old and she looks unnervingly like Jessica. I wonder if this is the moment when they had to turn the film off. Daisy glances mischievously at the camera, as if she knows she's not supposed to acknowledge it's there. Then she spots the bike, propped up by the tree and covered in pink ribbons. The next shot shows both children surrounded by mounds of wrapping paper. Daisy is talking to camera, pointing one at a time to the presents she's got and explaining what they are. Leo is to one side, not looking at the lens, stolidly opening present after present. It's clear from the contents that some of these are not for him. The next shot is outside the front of a small 1960s semi with a blue garage door too small for any modern car. First we see Daisy on the new bike, riding towards us, and later, both children in the snow, wearing bobble hats and mittens and playing snowballs with Barry. Daisy looks unbearably sweet in a pair of tiny Ugg boots. At one point Barry wrestles Leo laughingly to the ground and they roll about together, but Leo fights him off and runs towards the camera crying. Then we see the two kids circling round and round a snowman; Daisy is carefully patting the snow smooth, while a few feet behind her, Leo is purposefully digging chunks out of it with a small red trowel.

❧ *Chapter six: Summer holidays again* ❧

A small suburban garden; it's obviously still the same house. The grass is tired and brownish. There's some sort of industrial building visible behind the house beyond the back fence – perhaps the canopy of a petrol station. Or perhaps I only see that because it's what I saw, every day, for the first fifteen years of my life. The Masons' blurry footage is like a parody of my own past.

Barry appears now in a pair of tight black Speedos that leave nothing to the imagination, his chest out and his hands on his hips. He looks like he's oiled himself. We see him lifting weights and striking a pose to show his muscles. He's laughing. Then the perspective shifts and we see Sharon in a loose-fitting kaftan thing. She's holding a drink with a straw and an umbrella in it, and she raises her glass, but she looks listless and she's clearly put on a lot of weight. Then the camera pans to Gerald Wiley in the adjacent deckchair, stiff in a cardigan and a shirt and tie, and then to Daisy, sitting on her grandmother's knee. She looks uncomfortable, as if she feels out of place. It's a strange expression to see on the face of such a young child. And then the camera pans to the side, and we see Leo in a paddling pool, splashing in a monotonous, repetitive way that appears to bring him no pleasure. As Sharon comes over to lift him out, he begins to scream, and I realize that he has not looked directly at the camera once.

* * *

Sent: Sun 24/07/2016, 10.35 **Importance: High**
From: AlanChallowCSI@ThamesValley.police.uk
To: DIAdamFawley@ThamesValley.police.uk

Subject: Case no 372844 Mason, D

Attached herewith the results of the forensic tests on the black Nissan Navara belonging to Barry Mason. It has not been possible to test Sharon Mason's car, which has sustained extensive fire damage.

To summarize:
The interior and exterior of the pick-up were tested for blood and other physical evidence. Nothing untoward was found. There were no traces of blood in the flatbed,

nor any DNA. If it was used to transport a body, the remains must have been extremely carefully wrapped in some impermeable covering. I note that Mr Mason owned a number of high-viz vests and other similar items of protective clothing for use on building sites, which could in theory be used for this purpose, though the jacket found in the car definitely had not been: the only DNA was Barry Mason's. There was also a hard hat and a pair of black safety boots with steel toecaps, likewise bearing only his DNA. There were other high-viz items in the house, but the damage caused by the fire has rendered them useless for evidential purposes.

The car showed no signs of being recently valeted (indeed, rather the opposite). The DNA of Barry, Sharon and Daisy Mason was found on the seats, as well as that of another male, presumably Leo Mason. The latter principally took the form of bitten fingernails consistent in size with a child's hands. Samples from the other individuals were mainly hair and some skin, though there were vaginal secretions from two other unidentified females, mostly in the back of the car, as well as minute traces of semen, identified as that of Barry Mason.

There was only one unexpected finding. We have not taken a DNA sample from Leo Mason, but based on the fingernail fragments, I can state categorically that he is <u>not</u> related to the rest of the family. Leo is not the Masons' biological child.

* * *

'So why didn't you tell us Leo's not your son?'

I'm standing in Barry Mason's cell. It's Sunday morning. I can hear the bells from the colleges, each ringing to their own approximation of the time. And actually that's as good a thumbnail of the character of this town as you're likely to get. Barry is lying on his back on the bed with his knees up. He's badly in need of a shower. As for me, I'm badly in need of a shot to the brain. Because I can't believe it took me so long to work it out. Leo doesn't look anything like either of the Masons, and if nothing else, the timeline should have screamed at me – if they were married in December 2005 and Leo is ten, Sharon would have been pregnant at the wedding. Which she clearly wasn't.

Barry sits up and runs his hands through his hair, then he swings his legs round over the side of the bed.

'I didn't think it was any of your bloody business,' he says eventually. But the fight has gone out of him. 'Daisy's the one who's missing, not him.'

He rubs the back of his neck and looks up at me. 'Should I be talking to you without my lawyer?'

'It's not related to the pornography charge. But you can call her if you want. We've got an extension, by the way – we can hold you for another twenty-four hours before we have to charge you.'

He stares at me for a moment, considering, then sighs. 'OK, have it your way.'

'So why did you decide to adopt? You're clearly able to have kids of your own.'

274

'We didn't know that then, though, did we? Look, I only asked Moira for a divorce because Sharon was pregnant, but then she lost the baby and she was all over the place. The doctor said she might not be able to have another – they said IVF was the only option but the odds were against us. We'd be lucky if it took. So we decided to adopt.'

'But do the IVF anyway. Just in case.'

'Right.'

'How old was Leo when you got him?'

'About six months.'

'You were lucky – there aren't many babies available these days.'

He looks away.

'Mr Mason?'

'If you must know, they said he might have – problems. But when we saw him he seemed OK. Nice-looking kid. Took to Sharon straight away.'

And Sharon was desperate to have a child – desperate to keep Barry from changing his mind and going back to Moira. And the money. And his real son.

'And then Sharon got pregnant after all.'

'We could hardly believe it. Talk about bad timing. It was only a few weeks after the adoption went through. But by then it was too late. We couldn't give him back.'

I can't believe I'm hearing this.

'What sort of problems?'

'Sorry?'

'You said they told you Leo had problems.'

'They only said he *might have*. It was too early to be sure. He might just as well be perfectly fine. And he was – when he was a baby. Always really quiet, never gave us much trouble. Not like Daisy – she was always a bugger to get to sleep. Cried for hours – drove us both crazy. It was only later, when he was about four or five, that Leo began to get a bit, you know, weird.'

'And when they told you he might have problems – did they say why?'

'Apparently his mother was doing time and couldn't look after him properly. Had a drink problem, you know the sort of thing. That's why he'd been put up for adoption.'

I take a deep breath. It makes sense. The awkwardness, the mood swings. And what I saw with my own eyes, only two days ago. The question is whether that's *all* it is. Whether it stops there.

'What does your doctor say?'

He snorts. 'Sharon doesn't have any time for him – says all he ever does is poke his nose in. As far as she's concerned Leo's just a bit of a late developer and the doctor can't prove otherwise. She says how we bring up our kids is nobody else's business.'

And that adds up too. The last thing Sharon would want is for 'them' to think she was bringing up a less-than-perfect child. Or that she'd had to resort to adoption to get one.

'All that trouble he's been having at school – the lashing out, the bullying –'

Barry looks exasperated. 'Leo just needs to stick up for himself a bit more, that's all – not be such a wuss. Look, it's really not that bad. Honestly. Most days, you'd hardly even know. He's a nice kid. Docile.'

'Until recently.'

'Yeah, well.'

'Do you know why? Did something happen that might have triggered it?'

'Search me.'

'Does he know he's adopted?'

He shakes his head. 'No, we haven't told him.'

I count to ten. 'Don't you think it's getting rather late to tell him something like that? He's bound to find out sometime, and the older he is, the worse it will be.' I should know. My parents have never told me I'm not their biological son, but I've carried that knowledge round with me for over thirty years. I found out when I was not much older than Leo is now, rooting about in my father's desk where I knew I shouldn't have been. Snoopers learn no good of themselves. But that wasn't why I didn't let on; I knew, instinctively, the way children do, that this was something I could never raise with them, and even now, I never have.

Barry shrugs. 'Not my call, mate. And it's not worth arguing about it with Sharon. Believe me.'

Outside the cell, I strike the wall in frustration and jar my wrist. I'm still shaking the pain away when my phone goes. It's Everett.

'I wanted to call you last night,' she says, 'but I was worried it was too late. Look, I've been thinking about Leo. And I remembered that email from the doctor where he referred to Leo coming in for 'his check-up'. That's an odd phrase to use – makes it sound like he had them all the time. That's not normal, is it? And the doctor was really cagey – all that stuff at the end about needing authorization to release any information about the family. I think he was trying to tell us something. Under cover of doing the exact opposite.'

So she's got there too. She's sharp, Everett. She'll go far.

'I got an email from Challow this morning,' I say. 'The evidence in the car proves Leo is adopted.'

'Jesus – and they didn't tell us?'

'Don't get me started. It doesn't matter, of course, if that was all it was. But it's not.'

I tell her what Mason just told me.

'Shit,' she says. And then, quickly, 'Yesterday, when I was sitting with him, he said everything was "all his fault", but when I asked him what he meant he clammed right up. And then this morning, I came back from the shower and found him under the bed. He said he'd lost something and he'd lit a match to help him look for it. The underside of the mattress had already caught. It's a miracle the whole place didn't go up. He said he found the matches in the drawer.'

My turn this time. 'Shit.'

Find Daisy Mason Facebook Page

There is still no news of Daisy, despite an extensive police search in the area around her home. The police have questioned her parents, and there are now reports that an unnamed teenager is 'helping with enquiries'. If you live in the Oxford area and saw anything suspicious on the afternoon or evening of Tuesday 19 July, please please call the police. The person to ask for is Inspector Adam Fawley on 01865 0966552. This is especially important if you've been on holiday and haven't caught up with the news.

Jason Brown, Helen Finchley, Jenni Smale and 285 others liked this

TOP COMMENTS

Dora Brookes We just got back from a few days away and just saw this terrible news. I don't know what to do. I saw a man putting something into a skip on our street that afternoon, the 19th. We're about half a mile away from the Canal Manor estate. I know it was then because it was the day we left. He had one of those bright yellow protective suits on, and a hard hat. There's so much building going on round here I didn't think anything of it at the time. But now I'm wondering – could it have something to do with Daisy's disappearance? I went and had a look just now

and the house is empty and there's still no one on site. It doesn't look like work has even started, so why would a workman have been there? What do people think? I couldn't see what it was he put in the skip, so it may be nothing at all. But I don't want to waste the police's time
24 July at 16.04

Jeremy Walters I think you should call the police right away.
24 July at 16.16

Julie Ramsbotham I agree – don't worry about bothering the police – they'd rather know, I'm sure. Then they can check it out properly.
24 July at 16.18

Dora Brookes Thanks both – I will.
24 July at 16.19

* * *

Richard Donnelly lives in a big 1930s semi just outside Wolvercote. It's very much like the Rahijas' house, in fact, but minus the deprivation, the drugs and the general dreariness. When I draw up outside I can see him emptying luggage out of the car. He has the haggard look of a man who's just enjoyed two weeks of uninterrupted quality time with three small children.

When I introduce myself he becomes immediately wary.

'I told you, Inspector, I can't divulge anything about the Mason family without the appropriate authorization.'

'I know, Dr Donnelly. I'm not going to ask you to do that. What I propose to do is to tell you what we already know, and then ask if you can give me some general background. Just basic medical information. Nothing specific to the Masons.'

He considers. 'OK, I can live with that. Why don't you come through and I'll ask my wife to make some tea. Why is it you can never get halfway decent tea abroad?'

'It's the milk,' I say, realizing I sound just like Sharon Mason.

The back garden is desperately in need of both a water and a mow, but there's a bench under a pergola that has a view over Port Meadow. I can see four or five creamy coloured horses with a scatter of brown spots. They're standing so still, and in such perfect composition, that they hardly look real. But then a tail swishes and the illusion dispels. We brought Jake to see those horses once, after someone at Alex's office said one of the mares had had a foal. It must have been only two or three days old, skipping and leaping and frisking its little tail. We could barely tear Jake away.

'I had no idea you were so close to the Meadow.'

'In the winter,' says Donnelly, putting down two mugs, 'from my son's room, you can see the spires.'

I wait for him to pour the tea, and then I start. 'There are two things we know now which we didn't know when DC Everett first contacted you. The first is that

281

Leo Mason is adopted. The second is that his biological mother was an alcoholic.'

He says nothing, but I can tell from his face that this isn't news to him, even if it was to me.

'So, Dr Donnelly, what can you tell me about the long-term effects of Foetal Alcohol Syndrome?'

He looks sceptical. 'Purely theoretically?'

'Purely theoretically.'

He puts down his mug. 'Don't tell me you haven't googled it.'

'Of course. But I want to hear it from you.'

'OK, here's the official version. As you've probably gathered, the effects on the child can vary very widely but the common denominator in most cases is neuro-logical damage. That causes a spectrum of learning difficulties from mild to severe. There are also physical complications – there can be hormonal problems and organs like the liver and kidneys can be affected.' He hesitates. 'Stomach upsets can be another symptom. It's quite rare, but it can happen.'

Nuka the puker, I think. And then, how savagely observant kids can be.

'The most common physical sign is here.' He puts his hand to his face. 'That groove between your mouth and your nose? That's called the philtrum. In kids with FAS it's often underdeveloped. It's quite distinctive, when you know what you're looking for.'

It's what I noticed about Leo, almost the first time I saw him. But I didn't realize its significance. Not then.

'Can it be tested for? Physiologically, I mean?'

'No, there's no definitive test. And that can compound the problem. FAS can often be mistaken for autism or ADHD, even by an experienced practitioner, because some of the behaviour is very similar – these kids can be hyperactive and their physical coordination can be poor. They have the same struggles with empathy too, so they often have trouble establishing relationships and dealing with other people. Especially in groups.'

'So kids like that could be easy targets for bullies.'

'Sadly, yes. And they don't usually deal with it very well if it does happen. They're not good at thinking through the consequences of their actions, so they have a tendency to act impulsively, and that can just make a bad situation worse.'

Like going for another child's eye with a pencil. For instance.

Donnelly sighs. 'These kids need a huge amount of support. They need a stable home environment and trained specialists to help them develop the techniques they need to deal with their problems. There aren't any short cuts, Inspector. The parents of a child with FAS face years of patient, diligent care. And that can be a weary, thankless task.'

'But what if the kids don't get that support – what if the parents refuse to acknowledge the problem for what it really is?'

He glances at me, and then away. 'Sometimes it can take quite a while for the symptoms to become pronounced. In those circumstances the parents can be reluctant to rush to judgement – people generally don't like their children being labelled. In that case I would monitor the child closely and recommend a referral to the Community Paediatrician as and when I thought it necessary. Or helpful.'

'And can the parents refuse to have that?'

He flushes. 'Most people want the best for their kids.'

That's not an answer, and he knows it.

'But parents *can refuse*?'

He nods.

'So what happens then?'

'If – *in theory* – I were to find myself in such a situation, I would carry on monitoring the child and consider talking to the school nurse. I would also spend a great deal of time explaining to the parents how important it is to get their child expert professional help as early as possible. I would stress that the long-term consequences of failing to do that could be catastrophic – drug addiction, violence, sexual offending. There are some horrific stats from the US, where as usual they're far more advanced about these things than we are. I saw one report which estimated that people with FAS are nineteen times more likely to end up in prison than the rest of us.'

Which does nothing but confirm my worst possible fears.

I get up to go, but there's clearly one more thing on the doctor's mind. 'Inspector,' he says, looking me straight in the eye, 'kids with FAS often have an unusually high tolerance of pain. So what you can find – sometimes, with some children – is that they take out all that pent-up anger and frustration on themselves. In other words –'

'I know,' I say. 'They self-harm.'

* * *

Quinn is just turning off his computer when the call comes through. He wedges the handset against his shoulder as he shuts down his programmes, only half listening. Then he suddenly sits up and grips the phone.

'Say that again? You're sure?'

He ploughs into the paper on the desk, looking for a pen.

'What's the address? Twenty-one Loughton Road. Got it. Call forensics and tell them I'll meet them there. Yes, I do know it's sodding Sunday.'

Then he's up, seized his jacket and gone.

* * *

As I draw up outside my house, my phone beeps with an email alert. I open the file and scan it, then I call Everett.

'Can you get Leo Mason to the Kidlington suite for nine a.m. tomorrow? We'll need Derek Ross to be the appropriate adult, so can you call him and get that organized as well – tell him sorry, but there's no alternative. As for Sharon, she can watch on the video feed if she wants, but she can't be in the room. And if she wants to bring a lawyer, she can do that too, I'm not going to argue the toss on that one. But I want you there. If Leo trusts any of us, he trusts you.'

I'm just getting out of the car when the phone goes again. I can hardly make out the words for the panic.

'Slow down – where is she – which hospital? OK, don't worry. We'll deal with all of that. You just focus on Janet.'

I end the call and stand there for a moment. And when I go into the sitting room a few minutes later Alex looks up and asks me why I'm crying.

* * *

There's already a crowd gathering when Quinn gets to Loughton Road. A forensics officer is unravelling blue and white tape across the entrance to the drive and two more are removing items one by one from the skip. Old chairs, rolls of rotting carpet, broken bathroom scales, sheets of crumbling plasterboard. It doesn't seem to matter how affluent the area, crap still gets dumped in other people's skips. One of the uniforms directs Quinn to a small middle-aged woman in a loose dress and a pair of black leggings, standing behind the tape. She has her hair up in a messy bun – one of those women who grow their hair but never wear it down. She looks agitated and starts talking before he even gets to her.

'Oh, Constable – I was the one who called. I wish I'd known about Daisy before – I feel dreadful that it's taken so long to get in touch with you but we didn't have a TV in the cottage and I don't have internet on my phone. It costs so much, doesn't it, and you can never get a signal on Exmoor anyway –'

'Miss Brookes, isn't it?' he says, getting out his tablet. 'I believe you saw a man put something in the skip on Tuesday afternoon? When exactly, do you remember?'

'Oh, it would have to have been about five. We had wanted to leave earlier, it's such a long drive, but then I had to pick up some dry-cleaning and there was a queue and what with one thing and another –'

Jesus, thinks Quinn. Does she ever stop talking?

'So about five on Tuesday. What did he look like, this man?'

'Like I said to the other officer, he was in that bright yellow plastic they wear –'

'High-viz clothing?'

'Yes, that's right. A jacket and a hard hat, and even a face mask, you know, those white ones they use for sanding? The chap who took the Artex off our bathroom ceiling had one just like it. I should have realized, shouldn't I, that it was a bit odd – I should have called you before. I'm just so worried it might have made a difference – you don't think so, do you –?'

'Can you describe him? Height, weight?'

'Well, just *average*, really. He was bending over behind the skip, so I couldn't see very much.'

287

'OK, do you remember anything about what he put in the skip – anything at all?'

'I'm afraid I wasn't really concentrating, officer. Phoebe – that's our chihuahua – she was barking because she doesn't really like being in the car, and Elspeth was trying to quieten her down, and some horrible youth had just made a rude gesture at me on my way back from the cleaners because I tooted him when he walked across the road when the lights were on green. I don't think that's fair, do you? I had every right to be there –'

'The skip, Miss Brookes?'

She considers a moment. 'Well, all I can say is that whatever it was, he could hold it easily in one hand, so it wasn't that heavy. And it was wrapped in something. I'm sure of that. Not a plastic bag, though. It didn't reflect the light. I definitely remember noticing that.'

And so, from decided contempt, Quinn ends up in grudging admiration. And all the more so when a few minutes later one of the forensics team calls him over and lifts something from the skip. Something light enough to lift in one hand and tightly wrapped in sheets of newspaper.

* * *

When I get to the John Rad, it's almost dark. I spend ten minutes driving round in circles looking for the right department, and another ten finding somewhere to park. Inside, the corridors are deserted, apart from the odd weary nurse and cleaners pushing trolleys of mops and buckets. Up on the second floor, a motherly woman at the nurses' station asks me if I'm a relative.

'No, but I have this.'

She looks at my warrant card, and then warily at me. 'Is there some sort of problem we don't know about, Inspector?'

'No, nothing like that. The father – Mr Gislingham – works for me. I just wanted to see how Janet is.'

'Oh, I see,' she says, reassured. 'Well, we won't know for certain for a while, I'm afraid. She had severe abdominal pains and some bleeding earlier today, so we're keeping her in.'

'Could she lose the baby?'

'We hope not,' she says, but her face belies her words. At Janet's age, the odds probably aren't good. 'We just don't know yet. At this stage, there isn't much we can do but keep her comfortable and trust Nature to right itself. Do you want to see Mr Gislingham for a moment? You did make all this effort to get here.'

I hesitate. I haven't been in a maternity ward since Jake was born. We have a video of the birth – his tight little face hollering for his first air, his tiny fists opening and closing, and that tuft of dark hair he never lost even though they all told us he would. I've hidden the tape in the loft. I can't bear the happiness. Its unbearable fragility.

The nurse is eyeing me, her face full of concern. 'Are you OK?'

'Sorry. I'm just tired. I really don't want to disturb them.'

'Last time I looked, your colleague was asleep in the chair. But let's have a quick peek. He may be glad of a friendly face.'

I follow her down the corridor, trying not to see the cots, the dazed new dads. Janet's in a room on her own. When I look through the glass panel in the door the curtains are drawn and she's asleep, one hand curled round her belly and the blanket balled up in the other. Gislingham is on the chair at the end of the bed, his head thrown back. He looks dreadful, his face grey and shrunk in shadows.

'I won't disturb him. That's not going to do any good.'

She smiles kindly. 'OK, Inspector.' She pats me on the arm. 'I'll make sure to tell him you were here.'

She chose the right profession – she's just the person you'd want around you if you'd just had a child. Or if you'd lost one.

* * *

16 April 2016, 10.25 a.m.
94 days before the disappearance
Shopping parade, Summertown, Oxford

Azeem Rahija is sitting in his car outside the bank. On the opposite side of the road, the Starbucks is busy with Saturday shoppers. Azeem can see Jamie at one of the tables. He has a cup in front of him and a canvas bag at his feet. He's drumming his fingers on the table and he keeps looking up at the door.

Azeem lights a cigarette and winds down the car window. Across the road, a man pushes open the coffee-shop door. Mid-forties. Tight jeans, a leather jacket. He's talking on a mobile phone and gesturing a lot as he speaks. Two women at the corner table clock him as he goes past and he squares his shoulders a little. Jamie stares fixedly at him until he finishes the call and sits down, slinging the jacket over the back of the chair.

Azeem has no idea what they're saying but it's obvious it's not going well. The man keeps shaking his head. It looks like Jamie is asking him why. Then there's a long moment when neither of them says anything. The man gets up and points at the cup in front of Jamie. Jamie shakes his head. The man shrugs then turns and goes up to the counter to join the queue for coffee. He stops on the way to talk to the women at the corner table.

Azeem watches as Jamie reaches into the man's jacket and takes out the mobile phone. He glances up to make sure the man isn't watching but he's far too busy flirting with the women in the corner. Jamie taps at the screen for a while. Then he smiles. It's not a nice smile. He puts the phone back where he found it and when the man comes back some minutes later, Jamie gets up. The man makes a perfunctory attempt to get him to sit down again, but Jamie just brushes him off. He picks up his bag and makes his way through the tables to the door. He stops on the pavement a moment to light a fag, then dodges between the cars to the other side of the road. Azeem sees the man in Starbucks sit back in his chair and take a deep breath, then pick up his coffee spoon. There's no mistaking the relief on his face.

Jamie taps on the window and Azeem leans over and opens the car door.

'Bloody sodding shitty bastard,' says Jamie through gritted teeth, chucking his bag in the back seat.

'I told you, man. Wankers like him. Dey only care about demselfs.' Azeem watches a lot of American TV.

'Yeah, right,' says Jamie. 'I could do without the sodding *I told you so's.*'

Azeem shrugs. He hasn't seen his father in years.

Jamie takes a deep draw on his cigarette and looks across at Azeem. 'I did for 'im though. Good and proper.'

'What, you mean the phone?'

Jamie grins, his eyes narrowing. 'Yeah. The phone. Didn't even have a bloody password on it. Stupid twat.'

The two of them laugh and then Azeem starts the engine and pulls out screeching into the traffic, only just missing the rear bumper of the black Nissan Navara parked in front of them. A small boy in the back seat watches them go, then turns to look again at the man in the Starbucks window.

He's moved over to the corner table.

* * *

In the incident room the following morning, there are no jokes, no banter, in fact not much of anything. The muted room goes utterly silent as I take my place at the front. They probably think I'm bearing bad news.

'I suspect most of you already know that Janet Gislingham was taken into hospital yesterday. If I hear anything – anything at all – I'll let you know, but at the very least we should assume that Chris will be off work for the next few days, so we'll need to make sure we have cover. Quinn, I'll leave you to sort that out.'

Quinn gets up from where he's been perched on the edge of his desk. 'Boss, I also need to bring everyone up to speed with what happened last night. We got a call from a woman who saw a man in high-viz clothing dumping something in a skip the afternoon Daisy disappeared. She thought it was suspicious because there aren't any builders on that site yet. Anyway, we checked it out and recovered a package wrapped in newspaper. The *Guardian*, to be precise. Dated the day before, July eighteenth.'

'What was it?'

'A pair of extra-large cut-resistant gloves. The sort builders wear. Grey plastic stuff on the palms and fluorescent orange on the back. And there's blood too, I'm afraid. As well as some other stains on the back that are a reddish colour that I think are something else. Forensics are testing them now.'

I look around the room. 'So just when we thought Barry Mason might be looking less likely as a suspect, he's right back in the frame.'

'There's another complication too.' It's Everett this time.

'I just got off the phone from David Connor. You know – Millie's father? He's been talking to her again, and she told him something she hadn't told them before. About the day before the party. When the kids went round to the Connors to try on their costumes. Apparently Daisy begged Millie not to tell anyone.'

'Something about Daisy?'

'No, boss. About *Leo*.'

* * *

'How are you doing?'

Leo glances up at me and then down again. He's wearing a Chelsea football shirt that's too big for him and a pair of shorts. He has scabs on his knees and all down one leg. Derek Ross is sitting next to him on the other side of the table and Sharon is in the adjoining room, with her lawyer and the video feed. In her sundress and white shrug she looks like she's just popped in on her way to a regatta.

Everett passes a can of Coke across to the boy and smiles. 'Just in case you're thirsty.'

'Now, Leo,' I begin. 'I'm afraid I have to ask you some questions and some of them might be a bit upsetting. But if you do feel upset, I want you to let us know, OK? Do you understand?'

He nods; he's playing with the ring pull on the can.

'You remember the firemen who came to your house to put the fire out?'

Another nod.

'When there's a fire like that, the fireman in charge has to make a report, to find out what happened.'

No reaction.

'Well, they just sent me a copy of that report. Shall I tell you what it says?'

He won't look up, but the can suddenly buckles and the ring pull comes away.

'It says they don't think the petrol bomb came in from the towpath after all. They thought that at first, but now they've realized they were wrong. It's all about how the window broke, apparently. It's a bit like those cop shows on TV. Finding all the bits of glass and putting them back together.'

'*CSI*,' says Leo, still looking down. 'I've seen that. And *Law & Order*.'

'That's right. That's exactly what I mean. Anyway, after doing all that clever stuff the firemen now think the fire started inside the house. And they know which room it was, because they found petrol there. They didn't find it anywhere else. Just in one room.'

Silence.

'Do you know where the fire started, Leo?'

He shrugs, but his cheeks are flushed.

'It was in your room, wasn't it?'

Silence. Derek Ross glances across at him, but then nods at me. We can go on.

'Do you remember,' I say eventually, 'the day we first met? After Daisy disappeared. You told me you liked the fireworks at the party. Do you remember that?'

He nods.

'Is that what they looked like, Leo? You got woken up by the noise outside and when you looked out of your bedroom window you saw the petrol bombs go off in the garden, and you thought they were fireworks?'

Silence again.

'Shall I tell you what I think happened? I think you saw that one of them hadn't gone off, and you went downstairs and picked it up and brought it into the house, leaving the back door open. I think you got some matches from the kitchen and went back upstairs. And I think you lit the bomb up there, and that's how the fire started.'

His face is very red now. Derek Ross leans across and puts a hand gently on his arm. 'OK, Leo?'

'Can you tell us,' I say, 'what happened after that? Did you hear your mum calling for you?'

His voice is very small, so small I have to lean forward to catch it. 'She was downstairs.'

'But you didn't try to go down? Were the flames too big?'

He shakes his head.

'Weren't you frightened? Didn't you realize you could get hurt?'

A shrug. 'They wouldn't care. They only cared about Daisy. Not me. They wanted to give me back.'

I sense Everett looking at me. She knows as well as I do what I have to do next. Even though I hate myself for doing it, even though I can't predict the damage I might be causing.

'Leo,' I say gently, 'do you know what the word "adopted" means?'

He nods. 'Daisy told me. She said I wasn't really her brother. She said that was why no one loved me.'

Two large tears well in his eyes and start slowly down his cheeks.

'That was a mean thing for her to say. Were you having an argument?'

He nods.

'Was it the day she disappeared – is that when she said it?'

'No. It was ages ago. In half-term.'

So around two months ago. About the time Leo started acting up. About the time he started lashing out. Small wonder. Poor little sod.

'Do you know how she found out?'

'She was listening. They didn't know she was there. She was always doing it. She knew lots of secrets.'

I gesture to Everett. Her turn, now.

'Tell us about the day that Daisy disappeared,' she says softly.

More tears, silently welling. 'I was angry at her when she ran away and left me with those boys. I shouted at her.'

'So you had another argument? What did she say?'

'She said she had another brother. A real one. She

297

said Dad had a proper son he was going to see instead of me and he didn't need an adopted one any more.'

'Did that upset you?'

His eyes are down. 'I knew they didn't care.'

I can see the distress in Everett's eyes now. There's more pain in this room than one small boy can withstand.

'So what happened when you got home?' Everett says eventually. 'Did you see Daisy?'

His eyes flicker up to her face. 'It was like I said. I didn't *want* to see her. I don't know what happened. I had my music on.'

'Leo,' I say, struggling to keep my voice steady. 'You told us just now you were really angry at her. Are you sure you didn't go in her room when you got back? We'd all understand if you were still angry – she said some really mean things to you. I'd be upset if someone said those things to me. And sometimes, when people get angry, someone gets hurt. Are you sure that didn't happen to Daisy?'

'No,' he says. 'It was like I said.'

'You got angry at school, didn't you? With one of those boys who were bullying you. You tried to put a pencil in his eye.'

Leo shrugs. 'He was hurting me.'

'And didn't something else happen, the day before Daisy disappeared? When you were at the Connors' house, trying on each other's costumes?'

Leo flushes. 'I didn't mean it.'

'Mr Connor told us that you hit Daisy. That you went for her with some sort of wizard's wand.'

'It was a sorcerer. Wizards are for kids.'

'But that's not really the point, is it, Leo? Why did you want to hit her?'

'She'd been saying mean things about me. The girls were laughing.'

'So – did that happen again the day of the party? She said mean things again, and you got angry again, and you hit her? Did she fall over perhaps and hit her head? I'd understand if that's what happened. So would DC Everett. So would Derek.'

He shakes his head.

'And if something like that did happen to your sister,' I continue, 'I'm sure you'd be really sorry. Sorry and sad. And the natural thing to do would be for you to go to your mum and tell her. I'm sure she'd want to help you fix things. Is that how it was, Leo?'

I can only imagine what's going on right now in the room next door. But I don't care.

Leo shakes his head again. 'She's not my mum. Daisy's not my sister.'

'But did she help you – did your mum help you fix things after your argument with Daisy?'

'I told you. I didn't see Daisy. She was in her room.'

Everett and I exchange a glance.

'So it was like you said to start with,' I say. 'You got home and Daisy's music was on, and you never saw her again.'

He nods.

'You were in your own room, with your own music on.'

He nods again.

'So you were wearing your headphones.'

He hesitates.

'I had my music too.'

'Your music *and* your headphones?'

'Whatever. I hate them. I hate *all* of them.'

And he probably just wanted to drown it all out. And who can blame him. He's crying hard now. Really hard.

I reach forward and gently, very gently, take his hands and push back his oversized sleeves. The oversized sleeves he always wears, even in this heat. He doesn't try to stop me.

I look down at the lines across his flesh. I'm guessing it started soon after he found out he had no family. The doctor knew and I think the school suspected too. But neither of the people who were supposed to love and care for him noticed anything was wrong. Poor little Leo. Poor bloody Jamie. Poor abandoned lonely boys.

'I know what these are, Leo,' I say softly. 'I had a little boy once, who did this.'

I sense Everett stiffen beside me. She didn't know. No one knew. We didn't tell anybody.

'It made me very sad and it took me a long time to understand because I loved him so much, and I thought

300

he knew that. But I do understand now and I think I know why he did it. Doing this hurts less than all the rest of the hurt, doesn't it? It makes it feel a bit better. Even if only for a little while.'

Derek Ross reaches across and puts an arm round the sobbing little boy. 'It's OK, Leo. It's OK. We'll sort it out. We'll sort it all out.'

In the corridor, Sharon is already waiting. Waiting and blazing.

'How *dare* you,' she says, coming up far too close and pointing a long red nail. Those are new, too. 'How *bloody dare you* try to drag me into all this – if that stupid kid did something to Daisy, I knew *nothing* about it. Right from the start you've been insinuating I'm a bad mother, and now you're actually suggesting that kid killed my daughter and I helped him *fix it*? I helped him *cover it up*? What gives *you* the right – what gives you the bloody *right* –'

'Mrs Mason,' begins the lawyer, alarmed, 'I really don't think –'

'And if I were you,' she hisses, ignoring him and bringing her face even closer to mine, 'I would think twice before I started throwing accusations at *other* people about how they bring up their kids. After all, my daughter's just missing. *Your* kid is *dead*.'

* * *

4 April 2016, 10.09 p.m.
106 days before the disappearance
5 Barge Close, sitting room

Barry is watching an American cop show on TV. He has a can of lager on the table beside him. Suddenly the door flings open and Sharon storms into the room. She's holding his leather jacket in one hand and a piece of paper in the other.

'What the bloody hell is this?'

Barry glances up, sees what she has and reaches for his can. 'Oh, that.'

'Yes. *That*.'

Barry shrugs. The nonchalance is perhaps a little forced. 'She's just a little kid cutting out pictures from magazines. They all do it at that age. She doesn't know what it means.'

'She's not that little any more – she's eight.'

'Like I said, it's nothing.'

Sharon's face is red with fury. 'It's *disgusting*, that's what it is. You think I'm thick, but I've got eyes in my head. I see the way you pick her up – the way you have her in your lap – and now *this* –'

Barry puts down his can. 'Are you seriously telling me I can't pick up my own daughter?'

'Not the way you do it.'

'And what the fuck do you mean by that?'

'You know exactly what I mean. I see the looks she gives you –'

'She looks at me like I'm her bloody *father.*'

'– and all that whispering behind your hands and looking down your noses at me.'

'I can't believe I'm hearing this. How many more times do we have to go through the same old same old? No one's looking down their nose at you. You're imagining it.'

'And you're Daddy of the Decade,' replies Sharon sarcastically.

Barry gets up. 'At least I'm not jealous of my own kid.'

Sharon gapes. '*How dare you!*'

'Because that's what it comes down to, isn't it? It's just like it was with Jessica.'

'Don't you dare drag her into it. It's completely different.'

'It's *exactly the same.* You just can't stand being second best, can you? Being anything other than the centre of attention all the bloody time. It happened with Jessica and it's happening now. Your own fucking daughter. You never stop boasting about her when she's not there, but you never say anything nice to her face. You never tell her she looks nice or she's pretty –'

'My mother never told me I was pretty when I was a child.'

'That's *not the bloody point.* Just because your mother was a cow doesn't mean you have to be.'

'Daisy's quite spoilt enough without me joining in. She needs to learn she can't go through life expecting the whole world to revolve around her. She's not some *little princess*, despite what you tell her every hour of every bloody day.'

Barry walks to the fireplace, then turns to face his wife. 'Are you actually telling me you do it deliberately? That you do it to *teach her a lesson*?' He shakes his head. 'Sometimes I wonder whether you love her at all.'

Sharon's chin lifts. 'You give her far *too much* love. I'm just evening up the balance. She'll thank me in the end.'

'Jesus. After everything you had to go through to have her – what we *both* went through – that's what you come out with. Sometimes I think I don't bloody understand you at all.'

Sharon says something, but it's too low to hear. Her face reddens.

'What did you say?'

She turns to him and her chin lifts again in defiance. 'I said it's hard to love someone who despises you.'

Barry sighs theatrically. 'She doesn't *despise you* – she bends over backwards to *please you*. We all do. It's like walking on eggshells in this bloody place.'

'You don't know the things she says. Nasty bitchy things. You don't see it because she never does it when you're around. She's too clever for that.'

Barry puts his hands on his hips. 'Like what?'

'What do you mean?'

'You say she doesn't do it in front of me, so give me an example. Something she said.'

Sharon opens her mouth and shuts it again. Then, 'She said Portia's mother was setting up a book club and they were going to start with *Pride and Prejudice* but she'd already told Portia I wouldn't be interested.'

'Well, you're not, are you? You hate that sort of crap. You wouldn't go if they begged you on their hands and knees, so what's the problem?'

'It's the way she said it. Like I wouldn't be interested because I was too thick to understand Jane Austen.'

'You're reading way too much into all of this. She's only bloody eight –'

'And another time she said how Nanxi Chen's mother was a Roads scholar or something, and she'd told them I was once runner-up for Miss South London.'

'So? What's wrong with that? She's proud of you. And Nanxi would have been really impressed – she'd see it as Homecoming Queen or something. That's a big deal in the US.'

Sharon looks at him with contempt. 'You really don't get it, do you? Daisy would have made it sound like some pathetic cattle market full of useless airheads walking up and down in bikinis.'

Barry throws up his hands. 'I give up. I really do. I just don't think eight-year-olds think that way. You're her beautiful mum and she's showing off about you and all you can do is look for some nasty non-existent put-down.'

'How would you know what's she's doing – you're never here to see.'

'Christ, do you blame me.'

She moves towards him. 'So you're admitting it? That's why you're always getting back late? You're playing around?'

'I'm at the bloody gym. Or working.'

'So if I rang the gym, that's what they'd say, would they? That you're there three or four evenings a week?'

'You really want to do that, go ahead, knock yourself out. But before you do, ask yourself what that would look like — what would they think? Desperate housewife or what.'

'You've had enough of me. I'm getting fat and you want to trade me in for a younger model. Some skinny seccy with big tits. I see the way you look at women like that.'

'Oh for fuck's sake, not that again. Is that why you go through my jackets? Looking for receipts? Well, you won't find any. And for the last time, for the record, you are *not fat*.'

'I'm three sizes larger than I was when we got married. And after I had Daisy —'

'You can't blame it on that. Jesus, Shaz —'

'Don't call me that!'

There's a pause.

'I'm sorry.'

He swallows, takes a step forward. 'Look, I know you're not — not quite as thin as you used to be. But you know what I think about that. I don't think having

Daisy was anything to do with it. I keep telling you to go and see the doctor. You eat nothing and yet –'

There are tears in her eyes now. Tears of rage. 'And yet I'm still *fat*. That's what you mean, isn't it?'

'No, not fat. Just not like you were –'

'Before Daisy,' she says as she crushes the paper in her fist. 'Before I had bloody *Daisy* –'

There's a noise then, from outside the room, and Barry swivels round. 'Christ almighty, that's not her, is it – you know what she's like, listening at keyholes.'

He flings open the door to see his daughter disappearing up the stairs.

She stops at the turn and looks back down at him, her small face covered with tears. 'I hate her – I *hate* her! I wish she was dead so I could have another mummy – a mummy who'd love me –'

'Daisy, princess,' he says, starting up the stairs and reaching out for her. 'Of course we love you – we're your mum and dad.'

'I don't *want* to be your princess – I hate you – leave me *alone*!'

And then his daughter is gone and her bedroom door slams shut.

* * *

'So where are we on the forensics?'

It's 11.30 and we're back in the St Aldate's incident room. Including Everett, who's got Mo Jones to take her place at the B&B. She says she has to take her dad to the doctor's later, hence the delegation, but if she's had enough of Sharon, I can't say I blame her. Quinn puts down his phone. 'Just got some preliminaries. No prints on the newspaper but the blood on the gloves – it's definitely Daisy's.'

I take a deep breath. So she really is dead. There's no question about that now. I've known it a long time – I think we all have. But knowing, and finding proof, are not the same. Even when you've been doing this for as long as I have.

'There's also other DNA,' says Quinn into the silence. 'It's inside and outside the gloves, and it's a match for Barry Mason.'

A ripple of success goes through the room at that. Not triumph – how could it be, in the circumstances – but we all know there's no good reason for that man's gloves to be in a random skip, over a mile from his house, covered with his daughter's blood.

'And there's something else,' says Quinn quickly. It's a breakthrough – that much is obvious just looking at him. 'There are fragments of grit all over the gloves – grit and weedkiller. Seemed an odd combo for someone who just builds extensions, so some bright spark thought it was worth testing it against the aggregate they use for railway ballast. And it's *exactly* the same. And they've matched the weedkiller to the type Network Rail use too. It's pretty heavy-duty stuff – you can't just walk in and get it at B&Q.' People are looking at each other, the noise level is rising. They're all thinking the same thing: there's only one place around here that ticks all those boxes, and it's less than half a mile from where we found those gloves.

'OK,' I say, raising my voice. 'Quinn – get down the level crossing. Get the search teams to meet you there.'

'They've already covered that area once, boss,' begins Baxter.

'Well, they can cover it again. Because it looks like we missed something.'

Out in the corridor Anna Phillips comes towards me from my office, waving a piece of paper. 'I've found her,' she says, smiling.

'I'm sorry?'

Her smile falters a little. 'Pauline Pober? Remember? The woman who was quoted in that article about the Wileys – when Jessica died?'

'Oh, right. Where is she?'

'Hale and hearty and living in a village barely ten miles from here, would you believe. I've arranged for us to pop over and talk to her tomorrow morning. If it's all right with you, I'd like to go. I know I'm a civilian and all that, but having tracked her down, I'd quite like to, you know, see it through.'

I haven't the heart to tell her the agenda's moved on.

'That's great work, Anna. Really. And I'm happy for you to go and see her. But take an officer with you – just for procedure's sake.'

'Gareth – DS Quinn – is going to allocate someone.'

'Great. And make sure to let me know what she says.'

She must have picked up something up from my distracted manner, because a flicker of doubt crosses her brow. 'Right,' she says. 'Will do.'

* * *

When Quinn arrives at the car park by the level crossing, the wind's got up and there's rain in the air. He realizes suddenly how lucky they were that it's been dry since the gloves were dumped in the skip – a downpour could have wiped out the evidence. As he gets out, Erica Somer comes towards him from a patrol car parked ahead. Her hair's tied back but the wind is whipping it about her face. Quinn remembers her from the station. She was the one who brought in the DVD. Nice-looking. Very nice-looking, in fact. Though the uniform isn't helping. He wonders in passing what she'd look like in the sort of heels Anna Phillips wears.

He follows her across the car park to an area fenced off with metal security panels. There are signs all along it saying CONSTRUCTION SITE: KEEP OUT.

Somer pushes open the gate and pulls it to behind them with a clang. 'I asked the site manager to attend, sarge. He's over there, in the Portakabin.'

The man has obviously been keeping watch for them, because he comes down the steps as they approach. He has a rugby-player's ears and a shaved head.

'DS Quinn?' he says, extending a hand. 'Martin Heston. 'Your colleague here asked me for a schedule of the work we've been doing for the last two weeks.'

Full marks to Somer, thinks Quinn, as Heston hands him a worksheet.

'As you can see, we've been demolishing the old footbridge and laying new track for one of the lines.'

'And most of this has been going on at night?'

'Has to, mate. You can't do it with the trains running.'

'What about during the day – is there anyone around then?'

Heston gestures about him. 'Not when we're doing overnight work. No point paying people to sit on their arses. There are deliveries sometimes, and we have someone on site then, but that's about it.'

'What about security?'

'Don't need it, mate. All the kit's locked behind barbed wire on the other side of the track. We had to bring it in by train and that's the only way anyone's going to get it out.'

'So if a member of the public came here during the day, they wouldn't necessarily be seen?'

He considers. 'I suppose you might spot them from the other side, but there's a lot of trees in the way. When the level crossing was still open, there were people here all hours going across to the allotments. They used to park here and take their stuff over, but now they have to go via Walton Well. That's –'

'I know where it is.'

Quinn looks around. There's a pile of rusty garden equipment a few yards away. Wheelbarrows, hoes, empty bags of compost, rusting spades, broken terra-cotta pots.

Quinn opens out the schedule. 'So what was being done on the evening of the nineteenth?'

Heston points a thumb. 'We finished taking down the old bridge and worked on the footings for the new one.'

'Wait, are you telling me you've been digging bloody great holes in an area where any Tom, Dick or Harry can just walk straight in?'

Heston bridles. 'I can assure you we follow approved Health and Safety practices at all times – this area is completely cordoned off.'

Quinn looks back the way they came. There's fencing all right, but it's only loose panels, and he reckons he could force his way in. If he had to. If he had a good enough reason.

He turns back to Heston. 'Can you show me? Exactly what you were doing?'

They walk over to the new footbridge, where the pillars are beginning to rise above the ground.

'How deep were the foundations?'

'We'd planned for three metres,' says Heston, 'but when we started digging it just kept filling up with water. Port Meadow's a flood plain, so we knew it was going to be an issue, but it was a lot worse than we'd expected. We ended up going down more like six.'

'That's what you were doing that Tuesday night?'

'Right.'

'And if there'd been something in the bottom of that hole – something as small as a child – you'd definitely have noticed? Even in the dark?'

Heston blanches. He has granddaughters. 'Jesus – do you really think someone –? But the answer's yes – we'd have noticed. We had arc lights and we were pumping the water out the whole time, so we could see what was down there. No way my lads would have missed something like that.'

'Right,' says Quinn, folding up the schedule and handing it back. 'Two steps forward, three steps back.'

But Somer is still looking at Heston. Who isn't making eye contact.

'There's something else, isn't there?' she says. 'Something that wasn't to do with "your lads".'

Heston flushes. 'It's way off – I just can't see it happening –'

'But?'

He eyes her for a moment, then points beyond the foundations. 'When we took the old bridge down we heaped the waste over there – you can see where the pile was. Concrete, bricks, ballast, – you name it. Anyway, the contractor collected it all that night – we weren't allowed to do it during the day. Health and –'

'– Safety. Right,' says Quinn. 'And which contractor was it?'

'Firm in Swindon. Mercers.'

'So let me get this straight,' says Quinn. 'There was a pile of rubble over there that afternoon – the nineteenth. But that night this firm of yours –'

'Nothing to do with me, mate. I don't decide who gets hired.'

'OK, I get it. Anyway, they came that night and took the waste away.'

'Yes, but if you're suggesting someone could have buried something in there and the guy they had on the grabber didn't spot it, you're way off. It's not the bloody movies, that sort of thing just doesn't happen.'

'What *exactly* did they do with the waste, sir?' asks Somer quietly.

His shoulders sag a little. 'They trucked it back to their recycling depot. They crush it then turn it into gravel – stops it going to landfill.'

Quinn stares at him, then shakes his head, trying to dispel the picture it conjures. 'Jesus.'

'Like I said,' says Heston quickly, 'you're barking up completely the wrong tree. It just wouldn't happen.'

'Even though it was in the dark – and even though I'm guessing you're not so bothered with arc lights for a simple loading job like that?'

'I told you. It wasn't my lads. You'll have to talk to Mercers.'

'Oh, we will, Mr Heston. We will.'

As Quinn turns to go, Somer takes a step towards him. 'Was it luck then or did they know?'

'Sorry?'

'Whoever it was – who killed Daisy – was it just luck they came here the day the waste was being collected? Or was there some way they could have known?'

Quinn looks back at Heston, who shrugs. 'We leaflet the whole area every time there's likely to be worse noise than usual. Doesn't stop the complaints, but at least they can't claim they weren't informed.'

'So that would cover the demolition work?'

'Sure. That's one of the noisiest jobs. The leaflets went out the end of the previous week. Everywhere within a mile radius of the site.'

'Including Canal Manor?'

'You kidding? We get more complaints from them than anywhere else.'

* * *

At 1.00 Quinn calls from the site to update me. 'We had a closer look at the security barrier before we left. And I was right – on the far side, where they attached the panels to the car-park fence, it's just held together with cable ties. And someone definitely got in that way – all the ties have been cut through. No one noticed because the whole area's overgrown with brambles and whoever did it just pushed the panel back where it was before. And I'll bet my mortgage that's where those red stains we found on the gloves came from. I've got blackberry juice all over my sodding suit.'

I smile. I shouldn't, but I do.

'I'm going to drive to Swindon now,' he says. 'It doesn't sound good, but I need to see for myself.'

'You want forensics to meet you there?'

'Not yet, boss. Let's wait and see if there's something for them to find first.'

'OK, I'll send Everett to cover for you at the crossing.'

I lose him then as a train goes past in a shriek of hot white noise. Then, 'Any news from Gislingham?'

I sigh. 'I left a message. But no, no news.'

'Poor bastard. Let's hope that's a good sign.'

I hope so too, but my heart fears otherwise.

* * *

Interview with Barry Mason, conducted at St Aldate's Police Station, Oxford

25 July 2016, 1.06 p.m.

In attendance, DI A. Fawley, DC A. Baxter, Miss E. Carwood (solicitor)

AF: For the purposes of the tape, Mr Mason has just been arrested on suspicion of the murder of his daughter, Daisy Elizabeth Mason. Mr Mason has been made aware of his rights. So, Mr Mason, am I correct in assuming that someone in your profession would own a wide variety of Personal Protective Equipment?

BM: Yeah, what of it?

AF: We discovered a jacket, hard hat and safety boots in the back of your pick-up, and there were several similar items in your house.

BM: And?

AF: Do you own gloves of that type as well?

BM: Couple of pairs.

AF: Could you describe them?

BM: What, are you an insurance assessor now?

AF: Humour me, Mr Mason.

BM: I had one black pair, and one that was orange and grey. Satisfied?

AF: I have to tell you that a pair of orange and grey gloves was found yesterday in a skip on the Loughton Road.

BM: So?

AF: Tests on those gloves prove conclusively that you had been wearing them. Do you know how they got there, Mr Mason?

BM: No bloody idea. I can't even remember the last time I saw them.

AF: So you didn't put them in that skip yourself, on the afternoon of Tuesday 19th July?

BM: Of course I didn't. What is this?

AF: And did you seek to conceal your identity as you did so by wearing other items of protective clothing?

BM: This is crazy. That was the day of the party – I didn't have time, never mind anything else. And why the hell go to all that bother for a pair of sodding gloves?

AF: Because you wore those gloves to dispose of your daughter's body, and that's how they ended up covered with her blood.

BM: Hang on a minute – what do you mean, her *blood*? Are you telling me you've found her? Why the bloody hell didn't someone tell me –

EC: [*interjecting*]
Is this true, Inspector? Have you found Daisy?

AF: Not as yet. But we believe we know now where your client disposed of her body. Because the gloves he dumped in Loughton Road bear traces of a special type of aggregate. So special, in fact, that he knew they would lead us straight to where he'd buried her.

BM: [*to Miss Carwood*]
Is this for real?

EC: May I have a moment to confer with my client?

AF: Take all the time you need. Interview terminated at 13.14.

* * *

318

At the level crossing, the rain thickens suddenly from drizzle to downpour. Everett stops her car just outside the gate and leans over to the back seat for her waterproof. Even though the sky to the north is still a brilliant blue, the clouds are as dark as November overhead, and the wind is flaying the summer trees. It looks like the search teams have just started: one group is going through the stack of old wheelbarrows and garden junk, and the others are doing a fingertip search of the strip leading from the gate to the site of the waste heap. They definitely got the short straw: the rain is already turning the ground to orangey sludge.

She gets out and turns her collar up against the wet. A train is coming towards them from Oxford station, the passengers peering out of the misted windows at the police cars, the white-suited forensics team, the whole goddam circus. A teenager in one of the carriages is taking photos on his phone. Everett just hopes Fawley remembered to brief the press office.

There's a shout then, above the din of the train. By the time Everett draws level a forensics officer is gently dislodging something from under the rusted wheels of one of the wheelbarrows. It's so filthy it's hard to tell what it is, but then he opens it out and they can all see. Two bedraggled sleeves, shiny buttons, some sort of bobble effect round the neck.

'That's a girl's cardigan,' says Everett slowly. 'Daisy

had one of those. It was round her shoulders that day, on the CCTV. The last time anyone saw her.'

* * *

BBC Midlands Today
Monday 25 July 2016 | Last updated at 15:28

BREAKING NEWS: Father arrested in Daisy Mason disappearance

A statement from Thames Valley CID has just confirmed that Barry Mason has been arrested in connection with his daughter's disappearance. Daisy, 8, was last seen a week ago, and in the last few days there has been growing speculation that a member of her family may have been involved. Sources close to the investigation say that Mason, 46, will be charged with murder, and another unconnected offence, believed to be of a sexual nature. A further statement will be issued tomorrow morning, when details will be given of the charges. It is not clear as yet whether Daisy's body has been found.

The Mason family are thought to be in hiding after an arson attack on their home last week. This has been connected with the hate campaign being waged against them on social media.

* * *

Richard Robertson @DrahcirNostrebor   15.46
So it was the father after all – must have been
abusing her, poor little cow #DaisyMason

Anne Merrivale @Annie_Merrivale_   15.56
This whole #DaisyMason thing is just so horrible. I
hope they lock up her father and throw away the key
#Justice4Daisy 🏵🏵

Caroline Tollis @ForWhomtheTollis   15.57
@Annie_Merrivale_ Have the police said if they've
found a body? I can't find anything online
#DaisyMason

Anne Merrivale @Annie_Merrivale_   15.59
@ForWhomtheTollis I've not seen anything
either. OH says they don't necessarily need a
body if they can meet the test for 'presumption
of death'

Caroline Tollis @ForWhomtheTollis   16.05
@Annie_Merrivale_ They must have some sort of
evidence then. Something conclusive the father
won't be able to challenge #DaisyMason

Anne Merrivale @Annie_Merrivale_   16.06
@ForWhomtheTollis. I still keep wondering if

someone cd have offered her a lift home? Someone she knew and only found out later she couldn't trust?

Caroline Tollis @ForWhomtheTollis   16.07
@Annie_Merrivale_ But it'd have to have been someone Daisy would have gone away with and there just isn't anyone like that in the frame . . .

Caroline Tollis @ForWhomtheTollis   16.08
. . . Not that I've heard about anyway and if the police have proof against the father then that can't be what happened, can it @Annie_Merrivale_

Anne Merrivale @Annie_Merrivale_   16.09
@ForWhomtheTollis. I guess not. And it's not as if someone could have planted evidence or framed him. There's no one with a motive

Garry G @SwordsandSandals   16.11
#DaisyMason Told U so. It was the father. Bloody pedo

Scott Sullivan @SnapHappyWarrior   16.13
I heard a rumour the father's up for possessing kiddie porn. Hardcore stuff. God knows what he did to that kid #DaisyMason

Angela Betterton @AngelaGBetterton   16.17
Everyone at Daisy's school is devastated by the

news – she was so loved, such a happy child.
Memorial at the start of next term #DaisyMason

Elspeth Morgan @ElspethMorgan959   16.17
I so hope someone's looking after Leo in all this – who
knows, he may have been abused too #DaisyMason ✿

Lilian Chamberlain @LilianChamberlain   16.18
@ElspethMorgan959 It's heartbreaking, the whole
sad story #Justice4Daisy ✿✿✿✿

Jenny T @56565656Jennifer   16.20
@ElspethMorgan959 @LilianChamberlain I still say that
she didn't look like an abuse victim in that photo –
looks so happy, like she's looking forward to something

Lilian Chamberlain @LilianChamberlain   16.22
@56565656Jennifer I know what you mean, but
perhaps it was just the party? Something to take her
mind off it? #Justice4Daisy ✿ @ElspethMorgan959

Jenny T @56565656Jennifer   16.24
@ElspethMorgan959 I guess so. Just keeps nagging at
me, that's all @LilianChamberlain #DaisyMason ✿✿✿

*   *   *

'Boss? I'm at Mercers.'

Quinn sounds like he's in a wind tunnel. A gust

whips the words away but I can still hear the defeat in his voice, and in the background the thud and grind of heavy machinery.

'I'm guessing it's bad news.'

'I've texted you a picture. Has it come through?'

I reach for my mobile and open the photo. A wide space like an opencast mine, ringed with huge dunes of waste. Three lorries tipping out their loads in a billow of thick white dust, and in the centre, a huge yellow machine crushing the debris into a stream of something that looks like not much more than sand.

I pick up the handset again. 'Shit. I see what you mean.'

'They don't even know exactly where the stuff that came from Oxford ended up. And even if they did, God knows how many tons of other crap has been dumped on top of it since then. Needle and haystack is so far off it's laughable. It's a complete fucking non-starter.'

He doesn't usually swear. Not at me, anyway.

'Add to that the fact that they're absolutely refusing to accept they could have overlooked a body. However small it was, however carefully someone had wrapped it. They won't budge.'

'But they can't prove it.'

He sighs. 'No, of course they can't. But we can't prove it either. So the question is, do you think we have enough? Will the CPS be prepared to charge him, even though we don't have the body?'

'Ev just called – looks like they've found some physi-cal evidence at the crossing. And there could be something else too. I'm waiting for Network Rail to get back to me.'

His voice lifts a little. 'I'm on my way.'

* * *

Twenty minutes later the email comes through. I down-load the video attachment and watch it, then I call the team into the incident room and we watch it together. There's relief, and there's consensus, and there's even a tear or two. No high-fives, no excess, but a pride that the team done good. And they did. Baxter offers to leave a message for Gislingham ('that was solid police work, tracking down that Ford Escort'), and in the middle of it all a call comes through from the ACC asking when we can brief the press.

* * *

Just after three, Emma Carwood arrives, and we get Mason up from the cells. I've loathed that man pretty much since I laid eyes on him, but a small part of me is actually sorry for him when the custody sergeant leads him in. He looks like he's been hollowed out from the inside. Like the bones have gone and it's just the skin holding him up. No more walk of the cock now. He takes his seat like an old man.

'Mr Mason, this interview is in continuation of the one suspended at 13.14. It is now 15.14 and I am restarting the tape. Those present, Detective Inspector Adam Fawley, Acting Detective Sergeant Gareth Quinn, Mr Barry Mason, Miss Emma Carwood.'

I lift my laptop on to the table and swing it round to face Mason. Then I open the video and start the film. He stares at it, rubs his eyes, and stares at it again.

'I don't get it. What are you showing me this for?'

'This, Mr Mason, is footage from the cab camera of a CrossCountry train. This particular train left Banbury at 16.36 on Tuesday the nineteenth of July, arriving at Oxford at 16.58. As you will see, at 16.56, the train starts to slow as it approaches the station, and you will briefly see the area around the old level crossing.'

Mason puts his head in his hands and digs his nails into his scalp. Then he looks up at me. 'You've lost me. This is all some hideous bloody nightmare. I haven't a fucking clue what's going on.'

I change the player to slow motion and we see the allotments come into range on the right, and the heavy machinery parked alongside. Then I press Pause and point at the screen.

'There,' I say.

On the left of the track there's a figure in a hard hat, high-viz jacket and trousers. He has his back to us but he's clearly pushing a barrow across the car park towards the new footings, and the heap of rubble beyond. There's a tiny moment when we can see a flash of orange glove, and then the train has passed and the image is gone.

Barry Mason looks none the wiser. 'I still don't get it.'

'That's you, isn't it, Mr Mason?'

He gapes at me. 'You're having a laugh – no, of course it *fucking well isn't me*.'

'You own high-viz gear like that, don't you?'

'Yes, but so do thousands of other people. That doesn't prove anything.'

Emma Carwood intervenes. 'Are you seriously alleging that my client drove to the level crossing, unloaded his daughter's body into a random wheelbarrow and then disposed of it in that pile of whatever it is, all in broad daylight, without a single person noticing anything?'

'I think you'd be surprised how easy that would have been, Miss Carwood. The locals are so used to contractors on that site they probably wouldn't have given him a second glance.'

'And the wheelbarrow in question – do you have it? Have you examined it?'

'Our forensics officers have collected several wheelbarrows from the site and are analysing them now. As well as two further items that we believe have a bearing on the case. We will, of course, keep you fully informed. May I resume?'

She hesitates, then nods.

I turn to Mason. 'So, Mr Mason. As we have already informed you, we have found a pair of gloves carrying your DNA and your daughter's blood. The same sort of gloves the man in this footage is clearly wearing. We also found particles of railway ballast on those gloves. Are you really still claiming this man isn't you?'

'Yes I bloody well am – I was nowhere near there at the time. I've told you a thousand times, I was driving about and then I went home. That's it.'

'We've found nothing to corroborate that story, Mr Mason.'

'I don't fucking care, that's what happened.'

'OK,' I say, 'let's just accept, for the sake of argument, that your story is true. Explain to me how gloves bearing your DNA ended up in a skip in Loughton Road.'

'I could have left them somewhere – anyone could have picked them up.'

'When did you last see them?' asks Quinn.

'I told you, I don't know. I don't remember.'

'Fair enough,' I reply, 'let's accept that as well. Just for the sake of argument. Next question: how did your daughter's blood get on them?'

He swallows. 'I don't know.'

'No explanation at all? Come on, Mr Mason, an accomplished liar like you – you must be able to do better than that.'

'There's no call for sarcasm, Inspector,' says Emma Carwood.

'Look,' says Mason, his voice breaking, 'have either of you got kids?'

I open my mouth but no sound comes. 'No,' says Quinn quickly. 'Not that it's in any way relevant.'

'Well, if you did,' he says, 'you'd know that they're always getting into scrapes – falling over, grazed knees. Daisy has nose bleeds all the time – the blood gets all over the sodding place. Those gloves were just lying about in the house – there are all sorts of ways it could have happened.'

'I believe you tested my client's car, Inspector?' says Emma Carwood. 'As well as the high-viz clothing he had in the back? As far as I know, you found no incriminating evidence whatsoever. No fluids, no DNA, nothing.'

Quinn and I exchange a glance. It still bugs me. That he left no trace in the truck. He doesn't strike me as that meticulous. Though as Quinn was quick to point out, everyone's that meticulous if there's enough at stake.

I change tack. 'Has your daughter ever been to the car park by the level crossing, Mr Mason? For a walk on Port Meadow, perhaps?'

He puts his arms on the table and drops his head into them. 'No,' he says, his voice muffled. 'No no no no no.'

Emma Carwood leans over and touches him on the shoulder. 'Barry?'

Then suddenly he sits up. There are the marks of tears about his eyes, but he wipes his face with a sleeve and sits forward.

'Show me that bloody footage again,' he says quickly, pointing at the screen. '*Show it to me again.*'

'OK,' I say as I slide the cursor back three minutes and press Play.

'Slow it down,' he says after a moment. 'There, *slow it down.*'

We're all staring, watching the screen. The entire sequence only takes two or three seconds. We see the figure with the barrow take a couple of steps, his head down. That's all.

Barry Mason sits up, like a man come back from the dead. 'That's not me, Inspector. And I can prove it. Do you hear me – did you get that on your bloody tape? *I can prove that isn't me.*'

*   *   *

It's 5.45 and Quinn and I are standing behind Anna Phillips as she taps her keyboard.

'Are you sure we can't get a better close-up – see his face?'

She shakes her head, her eyes still on the screen. ''Fraid not. I've tried, but he has his back to us the whole time.'

'Bloody hell,' says Quinn under his breath. 'That's all we sodding need.'

'But what Mason said – you think he's right?'

'Give me a second,' she says, frowning into the screen. 'I've downloaded a photogrammetry app – I haven't used one before but I'm hoping it'll give us some sort of answer.'

'What the hell is photo-whatsit when it's at home?'

'It creates three-dimensional models from ordinary photos. It's pretty impressive actually – look.'

Three clicks and the still from the train camera opens up into 3D. A plastic replica of reality hangs suspended in a bright blue universe, like one of those cross sections you used to get in geography books. I can see the figure with the barrow, the railway line, the trees, the far edge of the car park, even the bushes along the track. Anna moves the cursor around and the image rotates. Left, right, tilt up, tilt down.

'It's accurate enough to give you proper measurements,' she says. 'Heights, distances between objects, that sort of thing. I could probably tell you how fast the train was going if you gave me long enough.'

'I just need to know if what Mason said is right.'

More work on the keyboard and grid points appear all over the image. One more click and the 3D image disappears, leaving only lines between the points, and numbers at each intersection. Anna sits back.

'Afraid he is. Perhaps not to the millimetre, but yes. He's right.'

*　*　*

At 11.15 the following morning, Anna Phillips draws up outside the Victorian two-up two-down owned by Pauline Pober. There are hollyhocks in the front garden and borage plants swarmed with bees. DC Andrew Baxter loosens his tie and looks out of the car window. The night's rain has blown over and the sun's already hot.

'This has Wild Goose Chase written all over it,' he says testily. 'We've arrested Mason now, so what's the point?'

Anna turns off the engine. 'Judging by what I saw yesterday, that Mason arrest isn't as cut-and-dried as we might have thought. And in any case, I told Mrs Pober we were coming. It would be rude to just not turn up.'

Baxter mutters something about old biddies and cats, which Anna decides not to hear. They get out and she locks the car, and as they go up the path, a curtain twitches next door. Anna was brought up in a village like this – she knows what piranha bowls they can be.

But far from being on the watch for their arrival, Mrs Pober takes a good three minutes to answer the door. There's a dark smear across one cheek and a rather unpleasant – and very distinctive – smell.

'So sorry,' she says, smiling broadly and wiping her hands on a pair of grubby trousers. 'The bloody drains are blocked again, so I had to get the rods out. Come through to the back. The air's a bit better out there, if you catch my drift.'

Anna suppresses a smile at the expression on Baxter's face, and the two of them follow her through the cottage to a small but dazzling garden. A square of lawn with flowers jostling for space in the borders. Lavender, clematis, penstemons, carnations, blue geraniums.

'We had a garden three times this size before Reggie died,' she says. 'This is all I can cope with on my own.'

'It's lovely, Mrs Pober,' says Anna, taking a chair.

'Oh, *Pauline*, please,' she says, flapping off a wasp. 'Do you want a drink? I have some cold Stella in the fridge.'

'Er, no thanks, not while we're on duty,' says Baxter in martyred tones.

'So how can I help you, officers? You said on the phone it was about that terrible accident in Lanzarote all those years back?'

'That's right,' says Anna. 'We were wondering if there's anything you could tell us – anything that wasn't in the press.'

Pauline sits back and wipes a hand across her brow. 'Well, it was a powerful long time ago. I'm not sure how much help I can be.'

Anna looks at Baxter, who makes it quite clear that pursuing this particular feral poultry is her responsibility, not his.

Oh well, she thinks, in for a penny.

'Did you have any contact with the Wileys before the accident, Pauline?'

'I remember they were on the same flight as us. We'd done a fair bit of travelling by then, Reggie and me, but you could see they were complete novices. They'd brought this huge bag of sandwiches to eat on the plane, and a *thermos*, would you believe! Of course, this was long before 9/11. Mrs Wiley was clearly very apprehensive about flying. They were a couple of rows behind us and I could hear her all the way – I don't think she was talking to anyone in particular. Just wittering away to relieve the nerves.'

'What about the girls – Sharon and Jessica?'

Pauline smiles. 'That Jessica was a little love. As soon as the seat-belt sign went off she was up and down the aisle the whole time, dragging this huge teddy bear behind her. She kept going up to people and asking what their names were. Terribly sweet. You could see the parents doted on her.'

'And Sharon?'

Pauline takes a deep breath. 'Well, fourteen isn't an easy age is it? Exams starting and periods and all that.'

Baxter's face is a sight to behold.

'And you were at the same hotel as well?'

'Yes, and we did spot them occasionally, but to be honest, we'd gone for the birdwatching, not the beach. Reggie could never stand sitting around doing nothing. I used to say he had a bee up his bum.'

Anna grins. 'I know a few blokes like that myself. So you didn't really see much of the Wileys?'

'They definitely kept themselves to themselves. I got the impression they'd never been to a hotel before either. It was little things – like not knowing it was a buffet for breakfast, and what to do about tips. And I didn't see either of the parents in a swimsuit all week,

334

even on the sand – it was slacks and a shirt for him and a sundress for her. It was sad, really, thinking about it now. It was as if they knew they should be enjoying themselves but hadn't the first clue how to actually go about it.'

'What happened that day – the day of the accident?'

'Now that I do remember – it's not something you're likely to forget, is it? The hotel had laid on a beach party. They did it every Friday. Games for the kids and ice cream, and then a barbecue for the grown-ups in the evening. All perfectly nice. Some of the children were playing with the inflatable dinghies and I remember seeing Sharon and Jessica together in one with an octopus on the side. It was all part of the theme, I suppose. Anyway, sometime later, one of the young waiters started asking where they were and it turned out no one had seen them for a least half an hour. And then, Lord, all hell broke loose. Mrs Wiley was screaming and Mr Wiley was shouting at the staff, and then someone said they thought they could see the dinghy out beyond the swimming area and Mr Wiley had torn off his shirt and run into the sea before anyone could stop him.'

She shakes her head, remembering.

'A lot of the younger dads went into the water after him, and that was just as well, because he only got a few yards out before he was completely out of breath. Someone had to help him back. It was two of the waiters who got out to the dinghy. Only by that time both the girls were in the water.' She sighs. 'I guess you know the rest.'

'How were the Wileys afterwards?'

'What do you call those things that won't die? Zombies. That's it. Zombies. They looked like their whole world had caved in. Back then, you didn't get the sort of support the travel companies offer these days, so those poor people just trailed about in the hotel till their flight home. Turning up to meals and not eating. Sitting in the lobby staring into space. It was pitiful.'

'And Sharon?'

'Oh, she was very shaken. I was there when they brought her back to the beach. She must have swallowed a lot of seawater because she was horribly sick. But after she came back from the hospital, I don't think I saw either of her parents speak a word to her. Apart from once. There was some activity or other in the hotel – I've forgotten what – and Sharon must have wanted to take part, because suddenly, in the middle of breakfast, her father stands up and bellows at her that she should show some respect – that it's all her fault and he wishes she'd died instead of Jessica. And then he threw down his napkin and walked out. That was the last time I saw them.'

She sighs. 'That poor girl. That poor, poor girl. I often wondered how things turned out for her.'

There's a silence, and then suddenly Pauline edges forward in her chair, looking at the two of them in open suspicion. 'That's why you're here, isn't it? I can't believe I didn't realize – Sharon – that's the name of that woman whose daughter has gone missing. Daisy – that's her, isn't it? That's why you're here.'

'Well,' begins Anna, but Pauline's still speaking.

'You don't think it was an accident at all, do you? You think she killed her sister, and now she's killed her little girl –'

'We don't know anything for certain, Mrs Pober,' says Baxter. 'It's an ongoing investigation –'

'I know what that means, young man. It means you think she did it but you can't prove it. And now you want *me* to help tip the balance against her.'

'We just need to have all the information we can,' says Anna gently.

Pauline gets to her feet, visibly trembling. 'I think you'd better go now.'

It's an uneasy exit for all three of them. At the front step, Anna turns to offer her thanks, but the door is already closing.

'Mrs Pober? Can I ask one more thing – it's not about Sharon, I promise.'

The door opens a little, just a little.

'You said the beach party had a theme. Something to do with the decoration on the dinghy?'

Pauline nods, but she's on her guard now. 'It was the *Octopus's Garden.*'

'Like the Beatles song? So there were fish decorations, shells, seahorses – stuff like that?'

'That sort of thing, yes. And the younger children could dress up if they wanted.'

'Really?' says Anna, taking a step closer. 'It was fancy dress, was it? What was Jessica wearing?'

* * *

27 July 1991
Hotel La Marina, Lanzarote

The girl wakes early on the first morning of the holiday.
Everyone else is still asleep. She slips out of the small
roll-away bed she is sharing with her sister and dresses
quickly, careful not to wake her parents. Her father
is lying on his back, snoring, and her mother's face
looks fretful, even in sleep. She picks up her yellow
flip-flops and closes the door quietly behind her. She
hesitates for a moment, trying to remember which way
the stairs were. There's a lift too, but she's never used
one of those, and she's frightened of getting stuck in it
on her own. Her father made them walk up three flights
when they arrived last night, huffing and blowing and
stopping at every turn on the stair.

When she gets downstairs, the reception area is deserted. There's a sign at the desk with a bell to ring in
emergencies, and somewhere, some way away, there's
the sound of tables being laid for breakfast. But that's
not what she's looking for.

The first two doors she tries are locked, but at last
she is out. At last she is free. When she gets to the beach
she takes off the flip-flops and goes barefoot, tenta-
tively at first, but then quicker, running, towards the sea.
The sun is still new, the air is still fresh, and she alone
owns this whole big beautiful day. The huge blue sky, the

sparkling waves nibbling and foaming at the flat damp sand. She hasn't been so happy for years – not since her sister was born. Not since everything changed.

She closes her eyes and puts her face up to the sun, seeing the redness inside her eyelids, feeling the warmth on her skin. When she opens her eyes again, there's a woman walking slowly along the edge of the water. She has a little girl with her, in a pink floppy sunhat and a little flowered dress. The woman is holding the child carefully by the hand as she jumps the waves, squealing and splashing. When they draw close enough to speak, the woman smiles at her. 'You're up early.'

'I was too excited to sleep. I've never been abroad before.'

'It's so nice to have the beach to yourself, isn't it? We live just round the bay. We love the early mornings.'

The woman bends down to the little girl and straightens the hat. The little girl puts up her arms to her mother and the woman lifts her, high, high into the sun, then kisses the laughing delighted child and swings her round and round and round in the glittering air.

The girl watches, barely breathing, like one gasping for a glimpse of heaven.

At last the woman sets the child gently back on the sand and they continue their walk. They're almost out of earshot when the girl finds herself calling out to her, 'What's your little girl's name?'

The woman turns and smiles again as the wind rises

for a moment and catches at her hair, and her long earrings, and her white cotton dress.

'Daisy,' she says. 'Her name is Daisy.'

* * *

'So it is your contention, Mrs Mason, that your husband was responsible for the death of your daughter?'

Sharon folds and unfolds her hands in her lap. She has no handbag, not today.

'His gloves were found in that skip. They had her blood on them, and his DNA.'

It's 9 January 2017, Oxford Crown Court, number two. The sky outside is dark and rain is splintering against the skylight above. Despite the fact that the room is freezing, the public gallery is packed: it's the first time Sharon Mason has taken the stand. She's wearing a plain navy dress with a white collar and cuffs. It's probably not her own choice.

The prosecuting barrister looks up from his notes. 'In fact, a subsequent test also found traces of *your* DNA, did it not?'

'Only on the outside,' she snaps. 'He was always leaving them lying about. I was always having to tidy them away. I never *wore* them.'

'But even if you had, there wouldn't necessarily be DNA inside, would there, Mrs Mason? Not if you'd worn plastic gloves underneath. Rubber gloves, say. They're very easy to obtain.'

She lifts her chin. 'I don't know anything about that.'

'As we have heard from Detective Inspector Fawley, during your interrogation you contended that it was your husband who killed Daisy, and disposed of her body. You said he had been molesting her, and must have killed her either in a fit of rage or to prevent her divulging the abuse. Is that correct?'

She says nothing. There is a murmur in the public gallery, a glancing at one another.

The barrister pauses and scans his notes, then lifts his head. 'Well, let us examine the evidence, shall we? Exhibit eighteen in your bundle, my Lady,' he says, nodding to the judge.

'Thank you, Mr Agnew.'

Agnew turns to the jury.

'As we have heard, the police have used special simulation software to analyse the footage taken by an on-board train camera, which passed the Oxford level crossing at approximately five o'clock the afternoon Daisy disappeared. I believe we can now show the jury on the large screen?'

An usher switches on a computer display and a still from the video appears.

The barrister picks up an electronic pointer and directs a red light on to the screen. 'I draw your attention to what you can see here. It is the Crown's case that this barrow contains the body of Daisy Mason, and this has been confirmed by expert forensic examination of blood spots discovered in a wheelbarrow found discarded at the site. Let me be absolutely clear: the person you are looking at here is Daisy's killer.'

He looks around. The air is electric.

'The quality of the video does not, unfortunately, allow for a more detailed close-up. However, I am pleased to say digital technology has not entirely deserted us.'

He presses the remote control again and the photogrammetry image appears. Various labels have been posted on to the model – *Line of railway track*, *Allotments*, *Waste heap*. The barrister pauses, allowing everyone to take this in.

'This technology has been employed successfully in both criminal investigations and legal proceedings, and has proved to be reliable. The findings I am about to show you have also been independently verified by undertaking a physical reconstruction on the site in question, details of which you will find in your folders.'

Another click and the model is overlaid with a grid of lines and numbers.

'As you can see,' he continues, 'this particular software allows us to recreate a two-dimensional photographic image in three dimensions. In virtual reality, if you prefer. And because some of those objects are of a known size – the fencing, for example – we can use the model to deduce the width – or height – of other objects, whose dimensions are *not* known. By using this software, the police have proved conclusively that the person shown here is no more than 1.7 metres in height.' He looks across at the jury. 'Approximately five feet six inches.'

The court erupts. The judge calls for silence.

The barrister turns to Sharon. 'How tall is your husband, Mrs Mason?'

Sharon shifts in her seat. 'Six foot two.'

'Six feet two inches. Or 1.88 metres. Approximately. So I put it to you, it is absolutely impossible that the figure shown here is your husband.'

'I wouldn't know. You'll have to ask him.'

He smiles. Like a cat. 'Perhaps you could tell us how tall *you* are, Mrs Mason?'

Sharon glances at the judge. 'Five foot six.'

'I'm sorry,' says the barrister, 'I didn't quite catch that.'

'*Five foot six.*'

'So *exactly* the same height as the figure shown in this image.'

'It's just a coincidence.'

'Is it?' He gestures with the pointer again. 'Can you describe to me what you see here? What footwear is this figure wearing?'

Sharon narrows her eyes, 'Looks like training shoes.'

'I agree. Blue training shoes. Rather odd footwear for a construction worker, wouldn't you say? Surely they'd be wearing safety boots or something of the kind?'

'I have no idea.'

Agnew raises an eyebrow, then, 'You're a runner, I believe, Mrs Mason?'

'I'm not a *runner*. I *go jogging*.'

'On the contrary, we have been told you used to run every morning, for several miles at a time.'

She shrugs. 'Most days.'

'And you wore training shoes?'

She shoots a look at him. 'What else would I wear?'

'And how many pairs do you have?'

She's flustered now. 'I had an old pair for the winter, when the ground is muddy. And a newer pair.'

'And what colour were they – the newer pair?'

A hesitation. 'Blue.'

'The same colour as these, shown here?'

'I suppose so.'

'So are we to believe that that, also, is just a coincidence?'

Sharon gives him a poisonous look, but says nothing.

'We were told, were we not, by the expert witness, that the training shoes recovered from your house had tiny traces of railway ballast embedded in the soles?'

The defence barrister rises to her feet. 'My Lady, it has already been established, and confirmed by witnesses, that my client went running on Port Meadow and used to use the level crossing to get there, before it was closed off. There is thus a perfectly innocent explanation for the presence of the ballast on the shoes.'

She looks at the jury, underlining the point, then returns to her seat.

The prosecuting barrister removes his glasses. 'Notwithstanding Miss Kirby's intervention, I put it to you, Mrs Mason, that the image we have on the screen is an image of *you*. Wearing your husband's high-viz clothing, your hair and face concealed, pushing a barrow containing your daughter's body. You wore *his* clothing and *his* gloves – gloves you later disposed of in Loughton Road. But his boots, as a size eleven, would have been impossible to walk in, given you are only a size five. Hence the training shoes.'

'It's *not* me – I told you – I wasn't there –'

'So where were you? At five o'clock that day? The time shown on the screen.'

'At home,' she says, folding her hands. 'I was at home.'

'But that's not quite true, is it? You told the police that you left your children alone in the house that afternoon, and were absent in your car for at least forty minutes. And this,' he jabs the pointer, 'was at exactly the time shown on the video footage.'

'I went to the shops,' she says sullenly. 'For mayonnaise. For the party.'

'But you *claim* you couldn't find any so there are no computer records of any such purchase. And no one remembers you at the store you said you went to, do they?'

'That doesn't prove I wasn't there.'

'Nor does it prove you *were*, Mrs Mason. On the contrary, it is the Crown's case that you spent those forty minutes driving to the car park by the level crossing and burying your daughter's body in rubble of the old footbridge. Waste which you *knew* – having conveniently

345

received a leaflet through the door – would be collected that very night.'

He clicks the remote and an image of Daisy appears on the screen. She is smiling, in her party outfit. A charming gap-toothed smile. It's three days before she disappeared. Then he holds up a plastic bag.

There are gasps from the public gallery and one or two of the jury put their hands to their mouths.

'Exhibit nineteen, my Lady. DNA analysis has proved that this tooth belonged to Daisy Mason. As we have heard, it was found in the gravel near the site of that waste heap, by a search team from the Thames Valley Police.' He takes his pointer again and gestures at the screen. A red label appears, marking the spot. Then he turns to the jury. 'I am sure, ladies and gentlemen, that Daisy hoped to leave this under her pillow, like any other little girl. Perhaps you have children yourself, who have done the same. But there will be no fairy coming to collect this, will there, Mrs Mason?'

The defence barrister rises to her feet. 'Is this really necessary, my Lady?'

The judge looks over her spectacles at the prosecuting barrister. 'Move on, Mr Agnew.'

He bows. 'So, Mrs Mason, let us recap. If it was your husband who killed your daughter, there are only two possibilities. Either he killed her after he got home at 5.30 or he came back earlier in the afternoon, while you were on your fruitless quest for mayonnaise. We can eliminate the first of these alternatives, not least because the time does not tally with the video evidence. And in any case, had he killed her then, it would have happened when you were in the house, and you, by definition, must have helped him cover it up, by failing to report the crime to the police. I assume you were *not* so complicit, Mrs Mason.'

'No.'

'We are therefore left with the forty minutes when you were absent from the house. Between approximately 4.35 and 5.15. During that time, your husband would have to return to the house, find you unexpectedly absent, take the opportunity to kill his daughter and wrap the body so diligently that no trace whatsoever is left in his pick-up truck, and leave. All in forty minutes. He would then have to drive to the car park, put Daisy in the wheelbarrow, where – somewhat inexplicably – he *did* manage to leave forensic evidence – and hide her body in the waste heap, before dumping the gloves in the skip, removing his high-viz clothing and returning to the house by 5.30. That's quite some going. Has he ever thought of entering *Supermarket Sweep*?'

There's some low-level laughter from the gallery, but the judge is clearly not amused. Agnew resumes.

'Only there's a flaw in this story, isn't there, Mrs Mason? Because the person who buried the body, at that time and in that place – the person we can see on this video – *couldn't possibly be your husband.*'

Sharon refuses to meet his eye. There are two spots of livid colour in her cheeks, but her face is white.

347

'So who is it, Mrs Mason?'

'I have no idea. I told you.'

'I put it to you that you know exactly who this is. It's *you,* isn't it?'

She lifts her chin. 'No. It's not me. How many more times. It's *not me.*'

*   *   *

19 July 2016, 5.18 p.m.
The day of the disappearance
Loughton Road, Oxford

The woman pulls the car over to the side of the road and switches off the engine. So far, so good. The 16.58 was on time, and even if no one on the train noticed her, she's pretty sure all drivers' cabs have cameras these days. And what with the wheelbarrow and what she's wearing, surely the police will have enough.

Only the gloves to deal with now. And for that she needs another witness. A middle-aged female, for preference. A busybody. They're the noticing type. Amazing how hard it is to get noticed, even if you're trying to be. People are so preoccupied. They're all so absorbed in themselves.

She unwraps the sheet of newspaper on her lap and checks the gloves. She could have left them at the crossing, but you have to give the police something to do in a murder case. Something to solve, like the pieces of a puzzle, so they can put them all back together and think they've found the answer. Because when it came down to it, there was no other way.

It had to be murder.

Daisy had to die.

* * *

'So, Mrs Mason,' says Agnew, 'you maintain that the person on the footage is not you. Even though this person is exactly your height. Even though this person has distinctive training shoes identical to yours. Even though this person is wearing high-viz clothes just like those your husband kept in the house. We are a very long way beyond coincidence, Mrs Mason.'

'Anyone can get clothes like that.'

Agnew takes a step back in exaggerated surprise. 'Am I to understand that you are *changing your story*, Mrs Mason? That you're now suggesting it was someone *else* who killed Daisy, and *not* your husband?'

'Well, it must have been, mustn't it?' She's veering towards sarcasm now. 'If it wasn't him it must have been someone else. It certainly wasn't me. It's *not my fault*.'

'I see. And I agree that it is not particularly difficult to obtain high-viz protective clothing. One can buy almost anything online these days, in relative anonymity. But how do you reconcile that with the timeline in this case? Your daughter disappeared sometime on the afternoon of July nineteenth. That we know. This

349

footage was taken shortly before five o'clock that afternoon. That we also know. The person shown here must, therefore, have *already had* that protective clothing to hand. Beyond those actually working in the construction industry, there are *very* few people to whom that applies. Apart from you, of course.'

The defence barrister rises and the judge nods to her. 'I anticipate your objection, Miss Kirby.'

'I withdraw that last remark, my Lady,' says Agnew. 'But I do have a further question for Mrs Mason. If you are now telling the court that it was some unknown abductor who took your daughter, why did you go to such lengths to incriminate your husband?'

Sharon refuses to look at him.

'You took two items to the police, did you not, with the express aim of suggesting your husband was molesting your daughter, and therefore, by extension, had a motive to kill her? The incriminating birthday card, exhibit seven, which you retrieved from the dustbin after your husband tried to dispose of it, and the mermaid fancy-dress costume you *claim* he had hidden in his wardrobe, exhibit eight.'

'He *did* hide it – that's where it was – that's where I found it.'

'You also told the police that you had no idea until that moment that your daughter might be being abused?'

Silence.

Agnew puts his glasses back on and whips through his pages. 'This assertion is in direct contradiction to

350

what your husband has already testified. He says you accused him of having some sort of incestuous fixation with Daisy as long ago as April 2016, when you confronted him about the birthday card. And yet you did not see fit to report any of this to the appropriate authorities.'

Again, silence. Sharon is gripping her hands together so hard her knuckles are white.

'It was revenge, wasn't it?' Agnew continues. 'Pure and simple. You found out your husband had been on a dating site, meeting other younger women and sleeping with them, and you saw your chance to get your vengeance by framing him for your daughter's death. You gave the police material that pointed to his guilt and you wore his high-viz clothing when you disposed of Daisy's body, so that if anyone saw you they would assume the person they were looking at was not a woman, but a man. Not you, but your husband.'

'He wasn't just cheating. He was looking at porn. At *kiddie porn*.' She leans forward and points at Agnew, stabbing the air. '*He's in prison for it.*'

Agnew raises an eyebrow. 'Ah, but you didn't know he was doing that then, did you? You didn't know that until *after* Daisy disappeared. At least that's what you told the police.'

'I didn't know he was on that dating site either,' she snaps. 'How could it be revenge if I didn't know? I'm not *telepathic*. I didn't even know he had that phone.'

'But you *did* know he was constantly coming back

late from work. You *did* know he was giving you increasingly lame excuses for those absences. And you accused him, for months, and with monotonous regularity, of having an affair. Can you deny that?'

Sharon opens her mouth, then closes it again. Her cheeks have gone very red.

'So let's run through it once again, shall we?' says Agnew. 'Just so we're all clear about this new story of yours. According to you, you are at home preparing for the party when your son and daughter get home from school. Daisy at 4.15, and Leo at 4.30. Daisy puts her music on in her room. You gather from Leo that the children had had some sort of argument but you don't go upstairs to check on Daisy. At just after 4.30 you go out for mayonnaise, leaving the children in the house on their own. At 5.15 you return, without mayonnaise. Again, you do not go up to check on Daisy. Or on Leo, for that matter. Your husband returns at 5.30 and likewise does not go up to see the children. Guests start to arrive for the party at seven, and all through the evening you see a neighbour's little girl running about in a daisy costume and have *no idea* – to use your own phrase – that she is not your daughter.'

Someone shouts abuse from the public gallery and the judge looks up sharply. 'Silence, or I will clear the court!'

Agnew takes a deep breath. 'When *precisely*, in all this, Mrs Mason, are you telling us your daughter disappeared?'

Sharon shrugs, avoiding his eye. 'It must have been when I was out.'

'So we're back to the famous forty minutes? You would have us believe some unknown paedophile – some random intruder – just happened to choose *that very moment* to break into the house?'

'She might have known them. She might have met them before and let them in. *You* didn't know her. She *liked* keeping secrets. She *liked* doing things behind my back.'

There's another ripple from the gallery at that, and anxious looks between the defence team.

'Indeed,' says Agnew, turning to look at the jury. 'Members of the jury might well wonder at a mother who says such things about her own child – her own *dead* child –'

Miss Kirby begins to rise again, but Agnew quickly forestalls her. 'I withdraw that last remark, my Lady. But I will, if I may, ask the defendant if she can cite an example – any example – of any *actual* duplicity on her daughter's part?'

'Well,' she flashes, 'she was seeing that nasty little half-brother of hers for a start. I didn't know anything about *that*.'

'And you are asking the jury to believe that?'

'Are you calling me a liar? We didn't know. *I* didn't know. I'd have put a bloody stop to it if I had.'

It was a trap, and she's walked right into it.

'I see,' says Agnew after a heavy pause. 'Are you in

the habit, Mrs Mason, of *putting a bloody stop* to things you don't like?'

It's the judge who intervenes this time. 'The jury will ignore that last remark. Move on, please, Mr Agnew.'

Agnew consults his notes. 'Regardless of whether you knew Daisy was seeing her half-brother, it wasn't Jamie Northam who came to the house that day, was it, Mrs Mason? Because we know for a fact that he was twenty miles away at a wedding rehearsal in Goring. Are you saying Daisy was meeting someone else as well – that she had a *second* secret assignation going on? Is that really likely – a child of eight with neither a mobile phone nor access to a computer? And even if such a person did exist, wouldn't Leo have known if they had come to the door that afternoon or broken in?'

Sharon glares at him; her anger is perilously close to the surface now. 'He had his headphones on.'

But Agnew isn't letting up – he's done his homework. 'But even so – surely he would have noticed – surely he would have told you as soon as you got back? After all,' he says, holding her gaze, drilling each word, 'you're his mother, *he's your son* –'

It's the last straw.

'That bloody kid is not my son!' The words are out before she can think them. 'And as for him hearing anything or doing anything, you've got to be bloody joking. There's *something wrong with him*. There always has been. He burned the sodding house down, for Christ's sake. If anyone's to blame it's his stupid mother. *Not me.*'

Kirby is again on her feet objecting, and people in the public gallery are shouting and pointing. It's nearly five minutes before order is restored. And all that while, Sharon sits there, her shoulders heaving.

'So you stand by your story,' says Agnew. 'That you never saw Daisy after she got home. You never spoke to her and you never saw her.'

She flushes, but she does not speak.

'In that case, how do you explain this?' He lifts another plastic bag from the desk in front of him. 'Exhibit nine, my Lady. A small cotton cardigan found under the heap of wheelbarrows in the car park. A cardigan which, as we know, has been identified as that worn by Daisy Mason on the day of her disappearance.' He presses his remote control again and the CCTV from outside the school appears on the screen. There are more gasps around the court: the police haven't released this before. No one has seen this footage. Agnew lets them watch. Lets them see Daisy alive, Daisy laughing, Daisy in the sun. And then he freezes the frame.

'This is the last sighting of Daisy Mason. The cardigan is tied round her shoulders and, as you can see, it is completely clean. Both sleeves are visible and there are no marks.'

He lifts the evidence bag again. 'I accept that the jury will find it hard to discern, in among the mud and filth, but analysis has proved that there are bloodstains on the left sleeve of this cardigan. This blood is not

Daisy's. It's from someone else entirely. That person, Mrs Mason, is *you.*'

He pauses, waiting for it to sink in. 'So perhaps you could tell us, Mrs Mason, how *your blood* came to be on this cardigan, when it was not present at 3.49, when your daughter left school. Do you still claim you never saw Daisy after she got home that day?'

She must have known this was coming, and yet she has nothing to offer. No story that will stand the slightest scrutiny.

'I cut myself,' she says eventually. 'There was glass on the kitchen floor.'

'Ah, the famous broken jar of mayonnaise. But that still does not explain how your blood got on to this cardigan. Can you enlighten us, Mrs Mason?'

'I found the cardigan on the stairs after I heard her come in. When I went to call up to her. So I picked it up and put it on the hook in the hall. I was tidying up. For the party. I didn't realize my hand was still bleeding or I'd have put it in the wash.'

'So when did you notice the cardigan was gone?'

She looks at him now and her chin lifts. 'When Leo got home. I just assumed she'd come downstairs and got it.'

'And you never mentioned this to the police? Not once – in all those hours of interviews before they arrested you?'

'It didn't think it was important.'

The courtroom is silent. No one believes her. But it's all she has.

There is a long, long pause.

* * *

19 July 2016, 4.09 p.m.
The day of the disappearance
5 Barge Close, kitchen

She knew he was lying. There was something about his voice, the noises on the line. The echoes were all wrong. He wasn't out in the open, at a site, he was in a room. A room with other people in it. She's got a long nose for them now. The backing tracks to his lies.

She puts the phone down carefully and stares at the kitchen floor. The mayonnaise is solidifying into a sticky glutinous mass, buzzing with flies. There's glass everywhere, tiny splinters crunching underfoot. When the front door opens five minutes later Sharon is on her hands and knees, collecting the pieces in a piece of kitchen roll.

'Daisy? Is that you?'

Sharon gets to her feet and reaches for a tea towel. There's blood on her hands.

'*Daisy!* Did you hear me? Come in here at once!'

Daisy eventually appears, dragging her school bag

357

along the floor behind her. Sharon's mouth hardens; there are two spots of livid colour on her cheeks.

'You did this, didn't you?' she says, gesturing at the mess on the floor. 'You were the last one in the kitchen this morning. It had to be you.'

Daisy shrugs. 'It's just mayonnaise.'

Sharon takes a step towards her. 'I've been out *all day* shopping and sorting things out for the party, and now I have to go out *again*, because you couldn't be bothered to tell me what you'd done. And what were you doing with it anyway? No one has mayonnaise for *breakfast*. Or is that something else your fancy friends do? Something else we're just too *thick* to understand?'

Daisy opens her mouth, but thinks better of it. She stares at the mayonnaise, and then at her mother. Her chin lifts in a gesture of defiance. The two of them have never looked more alike.

'You think you're too good for us, don't you?' says Sharon, moving towards her daughter. 'Don't think I don't know why bloody Portia and bloody Nanxi Chen aren't coming tonight. You're ashamed of us, aren't you? You look down your snotty little nose at your *own family*, just like those stuck-up little cows. How dare you – *how dare you –*'

Daisy turns to go, but Sharon lurches forward and grips her by the shoulder, pulling at the cardigan. 'Don't you turn your back on me, young lady. I'm your mother – you'll treat me with respect.'

Daisy twists out of her mother's grasp and they stand there for a moment, glaring at each other.

'Miss Madigan told us,' says Daisy slowly, her small face white to the lips, 'that respect is something you have to earn. You get it because of the things you've done. *You've* never done *anything*. You're not even *pretty* any more. That's why Daddy's looking for someone else. He's going to get a new wife and *I'm* going to get a new mummy.'

It happens before Sharon even knows what she's doing. The hand raised, the stinging slap, the red angry mark. She staggers a moment, horrified. Not just at what she's done, but at the look on her daughter's face. The cold, hard, triumphant look.

'You're not my mother,' whispers Daisy. 'Not any more. I'd rather *die* than be like you.'

Then she turns, picks up her school bag and walks away.

'Daisy? *Daisy! Come back here at once!*'

A door upstairs bangs shut and the music starts. *Thud thud thud* through the thin boards.

Sharon goes to the sink and pours herself a glass of water with a shaking hand, and when she turns again Leo is standing there, watching her.

'You've got blood on you,' he says.

* * *

When Agnew resumes, it's softly, almost kindly. 'There is another version of what happened that day, Mrs Mason, isn't there?'

Sharon turns her face away.

'Over the months leading up to your daughter's death you had become convinced your husband was having an affair. This jealousy, this suspicion, had become so all-enveloping – so dangerously obsessive – that you had lost all ability to think rationally. Every woman your husband looked at – every woman who smiled at him – fuelled the same terrible conviction. You had even started to see *your own daughter* as a potential rival – someone who stole love and attention you felt should rightfully be yours.'

Sharon's head drops. She's crying. Dry, miserable, self-pitying tears.

'And then, that afternoon, it all comes to a head. Your husband calls to tell you he will be later than he promised, leaving you to do all the work for the party. Not only that, you're convinced that he's not with a client, as he claims, but with another woman. Who knows, perhaps you hear a female voice or the sounds of a wine bar in the background. Whatever it was, it was enough to send you over the edge. You simply cannot take it any more. In this bitter, angry, resentful state of mind you go up to your daughter's room. And what do you find? You find her, still in her school uniform, with her pretty pink cardigan round her shoulders, about to try on a fancy-dress costume. A costume completely different from the one you had got for her, at great expense, and which you realize now she has carelessly given away. What did she say to you, Mrs Mason? Did she tell you her daddy was going to love her even more as a mermaid? Did she tell you he thinks she's prettier than you?'

Sharon's head jerks up. No, she mouths. No. It wasn't like that.

But he has not finished.

'For anyone else, for any other mother, such a moment would be so mundane as to be completely trivial. But not for you. For you, it is the trigger for a sudden rage which will have appalling and irreparable consequences. Because that costume brings back with the most horrible vividness another innocent little girl who stole attention you thought should have been yours. Another little girl whose father loved her better than he loved you. A little girl who was the very image of Daisy. Your sister, Jessica.'

'My Lady,' cries Kirby, springing to her feet. 'This is highly prejudicial –'

'Jessica,' continues Agnew, his voice rising, 'who died, at the age of two, in an accident no one could explain. Died when she was alone with *you*. Died when *you* were supposed to be looking after her. Is this another of your "coincidences", Mrs Mason, or did *two* little girls die *at your hands*?'

Sharon is shaking her head; the tears are furious now. Furious, incredulous and unforgiving.

'What was your sister wearing when she died?' He leans forwards. '*What was she wearing, Mrs Mason?*'

* * *

Find Daisy Mason Facebook page

This is just to thank everyone who's supported the campaign #Justice4Daisy. It's scarcely believable that her own mother could have been guilty of such a terrible crime, but now the verdict is in, at least there's the chance for some closure. Our hearts go out to poor Leo, who will be living with the consequences of the Masons' abuse for the rest of his life. We'll be closing this page in a week or so, but you can still contribute to the online condolence book.

Jean Murray, Frank Lester, Lorraine Nicholas and 811 others liked this

TOP COMMENTS

Nicola Anderson I heard Leo's been taken into foster care. No way he can stay with his father, even when he does get out.
1 February at 10.22

Liz Kingston I hope that now we've had a verdict Daisy can finally rest in peace and we won't keep seeing all those stupid stories of people claiming they've spotted her. I saw three people doing that on Twitter only last week.
1 February at 10.23

Polly Maguire I saw some of those too. One of them was convinced they'd seen her at Liverpool Docks, only it turned out it was a child with short red hair. Someone else

claimed they'd seen her in Dubai and another one somewhere in the Far East. Honestly, people can be so thoughtless. It doesn't help poor Leo, having all these horrible rumours floating around.
1 February at 10.24

Abigail Ward I agree, and I just wanted to say that the best memorial for Daisy would be to donate to the NSPCC. Violence against children has to stop. You can pledge money here.
1 February at 10.26

Will Haines I agree, or a charity helping kids with FAS. I've worked with these children and they need so much support. If that's really what Leo is struggling with, I just hope he gets the love he needs.
1 February at 10.34

Find Daisy Mason Great ideas – fitting tribute to two sweet innocent kids.
1 February at 10.56

Judy Bray I went past that level crossing on the train last week, and there were heaps and heaps of flowers. People had left pots of daisies. It was very touching. Some people in my carriage were in tears.
1 February at 10.59

* * *

Two days after the verdict, we have a day of sudden sunshine. A day in sharp frost-etched focus, beautiful in a way the soft edges of summer can never be. White wisps of mare's-tail cloud are racing across an impossibly huge blue sky. I buy a sandwich and wander over to the recreation ground. A swarm of little boys are running about after a ball, and there's a very elderly married couple sitting companionably on a bench on the far side. Funny how old men start looking like old women, and old women like old men. As if the differences of gender lose sway, and even relevance, as we near our common end. I don't hear Everett approaching until she's standing next to me. She holds out a coffee.

'Do you mind company?'

I do, actually, but I smile and say, 'Of course not. Have a seat.'

She sits hunched against the cold, her gloved hands curled round her cup.

'I just got a call from Gislingham,' she says. 'They're hoping they can take Billy home soon. The doctors are really pleased with how well he's doing.'

'That's great news. I'll drop him a line.'

There's a silence.

'Do you really think she did it?' she says eventually.

So that's it.

'Yes,' I say. 'I do.'

'You don't think she was convicted for the wrong reasons? I mean, because people hated them, and

364

because of Twitter and all that abuse, rather than because of the evidence?'

I shrug. 'There's no way of knowing that. All that matters is we got to the right result, however that happened. But I don't think there was anything wrong with the evidence. We did a good job – *you* did a good job.'

She looks at me a moment, and then away, across the park. A couple of seagulls swoop down low over the playground and one of the toddlers starts crying.

'There was one thing that kept bugging me.'

I take a sip of the coffee and breathe out a gust of hot sweet air. 'What was that?'

'Those gloves. The ones she dumped in the skip. They were wrapped in pages from the *Guardian*.'

'So? What of it?'

'When we were interviewing her, she just kept on and on – "we don't read the *Guardian*, we read the *Daily Mail*". She wouldn't let up.'

I smile, but not unkindly. This is coming from conscience, and that's something worth nourishing in this job. 'I don't think that means anything, Everett. She could have found a copy, bought a copy. It could even have been in the skip already. These cases always have loose ends – they'll drive you mad, if you let them. So don't let it worry you. We got the right person. And in any case, who else could it have been?'

She looks at me for a moment, then drops her eyes. 'I suppose you're right.'

We sit in silence a while and then she gets to her feet

and smiles down at me, 'Thanks, boss,' before making her way back to the station. Slowly at first, but as I watch, her pace quickens. By the time she's going up the steps she is herself again, brisk and poised and objective.

As for me, I get stiffly to my feet and make my way to the car and head out towards the ring road. Five miles the other side, I take a right off Kidlington High Street and pull up outside a small yellow pebble-dashed bungalow. There are tubs of snowdrops either side of the door and brightly coloured dog toys strewn over the front garden. The woman who answers my ring is in her forties. She's wearing a big Aran jumper and a pair of sweatpants, and she has a tea towel in one hand. I can hear an old eighties pop song on the radio in the background. When she sees me she smiles broadly. 'Inspector – how nice. I had no idea you were coming.'

'I'm sorry, Jean, I was just passing and I thought –'

But she's already waving me in. 'Don't stand out there in the cold. Have you come to see Gary?'

'It's not official – I just wanted to see how he's doing. And please, call me Adam.'

She smiles again. 'It's nice you still take an interest, Adam. He's gone down to the park to play football with Phil. Though I suspect the dog thinks it's all for his benefit.'

She wipes her hands on the towel. 'Give me a sec and I'll put the kettle on. They'll be back any minute and Phil will be gasping.' She smiles again. 'We've done up Gary's room since you were last here – you can have a look if you like.'

She disappears into the kitchen and I stand there a moment, then take a few steps forward and push open the door. There are posters of football players on the walls, odd socks rolled up under the bed, a Chelsea FC duvet cover, an Xbox and a stack of games. A muddle. A happy, ordinary, everyday muddle.

The door bangs then, as Jean kicks it open. She has two mugs of tea with her.

'What do you think?' she says as she hands me one.

'I think you've done a fabulous job,' I say. 'And I don't mean the decorating. All this – it's exactly what he needs. Normality. Stability.'

She sits down on the bed and smoothes the cover with her hand. 'It's not hard, Adam. He just needed to be loved.'

'How's the new school?'

'Good. Dr Donnelly and I spent a long time with his form teacher before he started, talking it all through. He's still settling in, but fingers crossed, I think it's going to be OK.'

'And he was happy going back to his original name?'

She grins. 'I think it helps that there's a Gary in the Chelsea team. But yes, I think leaving "Leo" behind is the best thing that could have happened to him. In every sense. It's a new start.'

She blows on her tea and I walk over to the window and look out over the back garden. There's a goal at the far end and a couple of footballs on the muddy grass. And on the windowsill, a little blue china dish. The sort you put keys in, or change. But there's only one thing in this one. Something silver that catches the light. It looks like some sort of amulet – something you'd wear on a chain or a bracelet. Hardly what you'd expect a boy to have. I pick it up and look quizzically at Jean.

'Oh, his sister gave that to him,' she says. 'And that reminds me. Gary wants to send an email to that nice DC of yours, Everett, is it? To say sorry about causing all that trouble at the B&B. That thing you're holding – that's what he was looking for when it happened. That's what he thought he'd lost.'

'Really?' I look at it again, turning it over in my hand. It's shaped like a bunch of flowers, or leaves, but hanging upside down. Like mistletoe, at Christmas. 'It must mean a lot to him.'

She nods. 'It's some sort of charm. To keep bad things away. Daisy's teacher gave it to her, then she gave it to Gary. It's odd, though, all the same.'

'Why do you say that?'

She takes a sip of her tea. 'Gary doesn't really want to talk about it and I haven't pushed him, but I got the impression Daisy gave it to him that day – the day she disappeared. It sends a shiver down my spine every time I think of it. I know it sounds crazy when you say it out loud, but it's almost as if she knew. But how could she, poor little lamb.'

Then there's the sound of keys in the door and the little house is suddenly filled with a clamour of voices and a chaos of mucky dog.

'Jean, Jean, I got three penalties!' he cries as he clatters through the bedroom door, with a leaping golden retriever half under his feet. 'One after the other – bang – bang – bang!'

He stops then, because he's realized Jean's not alone. His cheeks are pink with cold and his hair is shorter than when I last saw him. He has no fringe to hide behind now, but he doesn't need it: he looks me straight in the eye. I can see he's surprised, because he wasn't expecting to see me, but that's all. He's not scared; not any more.

'Hello, Gary,' I say. 'I just popped round to see how you are. Jean says you're doing great. I'm really glad to hear that.'

He bends briefly to rub the grinning dog behind the ears. 'It's good here,' he says, looking up at me again. And I can't think of any three words that could say more. Not just about the past, but about the future too.

'Three penalties?' I continue. 'That's not bad. Keep it up and you'll be as good as that player you like – what's his name – he takes penalties, doesn't he?'

He smiles then and I realize, with a ghost of self-reproach, that it's the first time I've ever seen him do it.

'Hazard,' he says.

When I get back into the car, I sit there for a moment, thinking. About Gary, who's been given a second chance, and Daisy, who wasn't. And about the second chance I never got, and I'd trade everything I've ever owned to receive.

Tomorrow it will be exactly a year. To the day. That day.

It had been raining for what seemed like weeks – the clouds never lifted. I got home early, because we wanted to talk to Jake and I didn't want to rush it. I didn't want him going to bed with it on his mind. We had an appointment with the child psychologist the following day. Alex had been dead against it, insisting our GP knew what she was doing, and Jake hadn't hurt himself for weeks. That our son wasn't a 'case' I could solve with my brain, and escalating things now might only make it worse. But I forced it.

I forced it.

I remember I brought the bins in, cursing the dustmen for leaving them strewn across the drive. I remember chucking my keys on the kitchen table and picking up the post, asking where Jake was.

'Upstairs,' Alex said, stacking the dishwasher. 'Playing music. Tell him supper in half an hour.'

'And then we'll talk to him?'

'And then we'll talk to him.'

On bad nights, I crawl those steps on my hands and knees, aware there is some terrible catastrophe only speed can save me from, but unable to move faster than leadweight in water. The door, standing half open. The darkening sky. The glow of the computer screen. The empty chair. Those terrible, exquisite seconds when I

stand there, not knowing. For the last time, not knowing. And then turning, assuming he must be in the loo,
in my study –

Hanging
There
The dressing-gown cord half buried in his flesh –
The red wheals on his skin –
Those eyes –

And I can't save him. Can't get him down. Can't get the
air into his lungs. Can't get to him five minutes before.
Because that's all it was. Five minutes. That's what they
said.

Those bloody bins.
My boy.
My precious, precious lost boy.

Epilogue

17 August 2016, 10.12 a.m.
29 days after the disappearance

The ferry sounds its horn as it picks up speed and heads out of Liverpool docks into the Irish Sea. The gulls dip and lift about the boat, calling and circling. Despite the sunshine, there's a sharp breeze up on the observation deck, where Kate Madigan is standing at the railings, looking at the clouds, at the other boats, at the people on the quay, getting smaller and smaller as the ship pulls away. Some of them are waving. Not at her, she knows that – people always wave at boats – but it adds, all the same, to the sense of an ending. To the feeling that an entire existence is receding with the water, yard by glittering yard.

Because there can be no going back now. Not ever. She takes a deep breath of exhilarated relief and feels the bright air fill her lungs like a cleansing of the soul. She still can't believe they got away with it. After all those weeks of lies, and concealment, and lying in bed at night, heart pounding, waiting for the hammering on the door. And even today, her hands were shaking as they drove up to the ferry terminal, expecting to see the police waiting, finally, to meet them. Barring the way to escape, denying them their precious new life. But there was nothing. Not that solid chirpy little DC; not that woman with the dull hair and the alert, clever eyes, and the questions that came a little too close to home. Nothing. Just a jovial P&O man to check their tickets and wave them smiling through.

And they *are* through. The risks she took; the planning, the care, the anticipation of all those deadly treacherous details, it's all worth it now. And yes, other people have paid the price, but as far as she's concerned they got no more than they deserved. A mother who withheld love and a father who perverted it. Who can say which had caused the greater harm? Which deserved the greater punishment? Her grandmother always used to say that God makes sure your sins will find you out, and perhaps in this case, it was true. The videos on his phone, the blood on the cardigan; neither could have been foreseen, but both were devastating. So whether by divine intervention, or her own, justice had indeed been done. The father caught in a mire of his own making and the mother in a snare that trapped her just as surely as it set her daughter free. And that was all that mattered, in the end: not who was convicted, but the fact of the killing – the belief in it. Because with that, all searching would cease. And as for the boy, well, she checked. Discreetly, so as not to draw attention. But then again, in her position, as his sister's teacher, it was natural she'd want to know. And she *did* want to know – she wanted to be sure. And they told her he's fine. More than fine, in fact. Everyone agrees it's the best thing that could ever have happened. Because now he's getting what he deserves too: a second chance. The same miraculous, odds-against, life-overturning second chance that she now has.

'*Mummy, mummy!*'

She turns to see a little girl running towards her, her face lit up with joy. Kate crouches down and holds out her arms, rocking the child tenderly and feeling her warm breath on her cheek.

'Do you love me, Mummy?' whispers the child, and Kate draws back and looks at her.

'Of course I do, darling. So much. So *very, very* much.'

'As much as your other little girl?' There's a little wobble of anxiety in her voice.

'Yes, darling,' says Kate softly. 'I love you both just the same. My heart was broken for a while, when she died, because she was so ill and I couldn't save her. Whatever I did, however hard I tried. But I *can* save *you*. No one will ever hurt you again,' she says, reaching to caress the child's soft red curls that are now so like her own. 'Because I'm your mummy now.'

'Nobody else would've believed me,' whispers the little girl. 'No one except you.'

Kate's eyes fill with tears. 'I know, darling. It makes me so sad you had no one else you could talk to – no one to love you like you deserve. But that's all over now. You've been so brave, and so clever. Taking those gloves, saving the tooth you lost – I would never have thought of any of that.'

She takes the child in her arms again and holds her, tighter now. 'I *promise* you they will never find you. I will *never* let you go. You won't forget that, will you?'

She feels the little girl shake her head. 'So,' she says, wiping her eyes and taking the little girl's hand, 'shall we say a last goodbye to England?'

They go to stand by the railing, in the sunshine. The little girl is round-eyed with excitement now, pointing, laughing, waving to the ferry that chugs past them going the other way.

A few feet along the deck, an elderly lady is sitting in her wheelchair, blankets tucked round her knees. She looks kindly at the little girl. 'You're having a nice time, so you are.'

The child looks across at her and nods vigorously, and Kate smiles. 'We're on our way to Galway,' she says gaily. 'I've got a new job there. Sabrina has been looking forward to this ferry trip for months.'

'Sabrina?' says the woman. 'Now that's a pretty name, so it is. It has a nice meanin' too. I always say it's good to have a name that means somethin'. Did your mammy tell you what it means?'

The little girl nods again. 'I love it. It's like a secret. I like secrets.'

And then she smiles. A charming gap-toothed smile.

Acknowledgements

Oxford must be one of the most fictionalized cities in the world, so you can imagine my trepidation in daring to add to the number of novels – and specifically crime novels – written about the place I'm lucky enough to live in. I hope the Oxford of *Close to Home* will ring true to anyone who knows it, and my readers will certainly be able to find many of the roads and buildings I mention on a map of the city – though it is also worth noting that many of the side streets and other specific locations are my own invention. And, of course, any resemblance to the real people who live here is entirely coincidental. Twitter usernames have been created with sixteen or more characters to prevent any accidental identification with real accounts. If there is any similarity to real individuals' usernames, this is not intentional.

A few words of thanks to the people who have helped to make this book happen. First to my amazing agent, Anna Power, and my delightful editor at Viking, Katy Loftus, and also to my eagle-eyed copy-editor, Karen Whitlock. To my husband, Simon, for saying 'Why don't you write a crime book?' on that beach in the

Caribbean. And to my dear friend Stephen for being, as always, one of my first readers.

As for the professionals, I'd like to thank Inspector Andy Thompson for his hugely helpful observations and advice, and Joey Giddings, my very own and very knowledgeable 'CSI'. I've learned so much from both of them, and *Close to Home* is a much better book as a result.

I would also like to thank Nicholas Syfret, QC, who was a mine of information on court procedure and the legal elements of the story.

Thanks also to Professor David Hills for his help with the technical aspects of engineering construction, and to Dr Oli Rahman for answering my medical questions so patiently (if he will forgive the pun). Needless to say, if any errors remain they are down to me, and not to the people who've been kind enough to help me.

TURN THE PAGE FOR A SNEAK PEAK OF

IN THE DARK

DI FAWLEY BOOK 2

CARA HUNTER

A woman and child are found locked in a basement room, barely alive.

No one knows who the woman is, and the elderly man who lives there swears he's never seen them before.

Nothing about this case seems to fit.

But DI Adam Fawley knows that nothing is impossible.

And that no one is as innocent as they seem . . .

JULY 2018

AVAILABLE TO PRE-ORDER NOW

Prologue

She opens her eyes to darkness as close as a blindfold. To the heaviness of old, dank air that hasn't been breathed for a long time.

Her other senses lurch awake. The dripping silence, the cold, the smell. Mildew and something else she can't yet place, something animal and fetid. She moves her fingers, feeling grit and wet under her jeans. It's coming back to her now – how she got here, why this happened.

How could she have been so stupid?

She stifles the acid rush of panic and tries to sit up, but the movement defeats her. She fills her lungs and shouts, flinging echoes against the walls. Shouts and shouts and shouts until her throat is raw.

But no one comes. Because no one can hear.

She closes her eyes again, feeling hot, angry tears seeping down her face. She is rigid with outrage and recrimination and conscious of little else until, in terror, she feels the first sharp little feet start to move across her skin.

* * *

Someone said, didn't they, that April is the cruellest month. Well, whoever it was, they weren't a detective.

Cruelty can happen any time – I know, I've seen it. But the cold and the dark somehow dull the edge. Sunlight, and birdsong, and blue skies, can be brutal in this job. Perhaps it's the contrast that does it. Death and hope.

This story starts with hope. May the first: the first day of spring – real spring. And if you've ever been to Oxford, you'll know: it's all or nothing in this place – when it rains the stone is piss-coloured, but in the light, when the colleges look like they've been carved from cloud, there is no more beautiful place on earth. And I'm just a cynical old copper.

As for May Morning, well, that's the city at its most eccentric, its most defiantly 'itself'. Pagan and Christian and a bit mad and it's hard to tell, a lot of the time, which is which. Choirboys singing in the sunrise on the top of a tower. Hurdy-gurdy bands jostling the all-night burger vans. The pubs open at 6 a.m., and half the student population is still pissed from the night before. Even the sober citizens of north Oxford turn out *en masse* with flowers in their hair (and you think I'm joking). There were over 25,000 people there last year. One of them was a bloke dressed as a tree. I think you get the picture.

So, one way or another it's a big day in the police calendar. But it's a long straw on the uniform roster, not a short one. The early start can be a bit of a killer, but there's rarely any trouble, and we get plied with coffee and bacon sandwiches. Or at least we were, the last time I did it. But that was when I was still in uniform. Before I became a detective; before I made DI.

386

But this year, it's different. This year, it's not just the early start that's the killer.

He just wanted a decent book to read ...

Not too much to ask, is it? It was in 1935 when Allen Lane, Managing Director of Bodley Head Publishers, stood on a platform at Exeter railway station looking for something good to read on his journey back to London. His choice was limited to popular magazines and poor-quality paperbacks – the same choice faced every day by the vast majority of readers, few of whom could afford hardbacks. Lane's disappointment and subsequent anger at the range of books generally available led him to found a company – and change the world.

'We believed in the existence in this country of a vast reading public for intelligent books at a low price, and staked everything on it'
Sir Allen Lane, 1902–1970, founder of Penguin Books

The quality paperback had arrived – and not just in bookshops. Lane was adamant that his Penguins should appear in chain stores and tobacconists, and should cost no more than a packet of cigarettes.

Reading habits (and cigarette prices) have changed since 1935, but Penguin still believes in publishing the best books for everybody to enjoy. We still believe that good design costs no more than bad design, and we still believe that quality books published passionately and responsibly make the world a better place.

So wherever you see the little bird – whether it's on a piece of prize-winning literary fiction or a celebrity autobiography, political tour de force or historical masterpiece, a serial-killer thriller, reference book, world classic or a piece of pure escapism – you can bet that it represents the very best that the genre has to offer.

Whatever you like to read – trust Penguin.